GARDEN

GARDENS OF DESIRE

by

Roger Rougiere

A Gentleman of Taste and Rich Endowments

First published in Great Britain in 1992 by
Nexus
338 Ladbroke Grove
London W10 5AH

Copyright © Roger Rougiere 1992

ISBN 0 352 32826 6

Typeset by Phoenix Photosetting, Chatham, Kent
Printed and bound in Great Britain by
Cox & Wyman Ltd, Reading, Berks

This book is sold subject to the condition that it shall not, by way of trade or otherwise, be lent, re-sold, hired out or otherwise circulated without the publisher's prior written consent in any form of binding or cover other than that in which it is published and without a similar condition including this condition being imposed on the subsequent purchaser.

CONTENTS

PART ONE
Roger Rougiere's Easy Exercises
1

PART TWO
Cecilia's Diary
81

PART THREE
Duets and Variations at the Organ
135

PART ONE

ROGER ROUGIERE'S EASY EXERCISES

Chapter 1

In which the sad loss of a father through an unpredictable prick is alleviated by the balm of a lady's prick of conscience

My father's premature death on a balmy June evening in 1811 was unhappily brought about by a change of musical rhythm. If only the Vauxhall orchestra had continued with its plodding four-in-a-bar, steadily and melodiously drifting through the trees to the sheltered spot where he lay atop his seventeen-year-old fancy of the moment, all would have been well. But without warning the rhythm changed to that of a galop in lively six-eight measure. At first laughing at the challenge, my father tried to ride the girl at this accelerated pace but all too soon found his upbeats and downbeats utterly confused. As the moment of climax approached he jerked himself right out of the clasp of the lass's lower lips and, while striving desperately to return, stabbed his eager member down upon the thorny tendril of a rose bush. Even today the mere act of writing it down brings filial tears to my eyes.

In spite of his discomfort my father proudly – in every sense of the word – attempted to remount; but the agonising effort, together with the shock of a sudden brassy fanfare from a military band marching past, was too much for his over-eager heart. He collapsed, and the girl had great difficulty in wriggling out from under his weight. Hastily adjusting her dress, she went off in search of a doctor.

I was much touched when she came next day to our house

in Bayswater and related all the sombre details to me. Many a young woman in such circumstances might well have hurried away from the scene, leaving her companion to breathe his last in that dark shrubbery of the pleasure gardens. Instead she had made it her business to find a physician and urge him out from one of the shady bowers in spite of his callous protestations that he, too, was occupied with a young woman and had reached the stage when it would be extremely injurious to his health to withdraw.

In any case he arrived at the scene too late. My father was declared dead of a heart attack, and to avoid the derision of our friends and neighbours I at once began spreading it about that this lamentable seizure had been due entirely to the execrable playing of the orchestra in Vauxhall Gardens, which had long been an offence to delicate musical ears. The girl who presented herself on our doorstep to tell me the sad truth was most charmingly agreeable to preserving this diplomatic version.

She was, indeed, agreeable in every way. I could understand my father's appetite for her, and as she described their intimate moments most earnestly and in meticulous detail I found myself dwelling upon the slow, half-smiling movements of her lips and guessing at what similar movements she might be capable of elsewhere. Also my attention was caught by the way she most appealingly touched her left breast when referring regretfully to the cessation of his heartbeat. I was conscious, with a burgeoning appetite of my own, of another beat; but, although fairly accomplished in answering to the needs of a number of older women, I was at that time rather shy of younger ones, especially ladies of such grace and such proportions. Besides, at a grave moment like this it would surely be improper to distract such a conscientious young creature from her solemn narrative.

That left breast was most inadequately confined within a meagre muslin dress, probably all that the poor child could afford. Her right breast, equally in danger of escaping, was clearly a fine match.

I made a mighty effort to concentrate on what she was saying.

Towards the end of her narrative, Polly – for such was the name with which she had introduced herself, though she seemed shy of adding a surname to it – shuddered slightly as a loud chord was thumped out on the piano in the next room. She glanced at the wall, perhaps reliving the unhappy drama occasioned by the Vauxhall discords.

'Pay no heed,' I said reassuringly. 'Merely one of my pupils going through a difficult passage.'

'Your pupils?' Her compelling hazel eyes studied me respectfully.

I explained that, although my father had undoubtedly reacted with the greatest sensitivity to music, I was in fact the true musician of the family, planning a glittering career as composer, conductor and pianist, but at the moment contenting myself with giving lessons on the pianoforte. The ill-tempered keyboard in the adjoining room had produced its aggressive sound because, I sensed, the middle-aged lady sitting at it was growing restive about my absence.

What I did not confide to the sweet-skinned, shapely creature sitting deferentially before me was the fact that Mrs Drabble, like a number of my other middle-aged pupils, expected exercises of another kind at the end of each lesson, and would be ready for one such in the all too near future. It was a regrettable chore, though it enabled me to charge extra in the guise of additional fingering exercises. Today I was assuredly not in the mood for it: not in the mood, that is, for the unsweet-skinned, unshapely Mrs Drabble.

Almost as if divining my thoughts, Polly murmured: 'How long will your pupil be on the premises?'

'Some twenty minutes.'

'I fear, sir, that that allows scarce time to conclude the agreement.'

'Agreement?'

'It distresses me that the late Mr Rougiere should not have received full satisfaction. Nor, alas, did we go on to supper as he had promised.'

I thought I now began to see what had brought the wench here. Although I had not yet received my fee from Mrs Drabble, and there was little enough ready money about my person, I began to fumble among the few coins in my pocket. She greedily watched the gropings of my hand with what I assumed to be a purely financial covetousness. 'I fear I cannot accompany you,' I said at last, 'but do enjoy a meal at such time as suits you.' I held out a guinea.

She accepted it, her warm hand lying on mine for a long moment. 'But,' she said, 'I am still in your debt. We did not reach the end. Would you not say, sir, that your father left you that bequest and that it is my duty to honour it?'

When the purport of her offer had penetrated my somewhat dazed consciousness I went into the next room, turned over the sheet of music before which Mrs Drabble was crouching, instructed her to depress the damping pedal which was such a gratifying feature of modern instruments, and went back to seek my own gratification. The twenty minutes available had shrunk to sixteen; but a part of me was doing the reverse of shrinking, and I now acknowledged that the poverty of Polly's garments did enable her to remove them in a time-saving matter of seconds. For a terror-stricken moment I was unsure of my ability to cope with a nymph so young and apparently so knowledgeable. The fear vanished the moment she pressed her nakedness against mine and reached down to appraise the length and strength of what she would have to cope with.

There were no thorns in this room. The artificial lilies in their glass dome presented no threat to my exposed person. One worn spring in the sofa was liable to protrude when fallen upon from a certain angle, but I was experienced in avoiding that angle. My only regret as I lifted Polly upon the sofa and she spread her long white legs to display the sweetest sweetmeat of my morning was that this piece of furniture should ever have had to be shared with the likes of Mrs Drabble. Certainly it would never have been possible to lift Mrs Drabble in such fashion: but in any event she was usually there ahead of me, creaking in anticipation.

Within another ten seconds I had forgotten Mrs Drabble.

Even if her playing had broken into a galop and she had trampled on the sustaining pedal rather than the damper, I would for once have been deaf to such musical misdeeds, and would assuredly not have been in any danger of succumbing to my poor dear father's syncope.

I marvelled that, whatever the shock of a changing rhythm might have been, my father could have involuntarily slipped out of Polly's clitoral clutch. The hot grip of her hand as she drew my prick towards her was painfully tight, but in no degree so tight as the clasp of those pulsing, biting lips which clenched around me. If there had been teeth within that ravening mouth, my manhood would surely have been summarily destroyed there and then. Only after I had driven into her seven, eight, nine times did she grow so responsively wet that I could move freely and appreciatively rather than smartingly.

She swung her head towards my right shoulder and scraped her teeth along my flesh. 'You touch me deeper than your father ever reached,' she murmured admiringly. It was not, I suppose, the most appropriate moment to refer to one who could no longer savour such material delights, but I was in no state to enter into a moral discussion, being already entered into what struck me as being infinitely more uplifting.

'Bitch,' I said quietly. It is a word which I have found the most apparently decorous, unresponsive women like to have spoken to them at certain moments in a certain soothing accent. Then came other words, and I now used these at a quickening pace, to which Polly responded with a quickening and soon uncontrollable threshing from side to side.

In the next room the piano fell silent. I cursed. Polly desperately reared up, carrying me upon her as she writhed to the arm of the couch and sprawled backwards over it, offering me the unconfined splendour of her breasts. I kissed her throat, her shoulders and her soft bubbies, and then fixed briefly upon first the blue hardness of her left nipple, then upon the right. As I bit her she fastened her nails into my arse. And then I poured myself into her and had to plunge my face deep into the cleft between her breasts so that Mrs Drabble might not think I was bellowing obscene criticism of her playing through the wall.

It was over. We came reluctantly apart, and I reached for an antimacassar from the armchair so that we might dry ourselves. Polly had dressed herself before I had even climbed into my breeches, and stood contemplating me with something like her original deference, mingled with another sort of appreciation. It was flattering to see in her expression how well I had pleased her.

She said: 'Thank you, sir. I'm much obliged. I don't like to leave things unfinished.'

'You've finished *me* for quite a time.' I made a joke out of it, but then realised that the joke would go sour any moment. Finished I truly was, and Mrs Drabble's expression would not be as contented as Polly's.

As I escorted the girl downstairs, our housekeeper appeared, heading as a matter of form to open the front door. Mrs Hiscock was dressed from head to toe in black, and had assumed a dark expression of decorous mourning. I half expected her to look with disfavour upon my young companion; and could only hope that she had no way of guessing at Polly's involvement in the death of the head of our household. But after a quick glance from one to the other of us, she almost allowed herself a smile, at odds with the funereal correctness of her dress. After all, it was Mrs Hiscock who, finding me at the age of twelve relieving the pressure upon my taut youthful member in the only way I knew, had taken me into her bosom – and elsewhere – and instructed me in more companionable ways of ejaculation. She was, I am sure, aware of the use to which I later put her tutelage when I offered musical tuition to ladies of an age similar to her own, and was not displeased by my practising what she had preached. Nor did she look displeased now when she saw me at last in the company of someone so much younger. She drew away, leaving me to make my adieus to Polly at the top of the steps.

Polly treated me to a businesslike smile. 'If you should wish to renew the acquaintance, sir, I am to be found most evenings after eight o'clock in the enclosure beside the Cascade. From there it is not too long a step to the arbours of Lover's Walk, as you doubtless know.'

In fact I knew little of Vauxhall Gardens, not having frequented its many pleasures with such assiduousness as my father had displayed since my mother's death many years before. Once or twice I had made a point of visiting it solely to listen to a new composition by Mr James Hook or to the voice of some much-lauded visiting soprano from Italy; but I had not lingered afterwards to partake of food or to gratify any other hungers. Now I felt that I might permit myself some diversion, especially if my father should chance to have left me any legacy other than that of a healthy lust.

The strength of this latter quality was much enfeebled when I went to tell Mrs Drabble that her lesson was over for the week. She looked peevish at having been neglected for so long, and suspicious about what she had seen through the window when moving away from the pianoforte.

'Who was that girl who has just left?'

'Like myself,' I said sombrely, 'a lonely orphan.'

'You weren't an orphan last time I was here.'

'One never knows when the grim reaper may appear at one's gates.'

'You don't have any gates – only a flight of steps.'

'I was speaking metaphorically.'

'Oh, of course.' She grew arch and expectant once more. In a moment of misguided flippancy many months earlier I had explained the concept of metaphors to her while resignedly accompanying her from the keyboard to the sofa, and one example had unfortunately become a favourite with her. 'We do just have enough time for a little *percussion* practice, don't we?'

Mrs Drabble, to put it bluntly, enjoyed having the sagging drumheads of her capacious bottom vigorously beaten upon before turning over and engulfing what she gigglingly referred to as her pet drumstick. At this moment I had the energy neither for the ritual taradiddles on her flaccid timpani nor for the production of an erect drumstick.

I took a deep breath and said: 'I'm so sorry I can't offer my full range of tuition today, but I do have this distressing matter of a family bereavement to attend to. My father died from listening to ineptly played music. I fear I must abandon music for some days until the anguish has worn off. I really ought to have found a way of telling you not to come today, but it was all so sudden.'

She was far from mollified. As I ushered her off the premises, assuring her that I would reduce my regular fee to take account of the inadequacy of my ministrations on this occasion, she made a belated attempt to offer sympathy and then, brightening, suggested that there were ways of forgetting my woes for a time and that she would be prepared to make a selfless contribution to this forgetfulness. Even if I had been capable of a response, I would have deplored her panting substitution on the sofa for the supple charms which had so recently assuaged my filial distress.

I was finally rid of her, and turned my attention to the funeral arrangements and to the pronouncements of the family solicitor.

My father had indeed left me a comfortable sum, together with the Bayswater house. I was an only child, and although there were two maternal uncles and three paternal aunts distributed somewhere between Australia and the Outer Hebrides, they had rarely been in touch with us and could not conceivably have any claim on the estate. I was now in a position not merely to cut down on the number of music lessons I had felt it incumbent on me to give in order to assert some degree of financial independence, but to abandon them altogether and devote myself at last to the beckoning world of the concert platform and the opera house. I was twenty-three years of age. By the time I was twenty-five, I trusted, my name would be a household word.

Having notified grief-stricken pupils of my decision and fought off three ladies (including, I need hardly add, the dread Mrs Drabble) who attempted to storm the steps and fight their way up to the first floor and the sofa, I devoted myself to practising some of the more dramatic passages of Beethoven's sonatas, and sketched out on music manuscript a few ideas for songs of higher aesthetic value than those generally performed at Vauxhall. At the same time I was aware that the introduction of such material on the Vauxhall bandstand could lead to further performance in more exalted surroundings. It was impolitic to sneer at what went on in those pleasure gardens.

After a decent interval I decided to pay a personal visit there, experience its musical possibilities for myself, and consider how to improve on them and so further my gloriously beckoning career. I would also make a point of politely seeking out Polly and offering her a bite of supper in one of the more reputable eating-places within the gardens.

Although there was a coach entrance at the corner of Kennington Lane, I remembered from my father's pleasantly tipsy soliloquies that by far the best approach was from the river. I therefore made my way shortly before nine o'clock one evening to Westminster Stairs, from which a barge had just set out on its brief trip across the Thames. The wait for the next was not long. Vessels of every size, each filled by a jostling crowd, plied a steady, profitable trade. I had decked myself in a new green coat with striped jockey waistcoat and gaiter pantaloons, and upon glancing at my companions felt that my attire was markedly superior to most of theirs. Indeed, I was worried that some of those shoddier men who were already rowdy and had taken of drink before even reaching Vauxhall might stain my garments; and as the barge swung in midstream and a light breeze blew along the deck I found my shoulders and lapels acquiring a deposit of powder lifted from the cheeks of certain forward young women.

It was a warm evening, though the sky was overcast. As if to defy this sullen blanket, the thousands of oil lamps in the gardens had been illuminated early and were glittering a multicoloured invitation through the trees. Through the clamour on board there drifted the faintest whisper of an orchestra playing. It grew louder as we approached, until the barge hove to, close to the landing-stage but not close enough. There was an almighty confusion of wherries and small private craft, jolting and bumping for precedence as their owners and passengers bellowed impatient commands and swore complicated oaths which suggested that at least a half of the population of London was illegitimate.

For a moment I had the impression that one of the women passengers had been disturbed by the rocking motion of our vessel. She was hanging her head over the side as if to dispose of the contents of her stomach into the already murky waters. A male companion had placed himself directly behind her and appeared to have clasped his arms firmly around her to ensure that she did not lose her balance and plunge in. It was only when I glimpsed the height to which the woman's rumpled skirts had been lifted, and the tendency of the man's breeches to slip towards his knees, that I realised how securely she was being pinned to the rail and how little danger there was of her going headfirst over the side.

After a good ten minutes of struggling for priority, our barge bumped against the landing-stage. Some uncouth revellers impatiently elbowed their way ashore, trampling on the toes of others and pushing a few women out of the way. I took my time, and was among the last to land.

Immediately within the watergate a hunched drab was selling flowers. For a moment I contemplated buying a small posy to lay on the place where my father had made his last stand; but perhaps that would not have been in the best of taste, especially if I had chosen roses. Besides, I would first have to find Polly to identify the precise spot; and it might well prove to be occupied when we got there. I abandoned the idea and walked on down a long dark avenue covered over with arching branches, emerging into the full radiance of the gardens.

Far down one radial avenue hung with lanterns I could see the flamboyant decorations of the orchestral rotunda. Lanterns dangled from every available tree until one explored the outer reaches, where they grew fewer and dimmer. Although the summer evening was not yet truly dark, there was nothing but secretive shadow in miniature caverns formed by the bushy enclosures. Nothing, that is, save for what might be revealed by unguardedly athletic enthusiasm. Through one interstice in the maze of hedges I spied the rise and fall of a white bottom – white save when, at the height of its upward convulsion, it was stippled gold and puce with the reflection of the nearest lamps.

I quickened my steps towards the bandstand, trying to prepare myself for the music I had come here to study, but finding that a certain stricture in my pantaloons was rendering a brisk stride decidedly uncomfortable. My thoughts had been diverted to Polly. A dark sprig of foliage reminded me of the little bristle of foliage around that generous orifice of hers. I made an effort to think of music, nothing but music, and of the dispassionate calculation I must bring to this evening's study.

Yet my treacherous footsteps led me towards the Cascade, above which was being stretched a long rope, while fireworks were being mounted in readiness to either side. I pretended to contemplate the preparations for what was evidently going to be a grandiose display later this evening; but in reality I was looking around for Polly.

There was no sign of her. It was a good omen, promising to save me from frivolity. I made my way past graceful pavilions and secluded supper boxes to the elaborate dome with its plume of feathers below which the orchestra was playing.

Just as I reached the colonnade through which one could stroll while listening, a voice of remarkable sweetness added itself to the strains of the woodwind and strings. It was a small voice, and not properly produced, but there was an exquisiteness about it which tugged at the heart. I emerged on to the promenade for a better sight of the singer.

And at once I was in love, consumed by desire, incapable of moving.

The folly of it – falling so abruptly in love with an unknown songstress, on a platform well out of reach, when there was so much uncomplicated diversion so ready to hand in every path and recess of the gardens!

* * *

She was slender but delectably proportioned. Her mauve dress combined a tightly laced bodice and a flounced skirt which rustled a mere two inches above her ankles as she swayed to the cadences of the melody. The high stomacher front of the bodice had a central scoop low enough to reveal, even from the distance at which I stood, a smooth throat, gently vibrating to the syllables of the song, and a graceful neck. As she sang she alternated between the most timid smile and a rounding of the lips into a provocative O. This did not improve her diction, but was most effective in enchanting the audience, which consisted mainly of men.

The theme of the song seemed to be of classical origin, which went well with the chaste timbre of her voice. As I strove to hear each phrase in full, however, I began to feel sure that such a virginal creature must be unaware of the innuendoes in each line. The verses concerned the exploits of Diana, goddess of the chase, but the suggestiveness of the words allowed for a most lecherous interpretation of the pleasures of this hunt: the splendour of the stallion, the stag brought down by Diana's attendant nymphs, the blooding, the capture of an illicit male hunting party on the goddess's sacred territory, and the celebratory mingling of dogs, bitches, hunters and huntresses afterwards. The very chastity of the girl's tone and the innocence in that ethereal face framed in the surround of her velvet, feather-trimmed capote gave a shameful added piquancy to the suggestiveness of what she was uttering. When she had reached the final stanza, depicting Diana riding to death one of the male huntsmen who had been mentioned in the previous line as lying sprawled on his back on the ground, and concluded with a shy little curtsey, there was a burst of violent applause – mainly, I observed, from elderly roués who combined awareness of the implications of her song with deplorable gloating at the tightness of her bodice.

The girl curtsied once more, and disappeared between a row of violinists. Enraptured, I saw from the programme that Miss Laidlaw would be singing again in one hour's time. It seemed an eternity. I could imagine no satisfactory way of filling the interval.

I wandered off, caught up in ecstasies of the imagination. So remote was I in my thoughts that I did not notice a young woman bearing down upon me from one of the avenues until she had taken me goodnaturedly by the arm and shaken me into awareness.

'You are short of a pupil this evening, sir?'

I doubted if there was much I could teach Polly. For a moment I fumbled with excuses for continuing on my way, but she was not really listening, and the musky smell of her armpits began to have a deplorable effect on me. Also, as if that lamentable song had become incongruously amplified the further away I was from the bandstand, its echoes were provoking visions in my head.

I must, in any case, find some way of occupying myself until Miss Laidlaw's next performance. Occupying Polly could be as good a way as any.

We made our way into one of the convoluted walks in which, as has been recorded by a distinguished critic, both sexes were accustomed to meet and mutually serve one another as guides to lose their way, the windings and turnings in the little wilderness being so intricate that the most experienced mothers often lost themselves in looking for their daughters, and perhaps gained even further experiences for themselves.

When we had found a bosky alcove, Polly showed an unexpected taint of prudery. There were so many people moving about in the byways that she refused to disrobe in case we were interrupted, and expressed a preference for a fairly brisk vertical consummation while clad as fully as was practicable. This was not at all to my taste. My limited experience so far had left me with a liking for certain basic amenities, and after feasting my eyes and ears upon the divine Miss Laidlaw my standards had, if anything, risen even higher. Without further argument I led Polly to one of the retiring rooms adjacent to the rotunda, rejecting the offer of an accompanying supper consisting of the much-praised Vauxhall ham in favour of the meat with which I had come provided, and made it my personal task to remove her garments.

The translucent coloured glass in the narrow window cast a deep red light upon us both. Polly's face seemed to be afire. So, I could not fail to notice with some self-satisfaction, was my own prized possession, a scarlet rod fully extended and tipped with the most becoming purple ferrule. Polly's shoulders glowed as she slowly sank to her knees. Thinking she was about to roll backwards in waiting for me, I was on the verge of moving down to join her when her head jabbed suddenly forward and she had engulfed my vivid cock as if to drench and extinguish that fire. I winced; and she laughed, sending a violent tremor along every inch of what she was embracing. Never did woman, surely, have two such hearty sets of lips.

Yet as I throbbed within her I saw in the eerie light the lips of another: the lips of Miss Laidlaw, rounded into that cajoling O. And so I fell back and freed myself, and pulled Polly's other greedy mouth into position to envelop me and give me some of the sensations lauded in that song of Diana. Wildly she rode, her breasts ruddy as in an inferno while they bounced and slapped to and fro; but still I was unchivalrously thinking of that other lovely, unattainable creature.

Unattainable? No, I would not have it so.

When we had finished, Polly gave me several of the most amiable and comradely of kisses before I could reach for my breeches. She asked if we were likely to meet again, with a mild puzzlement in her manner. Already she had sensed that my mind had not been exclusively on her. I made a half-promise, knowing that it was unlikely to be kept. I think that she, too, was aware of this. When I glanced back on my way to the bandstand she was still watching me with a regret which I found both flattering and embarrassing.

One of her more inventively placed kisses continued to sting for a full ten minutes, making it difficult for me to raise my thoughts to a sufficiently exalted plane while waiting for the concert to resume and the incomparable Miss Laidlaw to reappear.

Impatiently I had to endure a selection of waltzes, that rage which has replaced all the stateliness of the minuet and older, slower, graceful measures. The bouncing abandon of it prompted some couples who had already taken liberal potions of sherry wine to dance in the limited space below the bandstand. One man in tight cream breeches and grey jacket, with a tricorne hat tilted perilously to one side of his head, capered in front of a woman writhing and swinging her legs within a transparent skirt which offered tantalising glimpses of some unidentifiable garment beneath, shaped so tightly to her legs and bottom as to be almost an imitation of the man's breeches, though the rear cleft into which the material was moulded was far more appetising than any man's.

Then, at last, there was the angel again. Her head went back, her little bosom strained against the laces of her bodice, and she began to sing.

Chapter 2

In which it is shown that, if music indeed be the food of love, one should seek out the most appetising menu and reject inferior fare

The first item was one of Mr Hook's innumerable ditties. Called 'Sweet lass of Richmond Hill', it was not, I thought, among those likely to survive for the benefit of posterity. In spite of the minor inadequacies in her diction and breath control, Miss Laidlaw suffused the trivial piece with far more grace than it merited. Mentally urging her to treat this passage in more *legato* fashion, that one with an open throat rather than a pinched-in sort of *moue*, I swore to myself that she had caught my eye and that I was communicating mentally with her. I would happily have strangled the elderly goat who fidgeted beside me, waving meaningly at her and distracting her with gestures whose meaning left little in doubt.

At the conclusion of Miss Laidlaw's performance I knew that I must speak without delay. I hastened to the door at the sheltered rear of the rotunda used by singers and instrumentalists, only to find that three elderly men had already puffed their unsavoury way there. One of them eyed me indignantly as I edged closer to the door.

Two ladies came out, moving very quickly. One of them, now shrouded in light brown sarsenet pelisse, had a step as young and graceful as her voice. The other, an older woman hunched into a heavy mantle which made her even fatter than she obviously was by nature, raised one arm as she emerged, as if to defend herself against an expected attack.

One of the old men lurched forward, elbowing me aside, and spluttered: 'Madame, may I say what a great pleasure your daughter's dazzling interpretations gave me this evening, and beg as a further pleasure that the two of you might accompany me to – '

'Filthy old reprobate.' Mrs Laidlaw, for so she must be, turned the defensive arm into an offensive one, and sent the old goat tottering back into the bushes.

Taking his place, I drew myself up to my full height and offered a sweeping bow. 'A well-deserved rebuke, madame. May I, for my own part – '

'Filthy young reprobate.'

She had not had time to position her arm accurately for a subsequent blow, and I was able to move effortlessly into a position between herself and her daughter. The delightful child lowered her gaze and turned her head slightly away so that I could see nothing of her expression within the sheltering brim of her bonnet. But when I turned to address her mother, I was aware of Miss Laidlaw bending forward to size me up.

There was no time to lose. I had to put my case crisply and immediately. 'Mrs Laidlaw – if that is whom I have the honour of addressing – I am myself a musician of some standing, and a man of erect character withal. I would regard it as a privilege to give your daughter such musical advice as she needs to overcome a few minor imperfections.'

The woman glared at me. It seemed inconceivable that such a lumpish creature, with such a seamed, mistrustful face, could have conceived the delicate angel who stood beside us. She came a step closer and stared me even more aggressively in the face. When she spoke her voice was falsely genteel but hoarse from, one suspected, a liberal diet of hollands.

'She has had too many guineas spent upon her already.'

'I was not proposing a fee.'

The glare became even more accusatory. 'Then what is it

you have in mind? What are you hoping for in exchange? My daughter,' whined Mrs Laidlaw through primly clenched teeth, 'is a girl of strict upbringing, and not in the market for any kind of – '

'I have told you of my musical proclivities. I am a man of independent means, devoted to the service of the muse Euterpe, and dedicated to the encouragement and refinement of outstanding talent when I come across it.'

'Refinement.' The woman turned the word over on her tongue, obviously savouring it. 'It is true,' she grudgingly conceded, 'that in spite of my dear girl's undoubted aptitude, there are certain – ah – refinements lacking. Otherwise I would not be making do with the wretched pittances that this place' – hastily she amended this, in an even more throttled and prissy tone – 'would not be allowing her to accept a few engagements simply in order to practise and polish her style before such a frequently uninformed audience.'

The young Miss Laidlaw was by now contemplating me full face, quite frankly and quite delightfully. With disarming simplicity she said:

'My name is Cecilia.'

Before her mother could chide this forwardness, I said: 'But what else? Of course. The patron saint of music!' This seemed to appease Mrs Laidlaw, and in order to allow her no opportunity of raising any other possible objections I hurried on: 'We cannot talk in any civilised fashion in these surroundings. May I suggest that you both call upon me tomorrow at eleven in the forenoon, so that you may see for yourselves the respectability of my quarters and discuss our musical collaboration in detail?'

I handed the older woman my card and, with two elegant bows which I felt went off rather well, I chose this strategic moment to quit their company, feeling tolerably confident that they would appear in Bayswater at the appointed time.

On my way home I wondered idly whether a pagan goddess such as Diana and a Christian saint such as Cecilia had much in common other than a similar symbolic shape; and how long it would take to teach a diffident Cecilia those pastimes at which Diana the huntress had been a legendary success. Shocked at my own waywardness, I thrust such ideas from my mind and appealed to yet another mythic figure – Euterpe, muse of music – to keep my attention upon more uplifting matters. Unfortunately she must have been attending another engagement that day, and offered no solace when I was afflicted in the middle of the night by a most worldly, physical uplift. My desperation was such that I was tempted to call upon the worthy Mrs Hiscock for succour, which she would cheerfully have granted; but puritanically I steeled myself to endure the pain, conjured up the detumescent abstractions of a Bach fugue in my head, and assured the absent yet ever-present Cecilia that she was not the only one to experience martyrdom.

When, in the morning, I informed my housekeeper of the expected visitors, she looked dubious. 'I understood, Mr Roger, that you were accepting no more pupils.'

'This one is exceptionally gifted.'

Mrs Hiscock raised her eyebrows but said nothing. She was, however, on the alert well before eleven o'clock, and when the bell rang she was at the door before I could get halfway down the stairs. She looked thoughtfully at Mrs Laidlaw and then back up at me, and indulged herself momentarily in a frown of disbelief. Only when she saw Cecilia Laidlaw stepping into the vestibule from behind her capacious mother did she discard the frown and sigh very gently in my direction, as if relinquishing something cherished but knowing it to be in a good cause.

I took my visitors upstairs and sat myself close to the piano so that I could lean languidly against it and perhaps play a few passages to demonstrate a technical point or two. It became apparent that, whatever her reservations, Mrs Laidlaw had decided before coming here that my offer of guidance was too good a chance to miss. But she would not let herself be too grateful or compliant.

'I have no doubt my Cecilia will be a credit to you. But of course you are right in agreeing with me that her voice needs more rigorous supervision.'

'Which it shall have.'

'Also, it has to be admitted that her knowledge of musical theory and of notation is weak. She can carry a tune in her head, but when it comes to more advanced work she does not read the score fluently enough.'

'Before she leaves me,' I promised, 'she will be thoroughly familiar with both the theory and practice of the staff.'

'I understood it to be called the stave.'

'Ah, I keep forgetting that I am in the presence of a fellow expert,' I flattered her. 'It is true that some people refer to the stave, but the use of the word "staff" is optional, and I tend to favour it. But whatever we choose to call it, its function is essentially one which must penetrate the perceptions fully before the right sounds can be produced.'

'I shall expect you to work her hard.'

'We shall start gently and feel our way, but as time goes on I give you my word that I shall be hard on her.'

Mrs Laidlaw obviously expected me to begin without delay; and, equally obviously, intended to stay in the room throughout the whole proceedings. This was something I might have anticipated; but I had not given it enough thought to be capable of trotting out an excuse for our being left alone together. For the time being I had to devote myself to running Cecilia through her scales and criticising awkwardnesses of breathing – though it was sinful to criticise, when the very errors themselves produced such delectable frissons of the throat and mouth, and such mesmerically irregular distensions of the mounds beneath her corsage. When I made her sit at the pianoforte and read very carefully a sequence of crotchets, trying to pitch each one correctly, there was such a young, fresh scent in the nape of her flawless neck that I found my own breath control seriously at risk. And when I leaned over her to emphasise the gap of a crotchet rest between two black notes, I found myself staring involuntarily down into a shadowy gap between two white globes whose temptations made me dizzy.

At the end of the lesson Mrs Laidlaw congratulated me on my patience and chided Cecilia for some lapses of attention. I had not myself noticed these, apart from a few occasions on which she had looked at my hands rather than at the notes I was explaining, and moments of puzzlement as if she was not quite sure of the purpose of her being here at all.

I ventured to suggest that for our next assignation Cecilia might come alone, as it was possible that her mother's presence during the lesson distracted her and prevented her giving her whole self to the instruction. Mrs Laidlaw would have none of this, and when they left I had still formulated no practicable plan for separating the maiden from the dragon.

It was dear, dependable Mrs Hiscock who came to my rescue. On the next appointment – which I had insisted should be only three days later, since regular and concentrated practice was essential – she took Mrs Laidlaw under her wing, offering her a tray of tea and some of her own finest seed cake, and hinting that she might show the visitor around the whole ground floor of the house. This was a bait which no woman as inquisitive as Mrs Laidlaw could possibly refuse.

Cecilia and I went upstairs. I closed the door of the music room. There was a new chintz cover on the sofa: I had wished to expunge all last vestiges of the memory of Mrs Drabble and her kind. Sunlight streamed across the room upon the girl, and a ghostly reflection of her swam gently across the polished lid of the pianoforte.

She looked at me trustfully but questioningly, awaiting my instructions.

I said: 'First, let us loosen up your vocal cords with this little aria I have chosen.'

It was a simple little tune by Dr Arne, and should present no difficulties. She did in fact sing it most becomingly, but I now saw the opportunity of improving her delivery and, as it were, modulating to a more exalted level in our relationship.

Going step by step through the phrases of the melody, I made her sing a few notes at a time. Then, to demonstrate where her breathing was faulty, I put my hand on her throat and made her sing three F's from the top line of the staff.

When she had finished she looked at me imploringly.

I nodded, very grave about it. 'Most attractive. The fault is clearly not there. Will you repeat those notes, more slowly?' I slid my hand down to her breasts, easing the constriction of her bodice so that she might breathe more freely. 'Now take a deep breath. . . expel it on the note. . . inspire again.' Ah, truly did she inspire. 'A moment. Try a lower note.' And my hand moved lower.

Her lips were parting, forming that little O on which I doted. 'It must be further down than that. I feel strange.' She inhaled deeply, shudderingly, and got to her feet, swaying against me. 'I cannot explain it, but. . . is it perhaps something down there that I am holding back without realising it?'

She turned towards me and I put my hands on her hips to steady her. My outthrust, though contained within my breeches, could not have failed to make itself known to her. She looked curious rather than startled, and leaned more heavily against me.

'I have not known this before,' she whispered. 'Perhaps this is what has been lacking. I feel, somehow. . . that is, I would not presume to suggest your tutelage has been in any way neglectful so far, but. . . truly, I do have the strangest sensation that. . .'

She was still looking at me imploringly.

I put my hand up to her neck. Today her bodice was not tightly laced, but kept together by the much more negotiable modern hooks and eyes. I freed the mounds of her wondrous whiteness and reassuringly ran my index finger down the warmth of the valley between; and although she continued to stare at me with childlike trust and simplicity, her nipples were hard and upright when I allowed my hand to brush across from one to the other and back again. She allowed me to undress her, still subservient and unquestioning, her only movements being when she lifted an arm to ease the departure of her chemisette, and gently shook her bottom and lifted a leg to assist in the shedding of her last garment.

I was less gentle, more impatient, in my own disrobing.

She watched me attentively, rhythmically stroking the inside of her right thigh. When I advanced on her, eager to steer her towards the sofa, she reached out and tentatively touched my baton. Then she began stroking it, smiling at me in the hope of approval.

It was only gentlemanly to respond in kind. I ran my finger lower than it had yet been, and prised open her pink prize. I found that it could not enter all the way because of an obstruction. By this time I was too ravenous to continue gentle exploration with a mere finger. I thrust her against the edge of the couch, poised my baton, and stabbed into her. Her arms went round me and she whimpered into my ear. Then on the second downbeat I broke through, and she was clinging to me with arms, legs, and her unskilled but already quivering, seeking quim. On the next thrust I aroused not a whimper but a gasp of pleasure. She pulled her head back to gulp in a deep breath, and her mouth twisted from an O to a grimace, and back to an admiring O – a voracious 'Ohh . . . '

She was a willing pupil. Indeed, I confess that as an ensemble player – for in such performances there is little pleasure in being merely a soloist without any accompaniment whatsoever – she was soon teaching me a thing or two. Or three. Subtly she turned the tables, making me gasp with pleasure, and herself calling the tune. She feigned a teasing attempt to disengage, pulling away and softly biting, luring me to thrust more and more desperately in order to pin her down. Her little breasts danced so prettily – music of the spheres, indeed! – and even when I had most desperately impaled her to hold her still there was no way her arse would stop its own languorous dance. And all the while she talked to me silently but volubly down below, nibbling my baton as if to peel it away layer by layer.

Just as I felt I could no longer contain myself and that there was no pinnacle of pleasure still to be reached, she spread her legs more widely, lay quite motionless for a moment, and said demurely: 'You must be tired of just the one view. I have no experience in such things, but do you suppose it would be possible . . . '

Her voice trailed away. Slowly and with infinite care she began to turn over, gripping me ever more tightly so that I might not come out. As she brushed my cheek with her knee and then rested briefly on her right hip, I had a glimpse of the best of both worlds, dazzling my vision, transmitting what I would until this instant have thought an impossibility: an even greedier burning down at the throbbing tip of me. To one side was her sedate, meditative profile and delicately pale left breast; to the other, swinging gently over, came the edge of her shoulder, sparkling with a dewy sweat, and the wide swell of her left haunch. Then, still clutching me possessively, she had rolled dexterously over on to her face and presented me with the swelling shape of a cello made of yielding flesh rather than wood. Oh, the music of the human body! To be plucked, fingered, struck – and, like certain organs, capable of producing a grand swell. When I struck her lightly to produce an answering sound, she began rearing her bottom to encase me more securely. I bent to lick my way down the lovely cleft of her back, and would have been in danger of kissing my own cock had it not been so thoroughly sheathed. Again I touched her buttocks most affectionately. They were mounds of beauty to be fondled, gently scratched, not beaten.

Her voice muffled, she spoke in a reserved little tone like that of a pupil timorously seeking the master's approval.

'Is it as it should be, Mr Rougiere?'

'Your talent goes beyond what I had expected,' I said truthfully.

'I was not sure. It is not something I have practised.'

'If this is improvisation, then you have a rare gift. You accommodate yourself most skilfully to the beat. And I have nothing but praise for your variations.'

Downstairs I heard the sound of a door opening, and Mrs Hiscock's voice warningly raised. I glanced over the swirl of Cecilia's golden hair at the clock on the wall, of whose ticking I had been oblivious until this moment. We had left things dangerously late. Mrs Laidlaw was growing restless. We could continue our leisurely play no longer. As I drove down to end it, Cecilia moaned one gentle protest, then buried her face in the cushion. I pulled her head back.

'Sing!'

'But – '

'Your mother grows fretful. You must let her know you are making progress. Sing a scale. Keep singing!'

She twisted round again on to her back so that the sound would carry. Propped on my elbows above her, I was almost deafened. But the sight of her was the final stimulus I needed. Even if there had been no external necessity to finish quickly, I would not have been able to hold back any longer. I gave myself up – selfishly, I grant, but quite uncontrollably – to the pounding rhythm which ended in ecstatic delivery of what she had so inexorably set seething within me. At the last thrust she had reached the top of a scale in C major, of which the final note was forced out as a shriek, a full major third awry.

We sprang apart and I waved her towards the piano, noticing as I reluctantly quit the neighbourhood of the sofa that the flowered pattern of the chintz had been daubed with blobs and tendrils of red rather darker than the predominating roses.

I played a few arpeggios with my right hand, groping for my shirt with the left. She echoed the notes, dressing hurriedly as she did so, but with neat, precise little movements. As she smoothed the dress over her hips I lamented the disappearance of those hips into such a conventional camouflage. At last we were decorously positioned, pianist and singer – positioned too far apart for my liking, with a full yard between the piano stool and the hem of Cecilia's skirt, within which were shrouded those pliant legs which I was now convinced could fulfil their proper function only when I was between them. I hurriedly turned the pages to a simple little piece which would not tax my depleted energies, and indicated to Cecilia after the brief introduction that she should burst into song.

The sound of her voice came as a revelation. Charming as it had been before, it had never sounded even remotely as rich as this. There was a new resonance to it, a certainty, a rising grandeur and a quality of tone throbbing from the throat which filled the room with music: not with a mere sequence of predictable notes, a conscientiously practised melody, but the sheer essence of music itself.

Cecilia was just as aware of it as I was. When we reached the last bar she stared at me with an intensity bordering on the ferocious. Then, in her normal well-modulated speaking voice, though still with that husky overtone, she said: 'It is clear, is it not, what treatment I shall require immediately before every concert appearance?'

We went downstairs, where Mrs Laidlaw, having just been coaxed back by my artful Mrs Hiscock to sample a newly opened bottle of gin, greeted me with a sharply suspicious challenge. 'There was a great deal of silence today, Mr Rougiere.'

'We were concentrating on the staff,' I assured her.

Cecilia nodded bland confirmation.

Now her mother produced a more friendly smile than she had offered hitherto. Clearly she had been impressed by the quality of what she had heard in the belated cadenzas.

'My daughter has talent, yes? I'm sure she is performing better already.'

'Your daughter,' I said fervently, 'is a most accomplished performer.'

'But she must persevere.'

'Indeed she must. I am most excited' – it could not have been a more honest declaration – 'by the prospect of what she will be able to achieve, in my hands, in the future.'

After the two had left, Mrs Hiscock made her way upstairs and returned a few moments later, tut-tutting indulgently, with the chintz sofa cover and a cushion cover over her arm.

'Your first virgin!' she breathed sentimentally, and gave me a wistful peck on the cheek as she passed.

Chapter 3

In which it is demonstrated that artistic talent comes to the boil only when the fire below is adequately maintained by the sweat of the stoker

Demand for Cecilia's performances at Vauxhall intensified. I speak, of course, of her public musical performances, and not of the private preliminaries. Increasing numbers of elderly gentlemen braved the night air in order to warm their blood with impossible daydreams – or evening fantasies. At the same time, contributors of critical columns to the newspapers began to pay serious attention to her purely musical abilities, and there were even suggestions that she might soon expect approaches from the strutting impresarios of Covent Garden and the Royal Italian Opera House.

As her tutor I now invariably accompanied her to ensure that she was in good voice, though at first this presented some difficulties. Mrs Laidlaw still insisted on chaperoning her daughter up to the very steps of the concert platform and away from it, making it difficult for me to poke the waiting embers into flame beforehand.

I endeavoured to insist on the necessity of a brief rehearsal in my Bayswater dwelling before we set off each evening; but to gull Mrs Laidlaw this necessitated her sitting downstairs and hearing Cecilia singing the whole time I performed, and she was quick to ask why I was not performing as accompanist on the pianoforte while her daughter warbled. Another time I made an impromtu excuse for the orchestra leader to add an extra instrumental piece before Cecilia's appearance. We secluded ourselves in the band-room below the stage and, for lack of any other comforts, managed a brief performance in quick two-four time against a violoncello case propped at a forty-five-degree angle against the wall, Cecilia bracing herself by wrapping her legs round the back of the case.

Such shifts were far from satisfactory. I was compelled to suggest that, reluctant as I was to miss my own refreshing dips before a recital, we should accept the fact that it would not always be possible to indulge in our ritual. But Cecilia was quietly adamant about her required dosage, and was unwilling to forgo it. 'My voice needs warming up.'

'You keep your voice in a strange place.'

She was in no mood for flippancy, no matter how affectionate it might be. 'The warmth,' she said bashfully, 'percolates from below. It is a strange phenomenon which I do not pretend to understand.'

Neither did I. But I was not inclined to seek medical justification for something so manifestly agreeable to both of us. It was simply a matter of organising things in such a fashion that we could perform our preludes without unwelcome interruption.

'Roger,' she would whisper urgently, about ten minutes before the performance was due to start. 'It is time for the roger now, I think.' And while she was making this demand, the members of the orchestra would be tuning up, and a few yards away her mother would be poised like a ferocious guardian angel. My failure to respond was due not to reluctance but to bleak necessity.

Ideally we should have been provided with a silken couch and as much time as was necessary to establish our right key, tempo, and mood. A fire should be coaxed, not stormed at with bellows. Ah, the pleasures of leisure. . .! Time to inhale the scents of a beloved body, to lick and bite and stroke and cajole, to play the sweetest and most natural of all human games: impatience controlled, laughing together, a hand here and a hand there, leisurely tongue exploring moist mouth, slow-burning cock in cunt. . .

The problem was unexpectedly solved by the emergence of another problem.

The nightly congestion of carriages at the Kennington Lane gate was becoming such that delays in entering the grounds lengthened, tempers frayed, and there was many an ugly scene, followed by many an angry letter to *The Times* newspaper demanding that steps be taken to cope with London's traffic problems before the entire metropolis ground to a halt. On one occasion the carriage bearing Cecilia, her mother and myself was so caught up in the confusion that we did not reach the bandstand until half an hour after my angel's first perfomance of the evening had been listed in the programme. This did not at all please the management, and they were even less pleased when her singing during the second set proved shaky and quite lacking in her usual brilliance. The deficiency might be sympathetically attributed to the fluster of her belated arrival, but Cecilia and I were aware that a much more significant factor was the lack of the essential pre-performance inspiration: inspiration meaning, of course, to draw in.

It was suggested that we would do better to arrive by boat across the river. In spite of congestion at the piers, it was easier to weave a way through the various craft or to hail one and politely ask passage for a performer and her escort. And even if there were some difficulties, we discovered one major advantage in this approach. Mrs Laidlaw was prone to seasickness. Even the slightest rocking motion of a small craft on the Thames, especially when the wavelets became somewhat turbulent because of the threshing of competing oars, brought on a queasiness and a green pallor which reduced her to utter prostration within a matter of moments.

So once again I found myself approaching the pleasure gardens by means of the Thames. I felt a fleeting twinge of sadness as I recalled the trip I had made in honour of my father's memory and to be pleasured by the lass in whose arms he had expired. Thankfully, present anticipation soon swept away such past contemplation. Also I was travelling not on a crowded public barge, but in conditions of delightful intimacy. It had been easy to hire a small craft with a small shelter at the back, not so much a cabin as a low wooden canopy with a light curtain which could be drawn to minimise the onset of any unexpected shower or the spray from an inexpert sculler.

Our first venture in this fashion was thoroughly rewarding. Cecilia looked as demure as ever as she stepped gracefully into the boat and arranged herself on the sheltered seat. She was chastely dressed this evening as a shepherdess, already assuming the innocent smile which would go with her tuneful rural idylls. When she lowered her eyes it could to some extent have been the genuinely modest subservience of a performer awaiting the conductor's decision and the descent of his baton. At the same time it drew my attention to the fact that her petticoats had been so adjusted that none of their flounces would impede my direct entry to that shadowy cavern whose echoes would soon resound so blissfully from other openings. A chill breeze under the flapping curtain chilled my cods as I freed them from my breeches, hastening my desire to plunge my shaft into palpitating warmth before it, too, was cooled down. Cradled in the swaying motion of our vessel, I started with a gentle but rhythmic *adagio*, and as her breath quickened so I built up to a dancing *allegretto*.

It was now I discovered that not merely could my pupil hold the firmest, unfaltering high notes, but was also capable of holding in an unyielding grip this lower part of my anatomy. At the height of enjoyment, when I calculated that there was just one minute left before we reached the southern bank and it was time to bid *au revoir* to the mound of Venus by pouring my thanks into her, our boat grazed another and rocked violently. I was thrown to one side, in danger of being wrenched from that moist socket and squandering my seed on the rough planks of the boat. Her immediate intuitive reaction converted her soft inner nibbling into a grip of iron. She clenched on to the very tip of me and then seemed to inhale until she could draw me fully back in and clamp even more securely on to me. Even when we were only a few yards from the pier she could not or would not let me go, murmuring 'No, not yet' and at the same time squeezing even tighter. I fought to free myself as the babble of Vauxhall soared out above us, but only when she could feel my final *presto* throbbing and the gush I was aching to donate to her did she release me with a gentle moan and a last little convulsive bite.

She sang quite magnificently that evening, and was back in full favour with both management and patrons.

Word was indeed beginning to puff around the town. Offers were made. We accepted an engagement at the very reputable Hanover Square Concert Rooms, but turned down an invitation from a proposed rival to Vauxhall on the Chelsea bank. I watched carefully over the development of Cecilia's repertoire; and took pride in listening to the rapturous applause which greeted many of the pieces in which I personally had schooled her.

Apart from Mrs Laidlaw's intrusive presence there was only one thing to mar my enjoyment of life at this time. I had allowed myself to neglect my own career in order to foster Cecilia's, and although my pianoforte accompaniments to many of her recitals drew a certain amount of approval, I was receiving few invitations for individual performances. Conducting or accompanying her at the keyboard, on which she loyally insisted when many others would have been glad to usurp my position, I was often so exhausted by the task of fucking her up to concert pitch in hurried and inconvenient circumstances that I did not always turn in my own most energetic performance on the platform. Even if I had contemplated a partial return to private teaching in order to provide a creative contrast, it would have proved equally unsatisfactory, for much the same reason: Cecilia's demands made it impossible for me to satisfy those of others, and in any case the sweetness of Cecilia was such as to rob me of all taste for the sourness of middle-aged wantons.

In order not to strain her voice too much, Cecilia now gave in to her mother's injunction to limit her appearances at Vauxhall. I could hardly quarrel with this, since I was most anxious to do everything in the beautiful girl's best interests, though I regretted the longer intermissions between one waterborne shafting and another. I did however find, loth as I would have been to admit this to her, that these intervals allowed me a chance to improve my own status in the musical hurly-burly of Vauxhall. In an emergency I took over from a conductor who had fallen ill of what was called a muscular convulsion from having played too much music over too short a period, though his friends rumoured that it was more probably due to indulgence in a cheap distillation of gin from a Southwark back-street. I carried off the task with some style, was congratulated by the new intendant of the gardens and by Old Simpson, the awe-inspiring Master of Ceremonies for as long as anyone could remember. As a result I was asked what my fee would be to accompany a young Italian woman who had been engaged to sing the following night but had quarrelled with her pianist.

We came to a satisfactory arrangement, and during the following afternoon I ran through a few pieces with the young singer. She was dark of eye, feature, and voice, and very large indeed, with arms which in a dramatic scene could have embraced at least two tenors and a baritone. She spoke little English, and my only Italian consisted of musical markings and lines from a few of the better-known operatic arias and religious compositions. Nevertheless we reached cordial musical agreement on most points, and the recital went off with great aplomb, the sheer volume of her voice earning three rapturous encores, and the size of her breasts providing the elderly claque with much to think about, if they survived the homeward journey.

The next morning I was beset by a tight-lipped Cecilia, coming on impulse unchaperoned to my house, her sweet face unusually bitter and her voice more rasping than I would have thought possible.

The previous evening she had persuaded her mother to accompany her to the concert, just to experience what it was like to be in the audience as opposed to being on the platform. Also she had hoped to look fondly on me from a distance, and have at least a few hurried words with me and to make some assignation to rehearse a few new pieces and any new movements which might spontaneously occur to us. At the end, however, she had left in a rage. The Italian creature, she now assured me bitterly, could not conceivably have sung so well without having received the same treatment as I so assiduously lavished upon Cecilia herself.

I denied it.

Cecilia refused to believe me.

I went down on my knees and swore on all I held sacred that I had not laid a finger or any other part of my anatomy upon the Italian girl before the concert. As to what it was that I held most sacred, I demonstrated by unfastening Cecilia's laces and kissing her nipples most reverently until they hardened to a proud royal purple, while her heart softened and she accepted my word.

I had in fact been telling the truth. I had not touched the young diva before the concert. It was only afterwards that, in the oppressive heat of the evening when I was using the little combination of dressing-room and storeroom below the platform to change my shirt, the lady's flesh and mine had made contact. She made no pretence of trying to converse in English or in any other language needing words. Putting her meaty hands on my naked shoulders, she said something in Italian which I took to be complimentary and bodily heaved me back on to an ornamental iron table in the middle of the room. When she climbed upon me and freed her breasts to bounce them teasingly across my nose, I thought briefly that this display would have decimated our audience earlier this evening. Then I was allowed little further time to think. It was with difficulty that I managed even to breathe. Fortunately she was content to expend her own energy rather than mine, and when she had finished she bestowed an emotional, almost maternal shower of kisses on my brow, belly and balls (access to which had been simplified by the shrinkage of my drained cock), before thumping her feet back to the floor and waving me an amiable goodbye.

The following afternoon, with peace restored between

us, Cecilia and I set about rehearsing a number of new pieces which we intended to introduce at Vauxhall at the weekend, including two of my own settings of poems by William Shakespeare. I would have liked to try my hand at musical interpretations of some of Lord Byron's scandalous poems which were being secretly circulated throughout the town, but I had a feeling that he would require some share in the profits, and was not minded to suffer such deprivations. Cecilia took the rehearsals very seriously, though not seriously enough to accept my suggestion that while her mother refreshed herself with a pot of tea in Mrs Hiscock's company downstairs, we should refresh ourselves and her voice in proven fashion. That, she solemnly declared, should be saved for the night of the actual performance, when it would be much more efficacious. I was about to argue when I realised that even if she complied I would have to concentrate on maintaining a somewhat limited posture, since the decorative ironwork of that table to which I had been pressed was still etched into my back and would take many hours to fade.

In the middle of a particularly fine passage on whose beauty I could not but congratulate myself there came a tap on the door. I was extremely irritated by the coarseness of anyone who could interrupt such spellbinding music, and when Mrs Hiscock announced that a lady from Newcastle upon Tyne was downstairs wishing to speak to me, I suggested that she should forthwith start upon her journey back North.

'But she wishes to consult you on a matter of great musical interest.'

'You may tell her that I no longer take pupils.'

'I got the impression, Mr Roger, that she is a lady of some wealth. She was talking of making you an interesting offer.'

Cecilia drew herself up. 'How old is this creature?'

'A lady of some forty-five summers, I would estimate.'

Cecilia looked at me. 'Then you may see her for ten minutes. I shall occupy myself with breathing exercises.'

Knowing the beauty of her rise and fall in such exercises, I was reluctant to exchange her company for that of the plump and somewhat horse-faced woman who was awaiting me in the small drawing-room downstairs. She was by no means ugly, but there was a leatheriness about her skin which suggested any youthful charms she might have once possessed must have been subjected to a scouring wind while out riding to hounds or simply facing seawards during a hurricane. She wore a sarsenet pelisse with sleeves puffed out at the shoulders, and a huge poke bonnet like a coal scuttle, which must surely have made it as difficult for her as for a blinkered horse to see from side to side. Her accent was a strange sing-song, interlarded with what she supposed to be the fashionable drawl of the London salons.

'Mrs Armstrong,' she introduced herself. 'Mrs Wallace Armstrong of the county of Northumberland. And you are Mr Rougiere? The Mr Roger Rougiere who gave my friend Mrs Batchelor such inspiring lessons upon the pianoforte?'

The name of Mrs Batchelor at first meant nothing to me, but in any case I was not going to be inveigled ever again into giving lessons of any kind to ladies of this age and solidity. I said as civilly as possible: 'I fear that I am having to concentrate my energies nowadays on performance rather than teaching.'

'Oh, Mrs Batchelor – Mrs Robson, as she is now – cannot speak too highly of your performing talents.'

Was there a twinkle in those not altogether unattractive brown eyes?

'I regret to say that I do not recall this lady of whom you speak.'

'Oh, faugh! She would be so hurt to hear that you have forgotten her. She assured me that a mere twelvemonth ago you were rapturous in your praise for her fingering of trills upon the accidentals. You also commended her ability to transform a flat instrument into vitality by a natural ascent.'

Now I remembered. Mrs Batchelor had been a vigorous widow with surplus fat which had a tendency to quake rather than trill. My mind strayed instinctively back upstairs to the couch which I had had re-covered in Cecilia's honour. It was there that much of the widow's weekly practice had reached its final cadence, and there that I had achieved more than one natural ascent, not to mention some descents and sidelong modulations, according to the directions specified or implied by my pupil.

'Yes,' I admitted, 'I do recall the lady and her gifts. But I have not seen her in recent times.'

'She remarried,' said Mrs Armstrong, 'and is living in one of our more desirable suburbs. We are both members of the committee of the Philharmonic Fellowship of Newcastle upon Tyne. It is on her instigation that I have come to invite you to appear during our festival this coming June. We would arrange for you to be conveyed there in great comfort, and we are prepared to consider an appropriate fee for a certain number of performances.'

I turned this over in my mind. I had no wish for Cecilia and myself to lose ourselves in the grim northern provinces, but I did recall having read fine things about the lively musical climate created in Newcastle by the gifted Dr Avison. The fact that he so steadfastly refused offers to settle in London suggested that the town was not altogether inhabited by barbarians. At this stage in Cecilia's career perhaps a brief spell before a quite different, less cosmopolitan audience might have a beneficial influence on her. At least it would provide interesting contrasts.

I said: 'Obviously you have heard of our successes at Vauxhall. I shall have to consult my partner and –'

'We did not envisage you as an accompanist or duettist,' said Mrs Armstrong flatly, 'but as a soloist.'

Here, it seemed, was an answer to my recent worries about neglect of my own career. Somebody had a perception refined enough to wish to engage me on my own merits. It might be that a *succès d'estime* so many miles from London would count for little to the arbiters of metropolitan taste, but equally it might be a step up the ladder. After all, they had not scorned Dr Avison. Yet in the end it was a move I could not bring myself to make. Anxious as I was to further my own career as well as Cecilia's, I felt a deep-seated reluctance to be parted from her at this stage. I could not put words to my apprehensions; or perhaps I did not wish to. I knew only that I could not contemplate leaving her, even for a week, to the perils of London and those who might wish to usurp my place in her life – of which I suspected there were many.

All too soon I had alarming verification of this.

Chapter 4

How an old roué and a young buck in turn threaten a man's peace with his favourite piece

Mrs Laidlaw, not satisfied with her role as attendant dragon, suddenly took it upon herself to turn matchmaker. I fancy she was growing resentful of the fact that, in spite of her unrelenting presence in her daughter's life, her influence on that life was increasingly absent. Mrs Laidlaw was one of those women who have to be in charge at all times. Being a bystander was not good enough. Instead of gratitude for my part in advancing that very musical career on which she herself had staked so much, she felt an increasing dislike for what I had achieved. Rather than let Cecilia slip through her fingers into the hands of another, she would bring that promising career to an end.

Without a word of warning she yielded to blandishments which she had hitherto scorned. Many a prosperously attired old man had from time to time approached her with suggestions of taking Cecilia under his personal protection and, as a matter of course, making suitably generous provision for Mrs Laidlaw. Each and every one had been robustly rebuffed. Now she proposed to hand over her daughter to a rich Shropshire landowner who had attended our recitals whenever he was in town. I remembered him being carried to the front of the audience in a sedan chair which was then lifted high on his attendants' shoulders so that he might be as close as was practical to Cecilia's ankles.

There had, I also recalled, once been an undignified scuffle when a rival lecher of similar age complained about his viewpoint being obstructed, and the two men's attendants set about belabouring one another with cudgels. Now this pampered lump of lard, by name Osbert Merivale, had won Mrs Laidlaw's consent to the acquisition of Cecilia's ankles and every other part of her.

'You're a very lucky girl,' pronounced Mrs Laidlaw. 'I don't know what you've done to deserve it.'

Truly she did not deserve what was planned. It did not bear thinking of.

On the evening when the grotesque Merivale was to call upon the Laidlaws and go through the charade of making his formal proposal, I stamped up and down my music room, then went out and strode purposelessly through the Bayswater and Notting Hill streets. I had told myself that a walk in the open air would clear my head and enable me to come up with a scheme to thwart old Merivale's obscene designs. But by the end of that terrible evening I had thought of nothing.

Of course Cecilia refused his hand, as she had told me she would. But Merivale and her mother treated this as an irrelevance. She would do as her mother commanded. Such was the way of the world. Merivale promised to keep her in style, provide every comfort on his country estate for that mother also, and buy a pianoforte so that Cecilia could continue her music – purely as a hobby, it was understood.

What should we do? I should offer to marry her myself? Without an opportunity of consulting Cecilia on the matter, I put this to Mrs Laidlaw, who brushed it scornfully aside. Once I had been tolerably well-to-do in her eyes and by her standards, and perhaps if I had proposed marriage earlier she might grudgingly have acceded. But by comparison with Merivale I was virtually a pauper. She was not going to give up guaranteed luxury in the countryside merely in order to be pushed out of her daughter's life by the likes of me.

All our engagements had to be cancelled. Miss Laidlaw was spoken for, and would not appear in public again. Mr

Merivale had no wish for her to be exposed to the gloatings and droolings of anyone but himself.

Mrs and Miss Laidlaw went into the countryside for a week in order that they might be familiarised with the surroundings into which they would soon settle. I was left in London, bereft. Not for the first time I made vows to concentrate on a solo career. I began tentatively seeking engagements, and had renewed some useful acquaintanceships when Cecilia returned to town: alone, without her mother.

She was jubilant. There had been a splendid turn of events.

On their second night in the grandiose but damp mansion on a drizzling Shropshire hillside, Mrs Laidlaw had been woken by the sound of feet shuffling along the corridor outside her door. As one born and bred in London, she had an innate suspicion of anything in the rural wildernesses which might make noises in the night; or, even worse, go about its evil purposes without any sound whatsoever. Warily opening her door, she espied Mr Osbert Merivale in nightshirt, tasselled skullcap, silk dressing gown and Turkish slippers heading along the corridor for her daughter's bedroom door.

'She was furious,' Cecilia told me, with a note in her voice almost expressing admiration for that deplorable harridan. 'She was much concerned with my reputation.'

Her reputation . . . in the wilds of a country where Mr Merivale's writ surely ran more persuasively than that of any austere critic?

'It was clear to my mother,' Cecilia continued, 'that Mr Merivale wished to anticipate our wedding night. This provoked in her a mighty rage. In defence of my honour she snatched an old hunting-crop from the wall of the corridor – a family heirloom, I believe – and set upon Mr Merivale. "You shall have my dear one's maidenhead," she cried, "when you have concluded the rightful contract."'

Cecilia delivered this with such a demurely straight face that I truly do not believe she saw any irony in it. Whatever his purchase, Mr Merivale would surely not have found that highly valued part of it intact.

The thought of the wild assault was a tableau on which one could have dwelt pleasurably for many a rewarding hour. But I could not see why this had brought Cecilia so hastily back to London. Surely, after her tantrums were over, Mrs Laidlaw would not have abandoned every plan to ensure her daughter's prosperity and her own?

Cecilia continued radiantly with her story. It was not surprising that Mr Merivale, so lightly clad in but a nightshirt and dressing gown, should have let out a howl when the first blow fell upon his shoulders. What was surprising, however, was his plea after that first instinctive yelp.

'A moment,' he begged. 'I implore you, madam, wait until I have removed my apparel.'

When his gown and nightshirt had been tossed aside, he bent most humbly and presented her with his shrivelled back so that she might chastise him; and now when he howled it was with dribbling ecstasy. Cecilia watched through a chink between the edge of the door and the door jamb, and then decorously closed the door and went back to bed.

Next day the older two disappeared, returning late for dinner looking flushed and exhausted.

In short, Merivale had decided that he would prefer the older woman who so understood his tastes. No young filly could understand just how hard to lay on, or how to hold him firmly down when he pretended to protest. Without more ado Mrs Laidlaw accepted the revised marriage terms, and lost no time in dismissing her daughter from the premises. She would run no risk of the old goat changing his mind: the presence of such youthful flesh on the estate might be too much of a temptation to him if he wearied of the mother's charms.

So Cecilia was back in London, discarded by her parent, and wondering where she might most suitably lodge.

Very decorously, but with a twinkle in her eye, Mrs Hudson suggested converting what had been my late mother's boudoir and anteroom into a small apartment for my protégée. This was of course close to my parents' bedroom, which I had taken over upon my father's death, and it seemed to me that the situation might well be regularised now that Mrs Laidlaw showed no further interest in her daughter's future. When arrangements had been made and Cecilia was duly installed in her new quarters, I asked Mrs Hiscock to provide an especially elaborate tray of tea and cakes, and then went down on my right knee before Cecilia.

She looked puzzled and startled. Perhaps the flabby Merivale had attempted just such gallantry when asking for her hand, and had toppled over or done himself some other mischief before her very eyes.

I said: 'Dearest Cecilia, I ask you to do me the honour of marrying me.'

Now she looked not so much startled as distressed. 'Oh, no.'

'No?'

'I think it is too soon.'

In view of what had passed between us I found this a strange reaction. 'On the contrary,' I ventured. 'I would say that all the omens are favourable and that this is the time to set you above any possible reproach in society.'

'I feel I am still too young for marriage,' she said most earnestly. 'It is such a momentous step. I must learn much more before I can hope to make a man a satisfactory wife.'

I found this even more amazing. Trying to banish mental pictures of her on her back, on her front, on her side, head back or head down, I speculated that she might be referring to some neglect on her mother's part of domestic training, so that she knew neither how to fold sheets, embroider samplers, or make jams. I hastened to assure her that I would be only too happy to engage another member of staff to supplement Mrs Hiscock's talents and remove any drudgery from such young shoulders. Still she was not to be swayed. She was happy to be in my house; but was not yet prepared to be my wife.

How many men would have envied me! How many would have marvelled at my good fortune! Her exquisite body was here in my home, without any legal ties to besmirch our relationship. I resolved to drop further argument and to make the most of what was being offered.

The night of her installation in the rooms adjoining mine, I waited until movements had ceased and I could assume she was in bed. Shedding my garments, I walked through the connecting door, erect with anticipation.

She sat up in bed, her hair most becomingly loosened, and smiled. But when I tried to pull back the sheet and join her, she thrust me gently away.

'There is no concert tonight.'

'We shall make a fine duet.'

'No,' she said, still with the most affectionate smile. 'It is best, I think, to save such energies for evenings when they are needed to ensure the quality of the music.'

'A brief practice now will not harm our later exercises.'

'I am sure it is best to sleep now,' she said, and turned over with her back to me.

She was not to be moved. I could not fathom what had prompted her to adopt this puritanical attitude, but adopt it she did. My attentions were to be restricted to furtherance of her career. No music in the offing; then no fuck.

And for a while there was indeed no music in the offing. In the hiatus of her mother's marital negotiations and then renegotiations with Osbert Merivale, engagements had, as I have mentioned, been cancelled. No others had been sought on her behalf. Now it was time to start seeking again.

Not only did I need a resumption of musical activities. I desperately needed a resumption of activities with Cecilia. So I went out seeking engagements, and for a start was introduced by an old colleague to the secretary of a gentlemen's club, asking for a performance one Saturday evening. This was mildly surprising. My fleeting knowledge of such establishments as White's and Watier's was that women were not admitted and that the aristocrats and trumped-up dandies of the town spent all night gambling rather than listening to music. But I was in no mood for argument, and accepted. I was told they wanted certain songs which in fact Cecilia had not sung recently – those with salacious undertones and a coarse imagery which she might not comprehend but which her audience certainly would.

Before we set out I prepared to go to her quarters. This time she must accept the preamble to the programme.

Again I shed my clothes, and again was erect with an offer which I was sure would not be denied this time. After such a long interval she would surely want to have her voice tuned to its finest pitch.

I found Cecilia in the large oval tub which had been established in the space at the end of our shared corridor, behind a screen festooned with fragments of coloured pictures and costume design. Mrs Hiscock had just finished filling the bath from a huge, steaming metal can. Cecilia was poised above it, putting one foot in to test the temperature and then stooping to steady herself against the far side of the tub. I ran a glissando with my forefinger down her back from top to bottom.

Mrs Hiscock said: 'Would you like some more cold water, miss?'

'Thank you, no.'

'I think Mr Roger needs some cold water.'

'Thank you, no,' I also said.

Mrs Hiscock looked reminiscently down at me as I passed her. 'I swear it does look as if you need cold water,' she chuckled. Then she went out and closed the door.

Cecilia was chuckling, too. '*Mister* Roger,' she echoed. And then: 'So must I be polite and say it is time for the *Mister* roger?'

I refused to allow her to straighten up, but bent over and moulded myself to the flawless arch of her back. We wrestled joyfully for a moment, then her foot slipped and we collapsed into the bath, splashing water halfway across the floor. There were some preliminary difficulties in the round tub. Cecilia tried pressing herself against the contour of the vessel just as I had pressed myself to the contour of her back. But that made it awkward for me to find a similar shaping which would enable my aching sword to find its sheath. Then Cecilia slipped again, jarring me to one side, whereupon my sword broke the surface of the water like a thrusting Excalibur. The clumsiness of her movement was converted into a graceful lifting of the leg, so that I found my goal as surely as any salmon leaping up a weir.

We had such a long abstinence to make up for, and even after finishing and drying her with great tenderness I found I was capable of one renewed thrust which I liked to think would, by reason of its placing, improve the quality of her bottom notes.

The Cyprian Club was situated in a new terrace which a certain Mr Nash had been devising north of St James's Park. The ceiling was graced with a huge, sprawling painting of Aphrodite. By craning one's neck from different angles of the large room it was possible to see that her attendants, swimming around her, were taking instruction from the goddess in many complex ways. The men below were playing card games, smoking, and drinking, just as one would have expected. But the place was by no means devoid of women. Several in various degrees of déshabille were perched on men's knees and giggling as they chose cards, spilling drink over their bosoms, and at intervals were led away into other rooms which must have been numerous to cope with such constant traffic. A man would lean back in his chair, perilously close to collapsing backwards over it, indicate some twining of two-dimensional bodies on the ceiling, and mutter to his girl. The girl might shake her head in alarm, not fancying such an experience in three dimensions; but after a few more drinks most of them were prepared to attempt the contortions required, and were hurried off to consummate the deal.

As Cecilia began to sing those saucier little items from her repertoire, many of the men began to caress the women on their knees even more assiduously, and to pluck at such clothes as they still retained. Some older members of the audience grew very red in the face and, inexcusably, left in the middle of a song, dragging their wenches with them.

Viewing the scene with little enthusiasm from the pianoforte, I observed one young man of dissolute mien but finely etched features sitting alone, seemingly disconsolate.

Looking round with distaste, he appeared to have become disillusioned by the club, and perhaps to be wondering why he had bothered to join it. There was a raffishness about the whole place and its members which I found distasteful myself.

Then the secretary who had engaged us came between me and my partner just as she was concluding a song. As applause and coarse bellows came from the audience, his arm stole around Cecilia's waist, and I could see that he was murmuring in her ear. With his free hand he indicated a private door to the corner of the small dais on which we had been giving our recital. I had little doubt but that he was suggesting she should come and give a private recital in a room he had already set aside for the purpose. I rose from my piano stool and declared that it was high time for me to take Miss Laidlaw home.

There was a growl of discontent from the audience. When I tried to denounce the secretary, his cronies made it clear that they had no sympathy for my attitude. What the devil did we suppose she had been brought here for? Two brawny louts climbed on to the dais and pushed me aside as an irritating nobody – a mere underling.

All at once the rakish young man was in the middle of the scene. He put one hand on the secretary's shoulder and pushed him off the edge of the stage. One curl of his lip and the two louts somehow disappeared in a flurry of obsequious bows. The young man bowed also – most elegantly, at the same time raising Cecilia's right hand to his lips.

He introduced himself as Lord Alderley. Then, turning towards the disgruntled audience, he said in a rather high-pitched yet languid voice: 'I can only say that I regret having ever joined this rabble's club. My only reason was that, as you well know, it was my father who founded it. He would not have been happy to see the depths to which its membership has fallen. As his son, I apologise to this delightful young lady for the insults to which she has been subjected, and will now escort her home.'

There was the beginning of another threatening growl,

but he faced them all down and offered Cecilia his arm.

'If the steward will now have my carriage brought to the door. . .'

As we stepped out into the street, I thanked Lord Alderley and assured him that I could safely take care of Miss Laidlaw from now on. He insisted, however, that he should fulfil his promise to take her home; and, grudgingly, had to include me in this offer. The three of us made rather a tight fit in his curricle. In spite of his air of suave superiority, he looked momentarily taken aback when he realised that we lived in the same house. Then he tried to gloss over this. 'It had not occurred to me that you were brother and sister.'

'We are not, my lord.' I explained that Cecilia was virtually an orphan and had been taken into the care of myself and my housekeeper, though why I should feel it incumbent on me to explain anything to this young coxcomb I really did not know.

As he drove away, Cecilia looked after him for a long time with an admiring expression, until I hurried her indoors.

I made careful enquiries before accepting the next offer which came our way. It was for a costume ball at the Argyle Rooms in Regent's Street, likely to be a colourful and boisterous function but a reasonably respectable one.

There was to be dancing, for which I provided a small string orchestra. The premises already boasted one of Mr Broadwood's fortepianos, and on this I accompanied Cecilia during the intervals when dishes of meats and glasses of wine were brought to the tables under the balcony, and she was called upon to sing.

Halfway through the evening I began to feel lamentable stirrings as I looked down on women revolving slowly beneath the minstrels' gallery. During their gyrations I caught tantalising glimpses of exposed shoulders, and from that eminence my gaze could plunge into the clefts between some of the most delightful breasts I had ever seen in such quantity and quality. Even here, though in appearance so unlike the riffraff of the Cyprian Club, men and women occasionally moved away into far alcoves, or climbed the steps to the comparative seclusion of the balcony. That is one of the powers and at the same time one of the problems of being a musician: one can subtly inflame the passions of men and women moving to the beat of one's music, but never reap the reward of such stimulus oneself. Recovered from my pre-performance servicing of Cecilia, I was filling with an appetite which there seemed little chance of assuaging.

An exposed throat of the silkiest whiteness repeatedly drew my attention back to one of the shapeliest ladies. I felt a pang of disgust – blended with deplorable envy – when I saw a furtive, twitching gentleman luring her up to the balcony, only a few yards from my position in the minstrels' gallery. I could not see directly through the open French windows, but one of the long wall mirrors offered a partial view of what was going on outside.

The man, I took some satisfaction in observing, was poor at what he was attempting. He had pushed the comely creature's clothes up above her head and was trying to fumble his way through a succession of ruffles, without success. From the impatient movements of her arms I deduced that she was dissatisfied with these bunglings. Then the jerking of one arm became more and more agitated. The dress above her head had become caught up in the ironwork of a torch link projecting over the balcony. The man, all desire gone and chivalry non-existent, was clearly possessed by panic. He dashed back to the ballroom floor to rejoin a dumpy woman who was all too plainly – plain indeed – his wife.

In the mirror I could watch the lady struggling; and it soon occurred to me that there was a danger of her struggles bringing the fabric of her attire close to the torch flame.

The orchestra was at this moment playing a stately gavotte. The keyboard continuo was conventional and would not be missed. I slipped from the gallery and made my way along the balcony. Standing behind the lady, I gallantly assured her in an undertone that I was about to free her and that no one would ever know of her embarrassment.

'I am not ready to be freed.' Her voice was muffled by the silks and muslins in which she was enmeshed, but it was clear and commanding enough. 'Not until I am satisfied.'

'Madam, if you are not soon released – '

'The release I need is more than the unhooking of a fragment of dress. What tool can you provide, sir? What calibre of weapon?'

It was necessarily brief, but it met the needs of both of us. When I had withdrawn and was carefully rearranging her clothing for her, I was about to look into her face and see whether it was really a worthy match for the smooth-skinned buttocks between which I had been so hospitably clasped, when I heard a faint whimper close at hand.

Cecilia stared at me for a long, savage moment, and then turned and went away.

I had a terrible feeling that she was planning revenge, though I did not see that she had too much to complain about. Later I endeavoured to make a joke about it and challenged her to wipe the good lady's memory from my mind. She responded with frozen displeasure.

Our next engagement was of the highest importance. We were bidden to Almack's in the West, one of the most coveted of all social venues. I assumed the trivial misdemeanours of the past would be forgotten, and that evening went in good spirits to prepare Cecilia for the perfomance. But she refused to accept her rogering.

'I shall manage well enough. It is a ladies' club, and I shall not need to cater to the tastes of dribbling old men.'

'All the more reason,' I insisted, 'to perfect every last little nuance of your voice.'

'No. Not until the score is settled.'

Almack's had come into being as a club for ladies, run by ladies and devoted to suppers, gossip, and dancing. The partners invited for the dancing were those men who found female company more diverting than the company of their fellows, so busy wining and gambling that they had fallen into the habit of utterly neglecting their wives. Habitués of Almack's were less neglectful. While their husbands played cards and laid absurd wagers, the ladies found diversions of their own with more attentive men. It was widely known that the Marchioness of Tenterden had acquired three illegitimate children as a result of strenuous social activities at Almack's.

On the evening of our engagement it had been announced that the latter part of the proceedings, divided from the first by a musical interlude, would be a masquerade. It was Cecilia's task to sing during that interval. Her contributions were politely applauded, though there was some fidgeting in the audience which I attributed to the fact that she was not singing at her best. It served her right. She would know better than to spurn my treatment next time. But one young man was gazing starry-eyed at her.

It was Lord Alderley.

He was in the company of a rather horse-faced young woman but was utterly neglecting her so that he might concentrate all his attention on Cecilia.

One thing at least the occasion had in common with the deplorable Cyprians: people were beginning to drift away before Cecilia had even finished singing.

Then the second half began, and I learned the truth of the masquerade. The masks themselves were remarkably ornate and inventive: some of them veritable headdresses. A fanciful Eastern potentate bobbed his way past the richly feathered poll of an unidentifiable tropical bird. But between the masks and the pairs of polished dancing shoes there was nothing. Masks hid the face, shoes the feet. Nothing hid the breasts and tufts of hair, the swaying buttocks and the limp or pert penises. Nor, alas, were some deplorable pot bellies and sagging bosoms concealed.

I was asked to resume the music. I looked around for Cecilia: not that she would be expected to sing while we played for dancing, but I liked her to keep close to the ensemble.

She had disappeared.

When the rhythm of the dance reached the feet and other movable parts of those mixed anatomies, I noted that some couples clung ever more closely. It was not surprising that the Marchioness should have been blessed with the fruits of such coupling. I wondered how many more seeds might fall into the appropriate place this same evening.

About ten minutes must have elapsed when a beautiful young woman moved into the crowd. I say she was beautiful although I could not discern her face, shrouded as it was in a sinister black mask topped with two horns, suggesting a lithe devil. But her enticing breasts, dancing gently in rhythm with the sway of her lower dimpled cheeks, would have drawn any man's attention away from her face. The cockerel masks and Greek masks and leering satyr masks turned, and men's interest showed all too instinctively as she brushed between them.

Sickeningly I recognised that incomparable body. I was horrified that its beauties, which I had regarded as entirely my own territory, should be exposed to these vulgarians. Not merely was she exposing it, but flaunting it. When an ambitious young gymnast endeavoured to walk on his hands across the floor towards her, her lips and teeth pushed through the mask and dabbed and bit at his cock, until he fell over amid a roar of applause. Many others tried to seize her and dance with her. She suffered each of them for a moment, wriggling provocatively in their embrace, before twirling away and offering herself to another.

And each time, between each tantalising swing of her haunches, the devilish mask leered vengefully up at me, trapped as I was in the minstrels' gallery.

Finally she stood quite still as a young man with skin as smooth as her own approached. His mask was that of a Roman warrior, but I knew what very English features were concealed beneath it. Very gracefully Lord Alderley turned her from side to side, drifting his prick along her hips, touching and probing and playing her both front and back without concluding. I had to admire his self-restraint. Then the two of them left the ballroom; and an eerie, unnatural sigh followed them as they went.

That night it was Alderley who took Cecilia home again; not this time to our home, but to his.

I had lost her. Having once turned down the invitation to visit Newcastle upon Tyne, I now dismally decided to write and ask if the offer was still open.

Chapter 5

In which it is demonstrated that a talented performer can be as proud in the provinces as in Pall Mall

The wrench which I felt as the coach supplied by Mrs Armstrong carried me away through Edgware and on towards the unknown North twisted my vitals not just once but at regular intervals. My whole inside was being gnawed away by jealousy. Absurd jealousy, of course. No fit state for a man of the world. Yet more than once in the first few hours was I miserably tempted to order the coachman to turn back so that I might seek out Cecilia, wean her away from the young upstart Alderley, and sweep her into my arms.

Then I defiantly told myself that she would soon regret her impetuousness, and it would do her good to suffer a while.

Always supposing that she rather than I was the one who suffered, and was not having the abominable treachery to enjoy herself.

I tried to think of my music and the acclaim which lay ahead.

Unfortunately the jolting of the coach and the continual friction of the seat and cushions under my crotch began to produce an involuntary swelling which I could in no way relieve, and which inevitably conjured up even more tormenting visions of Cecilia.

We stayed one night at Stamford and another at York, at

both of which I was treated with great deference. Clearly the name of Mrs Armstrong, or the money behind that name, sent out ripples far beyond the waters of the river Tyne.

We reached the northern bank of that river after what seemed to me an eternity, and in the cool of the evening I was greeted by Mrs Armstrong on the steps of an elegant town house on the corner of what I had been informed was Hood Street. She wore a cream lamé dress with rosebuds, rather too youthful for the age of its contents, and a wispy lace fichu and coral necklace to soften her throat.

Gushingly she escorted me to my room, followed by a manservant with my meagre luggage. The two travelling boxes had belonged to my father and had seen better days. They were certainly not worthy of the princely accommodation into which I was led. Between the richly appointed bedroom and small sitting room was a changing room amply furnished with wardrobes, washbasins and jugs, and a gilt-framed mirror. Between a pair of silver-backed hairbrushes stood a porcelain pot of expensive pomade from what I knew to be the most exclusive establishment in London.

Utterly exhausted by that long journey, I had felt a tremor of apprehension lest my hostess should make some immediate physical demand upon me. As a confidante of Mrs Batchelor, and presumably of similar disposition, her motives for inviting me to Newcastle could not have been purely musical. Without being too cynical on the matter, I had mentally prepared myself for whatever subsidiary activities were called for. But to my relief there was not even the faintest hint of such things. I was left to refresh myself after the journey, and was then promised a light dinner so that I might get to bed early.

'We must make sure that you are at the peak of your prowess on the morrow, must we not?' said Mrs Armstrong, her stubby little fingers toying with the fichu above her ample bosom.

At dinner I was introduced to Mr Armstrong. He was a burly man with tufts of black hair receding from a red face and red forehead, so that wherever the light struck his head it produced a ruddy glow seeming to threaten apoplexy. He was amiable enough, shaking my hand with easy-going warmth and grunting some civilities; but during the course of the meal he made no attempt to join in talk of music and musicians, and did not hesitate to inform me that other engagements meant he would not be attending my first recital on the morrow. I got the impression that he would not be attending any subsequent concerts, either.

His wife paused during one disquisition upon the merits of a gifted local composer and collector called John Peacock, of whom I confess I had never heard, to tell me briskly and dismissively that Mr Armstrong was a shipbuilder. It was not difficult to deduce that the only music he really enjoyed was the clang of hammers and the rattle or rustle of money into his coffers.

In the morning, after a substantial breakfast, I strolled around the town, humming a few themes and going over in my head the items in my programme for this evening. I was, I have to admit, distracted from time to time by the impudent-eyed girls who walked with such a delightful swagger along every street. Many were red-haired, and many of Nordic, almost Viking proportions. I will not say that my nostalgic memories of Cecilia faded; but at least I realised that life could still hold other pleasures – or, rather, similar pleasures with a variety of partners. For their part, several of these radiant passers-by studied me with what seemed to be favour. One or two giggled at my Bond Street walking dress, with new grey nankin pantaloons and Hessian boots; but others smiled admiringly and slowed their pace as if inviting me to speak. I was not, however, too optimistic about Mrs Armstrong's allowing me to indulge myself while under her patronage.

In the afternoon I was introduced to the music room on the first floor above Hood Street and to a very modern pianoforte at which I could practise for this evening. I went through some pieces by Josef Haydn and Dr Arne, and also my own variations upon a theme of Spontini. These latter did not require too much conscientious rehearsal: if I played a few wrong notes, the audience would assuredly not notice, but would assume that I had introduced some daring modern harmonic experiment. Since the works of Herr van Beethoven had begun to circulate in our country, almost any gaucheness was allowable.

Mrs Armstrong's thoughtfulness was shown yet again when a carriage was provided to deliver me early to the door of the premises in the Groat Market, to give me time to accustom myself to the sound and feeling of the place. Mrs Armstrong tactfully assured me that she would not wish to distract me by her presence and conversation before the concert, but that she would accompany me on the homeward journey. I was somewhat awestruck on realising that I was in the very salon in which Dr Avison had given his celebrated subscription concerts, sometimes following them with decorous dancing and card playing.

By the time the recital was due to start, the room was gratifyingly full, though preponderantly with women. Glancing through a side curtain I could see a few men who had been dragged along by their wives. No more interested in music than Mr Armstrong, they lacked his size and power, and any objections they had dared to raise had been overruled. I was sorry for them, and vowed to introduce a few of Mr Thomas Moore's settings of Irish ditties to leaven the programme and perhaps wake them up with a recognisable melody.

Before setting foot on the platform I was introduced by Mrs Armstrong to her fellow sponsor of the concert series, a Mrs Robson; and at once recognised her, as she did me. This was the formidable Mrs Batchelor of days gone by, looking just as formidable and just as heavily playful. Although my hostess was, as I may have indicated, prone to gush, Mrs Robson was a positive fountain. Marginally smaller than her friend, in height if not in girth, she made up for this by bouncing up and down, chattering, dabbing at one with her fan, then with her fingers, and forever making arch little *moues* with her lips and laughing as if she had made a joke, or as if she remembered something daringly funny which she and I had once shared. Her fat little bosom was ceaselessly a-quiver, thrusting forward in unison with her fan and fingers.

I had the impression that before my arrival some arguments must have taken place between the two ladies as to who should house me and who should have the honour of introducing me. Possibly the loser of one claim became the winner of the other.

In any event, it was Mrs Robson who preceded me on to the platform and recounted at length my musical genius, from which she herself had had the good fortune to profit in the past, the good fortune of the people of Newcastle upon Tyne in having lured me into their midst, and the testimony this offered to the continuing growth and success of the Philharmonic Fellowship of Newcastle upon Tyne, for which she and her colleagues had laboured so assiduously. . .

I began to wonder if there would be time for my recital, let alone for any encores. Finally Mrs Armstrong cleared her throat so raspingly that Mrs Robson stopped, looked around, spluttered vaguely, and waved me on to the platform.

If I cannot claim that I lived up to the standards of genius with which Mrs Robson had endowed me, at least I knew myself to be at my best, inspired by the ambience to which I felt my talents entitled me. Perhaps the audience was too hushed and respectful and would have been so whatever I chose to play; but it did make a welcome change from the raffishness of London. The admirable Dr Avison had left his mark upon the place, and some of my unworthy apprehensions about the ladies who had invited me here began to fade.

At the end of the evening I flatter myself that I responded graciously and adequately to all the confused, adulatory remarks which were showered upon me. Mrs Robson, like an overfed terrier trying to push its way through a crowd of creatures even weightier than itself, kept trying to reach me, but was continually edged backwards and reduced to a high-pitched yapping on the outskirts.

Just when I was feeling the full weariness of the aftermath

of my strenuous recital, Mrs Armstrong came to the rescue. Majestically she took my arm, swept us through the crowd of admirers, assured them that they could look forward to many such a wonderful evening provided they had not omitted to subscribe to the full range of concerts, and bundled me into her waiting carriage.

In the tranquillity of the house she suggested that I share a soothing brandy with her. It was a particularly fine marque, imported by one of her husband's acquaintances. As we sipped it appreciatively, she commented with apparent casualness that Mr Armstrong would not be back until the early hours of the morning. He had even intimated that he might spend the night at his club.

'But for us,' said Mrs Armstrong, smiling over the rim of her glass, 'the night is young.'

Now I knew that my original suppositions had been correct. The lingering effects of yesterday's journey, the recital, and the brandy had left me ready for sleep. But Mrs Armstrong was looking at me with a roguish invitation which I found all too familiar. Trying not to sound too discourteously jaded, I said as lightly as possible: 'Am I to assume that a further small encore is required – perhaps one of my livelier variations?'

'I admired your fingering in that remarkably exultant cadenza.'

'I was endeavouring to produce the equivalent of a great organ swell.'

Mrs Armstrong squealed with ecstatic laughter. 'A great organ swell! Ah, yes, dear Mrs Robson – Mrs Batchelor, as *you* knew her – did tell me how rewarding your hidden depths of meaning could be.' As I hesitated, wondering whether I was to lead the way upstairs to my bedroom or be led by my hostess to hers, she uttered another hopeful squeal. 'Does the couch in this room resemble that which I believe you make such good use of at home?'

I looked at the piece of furniture to which she was gesturing. It was a large brown leather affair, with a bulky curving back crossed by three leather straps. It was very solid and heavy. If Mrs Armstrong was hoping to emulate one of Mrs

Batchelor's favourite virtuoso movements, such weight and security would not come amiss.

I finished my brandy and resignedly set the glass aside.

The flesh of her nude body looked much younger than that of her arms and face. I have found this to be gratifyingly the case with many older women. Wrinkles may disfigure the ageing countenance, and a coarseness may come into the hands and wrists and, alas, often into the folds of the throat. But shoulders and breasts and belly can emerge as smooth and unspoilt as those of a nubile sixteen-year-old.

I was greatly relieved. It would not be such an arduous experience after all. Tiredness was rushing away. I felt that I could rise to the occasion.

She was waiting for my directions. I set her against the back of the sofa, her feet only just touching the floor. Then I interposed myself between her ample thighs, and lifted her legs so that they rested on my shoulders. This produced an interesting surprise. I found myself looking upon a flamboyantly crested cunt whose usual pink lips were garnished with a brighter red frill, like that of a cock's comb. Yet I was the one with the cock. And I observed that as I moved it a fraction of an inch closer, deliberately keeping her waiting, that frill of hers began to quiver. I felt it to be like some carnivorous sea plant, all a-tremor, greedy to close upon me and devour me.

In fact at the moment I was a few inches too low to enter. I thereupon put my hands on the back of the sofa beside her buttocks, and swung myself up, raising my shoulders against the pressure of her legs until she was gleefully waving them in the air. It became, suddenly, an athletic game. I lunged at her, dabbed into her, and then swung out again, swaying to and fro on my extended arms. She began to gasp with frustration. I slowed the tempo of my pendulum, and courteously pleasured her for a few seconds before lowering my feet to the floor again and debating whether there might not be a more comfortable posture in which to conclude the evening's business.

Before I could reach a decision, there came a violent rapping at the door.

I took a step backwards, alarmed. Mrs Armstrong slid precipitately from the back of the sofa and by chance was impaled again on my prick, which rendered her less impatient to dash away across the room.

The door was flung open.

Mrs Robson stormed in and glared at us in a fine rage. I advisedly say rage rather than revulsion; for her expression made it all too clear that she was envious rather than morally censorious.

Her shrill abuse was difficult to interpret, but the general drift was unmistakeable. Mrs Armstrong had had no right. . . chairwoman's prerogative. . . prior agreements betrayed. . . mutual decisions. . . But she eased off when she realised that I had not discharged my final duties to her old friend. There was still hope. Withdrawn from Mrs Armstrong as a matter of politeness while we were exchanging views, my member was still at attention. Even the relief of realising that it was no jealous husband who had burst in upon us had not been enough to persuade it to stand at ease.

'Very well.' Mrs Robson began purposefully to disrobe. 'I will forgive you, Mildred, if I may now partake of the same delights.'

'I had not finished,' protested Mrs Armstrong.

'Whereas I have not even had the good fortune to start. We shall share, I fancy, as we have always shared – the duties of committee members, and now the pleasures. And Mr Rougiere and I will share some old memories.'

I suppose that I ought to have stood upon my dignity and refused to partake in such a double game. But while I could certainly boast a substantial standing at that moment, dignity was far from appropriate. Mrs Robson's squeakings and tremblings had reached fever pitch, and I grasped that the only way to put an end to the clamour was to put a stopper in both the orifices she was presenting to me. I therefore rammed my tongue into her upper mouth and my staff into her lower one. Even then she continued gasping, making the air bubble out around my tongue, while at the same time she produced a strange sighing flatulence below.

Over Mrs Robson's shoulder I was presented with the sight of Mrs Armstrong, propped against the sofa, watching with ill-concealed disdain.

'You will oblige me, Mr Rougiere – '

'In a moment,' I promised, extricating my tongue.

'You will oblige me,' said Mrs Armstrong inexorably, 'by not discharging yourself into that present receptacle. I shall expect to be the ultimate recipient.'

Mrs Robson emitted a wild denial which shook her whole body and sent ripples of protest from the tip of my prick into my guts. Her ejaculation was almost enough to provoke my own immediate ejaculation, but I restrained it while I tried, in the far from calm circumstances, to estimate my best course of action. It was difficult to remain objective when two determined ladies were trying each to claim sole possession by laying hands on the evening's outstanding attraction.

It was an embarrassing situation. I did not wish to antagonise either lady, but obviously there must come a time when I would be forced to finish in one or the other. The only other recourse was to alternate between the two, withdrawing from one and plunging into the other, to and fro and to and fro until I was so weary that my member would sag and prove incapable of offering either of them more than the last respectful droop of a flag being lowered at sunset. Then perhaps we could all three agree to an honourable truce. But here my body was betraying me. After three or four dips into one and then the other it was growing sore, especially since the fleece around Mrs Robson's cleft had all the gentle furriness of a hedgehog; but the chafing inflamed rather than discouraged. I was desperate to effect a delivery.

In the end it did prove a matter of desperation rather than calculation. Pinning Mrs Armstrong to the wall, since I no longer had either the time or the energy to go through complicated maneouvres against the couch, I managed to say 'With my compliments, madam' as she smiled in triumph – not at me, but across my shoulder at Mrs Robson – and I felt the warmth of fulfilment run through my stem and into her.

Mrs Robson began to squeak with vexation.

I said diplomatically: 'My hostess deserves something in return for her hospitality.'

Mrs Robson spoilt this by retorting: 'Perhaps it's all for the best. At least at Mildred's age she runs little risk of conceiving.'

Next morning I overslept. I forced myself to take a brief walk, and was once more stimulated by the glances of the Tyneside beauties; but resolutely averted my glance and thought of risking a purely classical concert of the most austere of Bach's keyboard music. That might cool ardour in certain places.

Turning back towards Hood Street, I was aware of a small coach and pair trundling dangerously close to the kerb. As I began to step away into the centre of the pavement, the nearside door of the vehicle was flung open and a large man with arms as thick as a collier's mooring cables sprang out at me. In a few seconds he had lifted me bodily from the street and tipped me into the dark interior of the carriage, with black velvet curtains fastened tightly across both side and back windows. Another man was waiting to take my right arm and settle me into the centre of the seat. As the door clicked shut, my attacker kept a hold on my left arm. Neither of them squeezed in any way hard or brutally; but they made quite sure that I could not struggle free.

'This is outrageous,' I protested. 'Is this the sort of hospitality the city of Newcastle offers its guests?'

Neither said a word.

I tried again, not pleading but stating facts. 'I am not a rich man. I have no more than a few guineas on my person. You'll gain nothing by this appalling behaviour.'

Still they held me, while the carriage rocked and racketed round corners. I knew nothing of the town's twists and turns, and could not even begin to guess where I was by now or where I was being taken.

When we stopped and I was bustled out, I was none the wiser. We had entered an alley almost too narrow for the door to be opened. But without ceremony I was pulled across the cobbles and in through the back door of some building I could not hope to identify. The men were abruptly gone; the door had closed; and again I was in darkness.

I had been kidnapped. Money or no money, somebody must absurdly suppose that I would somehow be worth the trouble. Alien rogues in an alien city: what would happen to me when they discovered their mistake?

Before I could blink my eyes in an attempt to get used to the gloom, a hand seized mine. I have to confess that I let out a gasp, and jumped. The hand moved gently up my arm.

'Welcome, Mr Rougiere.'

It was a voice laden with determination. It was a voice I knew, though huskier and less shrill than when I had last heard it.

I said: 'Mrs Robson, whatever possessed you to – '

'Possess me,' she murmured. 'Yes, that's what I want of you.'

'Mrs Robson – '

'With you I'll be Mrs Batchelor, if you like. If that is how you like to remember me. How *do* you remember me, Mr Rougiere?'

Her hand strayed down to mine again, and drew it towards her. My fingers discovered that she was naked.

'But where are we?' I demanded.

She leaned heavily against me, and urged me towards the foot of a flight of stairs which I could just begin to distinguish in a pallid light from above. At the top of the flight was an open door, and immediately within was a large bed, lit by two candles on a mantelpiece. There were two small chairs, on one of which a woman's garments were neatly folded.

In that subdued glow Mrs Robson looked plump rather than flabby, and the lines of her face and neck were suggestive shadows rather than wrinkles.

'Here we will not be interrupted,' she said, with a trace of her greedy giggle. 'I fear I could not invite you to my home. My husband is rarely off the premises for long, and is an extremely suspicious and intolerant man. But I could not bear to leave you entirely to the mercies of Mildred Armstrong. Least of all' – she was urging my right hand through her prickly copse, and tilting us towards the bed – 'after what we meant to each other in those dear days in London.'

I made a quick mental calculation as to the time it would take me to find my way back to Hood Street, lunch with Mrs Armstrong, and practise for this evening's concert. That left a not too limited space in which to renew my acquaintance with Mrs Batchelor/Robson.

As if reading my thoughts, she said: 'I have hired this room of assignation for one hour. You usually succeeded in teaching me a great deal in the course of an hour.'

Freeing myself from her eager clutch for long enough to shed my clothes. I waited for her to settle comfortably on the bed. It was comforting to know that there was no couch in the room on which she might wish to revive unduly strenuous memories.

She reached out and tapped me where it hurt, letting out a hoarse 'Ahh!' like a child being offered an unexpectedly juicy sweetmeat. Then, with unexpected deference, she said: 'I had of course not completed my education with you before our paths parted. I have since pondered over a technique to which you promised to introduce me when you were sure my elementary studies had reached a certain grade.'

I wondered what wild promises I might airily have thrown off.

'What did it mean?' she asked. 'We were discussing time signatures, and I had just mastered a little jig in six-eight time, and I remember your saying that six-nine might be the next step – or was it nine-six? I have tried to hear such a beat in my head, but I cannot grasp it.'

Pleadingly she grasped what was most readily available, and looked up at me, awaiting further instruction.

'Open your mouth,' I said, 'and close your eyes.'

She obeyed. I kneeled above her head, and lowered her coveted sweetmeat into her mouth. She was an apt pupil, with a discerning palate. At once she wrapped her lips round it, and when I lowered myself full on to her and began to tongue her quim she was quick to respond with a flickering of her own tongue.

Just when I felt I could bear it no longer, she surprisingly heaved herself up, tipping me off. Coyly wiping her tongue on a corner of the crumpled sheet, she said: 'Yes, that was most enjoyable. But. . . I prefer the old finale. For old times' sake, Mr Rougiere. . .?'

And so we finished happily and conventionally with me on top of her, worrying no longer about finesse but pounding into her fat, frenziedly appreciative body until I had delivered the final drops of mid-morning refreshment.

It turned out that she had kept the carriage waiting for me round the corner. I was taken back to Hood Street by an impassive driver whose stony features resembled those of an undertaker's mute rather than a coachman. Mrs Armstrong looked searchingly at me; but I avoided questions by beginning to hum a very complicated passage which would deter even the most resolute woman's efforts to interrupt.

The recital that evening was such a great success, and a review in the local journal of my previous performance had been so full of praise, that I was asked to stay on a further week. It was even suggested by both Mrs Armstrong and Mrs Robson, presumably as co-chairwomen but in fact on separate private occasions, that I might consider taking up permanent residence. I could become the leading musician in a large northern city, the cynosure of all eyes and ears, and the doted-on favourite of other organs, rather than one of a thousand struggling aspirants in the fleshpots of London.

I went out for another of my regular walks, but this time in the afternoon, in order to mull this over. On my way I observed Mr Armstrong a few paces ahead of me, slowing and turning up the steps of what I presumed to be his club. As he did so, two young women crossed the road and followed him. One of them paused halfway up the fine flight of steps, and I will swear that she smiled at me; and I was equally sure that she was one of the bold-eyed beauties I had passed more than once already. In the magnificent portico Armstrong turned to greet them, and then saw me. He beckoned me to the foot of the steps.

'Come in, young man. It's high time you played on something softer than ivory keys. Gather my wife has been trying to coax you to settle in these parts. Let me introduce you to some of the finer parts.'

The prettier of the two girls looked down at me hopefully. But I had to be firm. I said: 'I must do a full hour's practice when I get back to the house.'

'Then tomorrow. These canny lasses will share some other practices with you.'

'You're very kind.' I raised my hat.

Both girls looked flatteringly as if they would relish being kind to me.

But in the morning all my tentative plans and half-willing speculations were swept away. There came a plaintive message from London. Cecilia was in dire need of my services. Her letter was naive and would have meant little to the casual reader, if any had been so ill-mannered as to intercept and read it.

She had been commanded to sing before the Prince Regent, who had seen and heard her at one of Lord Alderley's routs. Her natural timidity at such a prospect was made all the worse in that Alderley had no ability to inspire her before a recital. There was only one person to whom she could turn, and most respectfully she begged me to return and take her through the necessary exercises before she appeared before His Royal Highness. She would be at our own dear lodging, awaiting me.

Did this mean, then, that she had already discarded Alderley? Or was it simply that she wished to use me so that she might dazzle the Prince Regent, and then would leave me again?

I thought of the ease in which I could continue to live in Newcastle, and of the relaxations to which Mr Armstrong could so easily introduce me.

I announced that I must return without delay to London.

Mrs Armstrong was outraged. Mrs Robson was outraged.

Neither would provide me with a carriage or help me in any way to leave the town. So I was compelled to expend a large part of what I had earned here in order to hire a coach to take me to London. It was an exorbitant sum, justified by the coachman on the grounds that he had no way of being guaranteed a return fare from London to Newcastle.

When we set out, the driver made it insolently clear that he was in no great hurry. He would not damage his vehicle or his horses. Desperate to get there, I saw myself arriving with too little time to spare. When at last we trundled into the purlieus of Bayswater I was terrified that Cecilia might already have set out for Carlton House, without the essential prerequisite for the kind of performance which would enchant the Prince Regent.

Was I going to reach her in time. . .?

Chapter 6

In which it is shown how little snobbery princes and princelings feel towards lower members of society when their own members are in sociable mood

Breathless with fear that I might have arrived too late, I bounded into the house, to be greeted by Mrs Hiscock with a sternly raised hand.

'She cannot be undone,' she pronounced.

I found this remark rather naive, since my sweet Cecilia had surely been well and truly undone long before this. I did not pause to argue the matter, but hurried on my way up the stairs. Cecilia was there in her room, her face contriving to be radiant at the sight of me yet at the same time troubled. She wrapped her arms lovingly round me, and I put my left arm round her while fumbling with my breeches to release what she had so urgently summoned me for.

'Too late,' she breathed with that sweetly scented breath of hers, which made me so glad to be home.

'There is time,' I panted. 'I promise to take only so long as you can spare.' I was indeed impatient to serve her with unceremonious haste after such a long absence.

But what she meant to convey was that she was already fully dressed, in a most lavish costume of white muslin with a long train, ostrich feathers in a band round her head, and beneath it all a fearsome armour of tightly laced stays giving Grecian form to a form which needed no such artificial aids. It must have taken Mrs Hiscock some considerable time to tighten all those laces and to adjust the fall of the dress and train. Forcing my way through such barriers would cause a great deal of disturbance, and a great deal of time would be needed to restore the ravages afterwards.

Yet I had arrived in a state of such readiness to meet her demands that, thwarted, I was now in acute pain.

Cecilia must have read the torment in my eyes. She took off a long white glove and closed her fingers affectionately around my anguished lance, plucking at the skin and drawing it to and fro over the end of me.

'You have come so far at my behest,' she said tenderly. 'It wouldn't be fair that Roger should suffer from no roger.'

She went down in a graceful curtsey which I supposed to be something she had been practising against the moment when she was greeted by the Prince Regent. But once down, she bobbed her head forward, not deferentially but rapaciously. Her fingers slid away and her lips took their place. She was in a hurry, but she managed to create ecstasy for me in a matter of less than a minute. Her tongue fluttered and stabbed, until at the climax she was triple-tonguing on the very tip of my pipe with a speed and dexterity which would have been the envy of any flautist or cornet player. Then, knowing exactly when to stop, her lips closed tightly around my pulsating muscle, and she gulped down the nectar spurting into her throat.

We made hasty farewells. It was my dearest wish to accompany her and hear how well she might sing this evening; but I was travel-stained and not dressed for the occasion, and in any event one did not walk uninvited into a royal reception.

I had intended to stay awake until she returned, so that I might question her about her performance; but tiredness overcame me and I slept for a full fifteen hours without once stirring. Next day Cecilia told me, proud yet modest, that she had never felt in better voice, that the Prince had been most attentive and revealed a knowledge of music far greater than most of the supposedly musical impresarios who had engaged us in the past, and that he had suggested her visiting him during one of his sojourns at Brighthelmstone.

Before I could voice some jealous doubts about this, she hastened to assure me that she had made one stipulation. She must bring her own accompanist, who was accustomed to her ways and knew every nuance of all her songs. His Royal Highness had seemed quite agreeable to this, and promised that he would send for the two of us when it pleased him to hear her again.

Her appearance before such a personage had immediately enhanced her reputation, and engagements were offered in such quantities that we had to turn many of them down. It was good to be able to pick and choose, eliminating the shabby and immoral, and concentrating on those with the highest musical potentiality. For myself, it has to be admitted, this was one of the most exhausting periods of my life. With such an increase in professional performances, there was a corresponding increase in the need for the pre-performance bellows to fan the flames. And if there were differences in the type of audience we could now select, there was also a difference in Cecilia's choice of treatment.

Since that evening when she had sung so superbly before the Prince Regent, the devouring crouch became her favourite position. Before each concert she would sink to her knees before my crotch. She vowed that the lubrication of her vocal chords by this method was far superior to the effect of any physick or lozenges. Naturally I continued to gratify her wishes, though I enjoyed this fulfilment less than others we had so healthily practised. Perhaps Mrs Hiscock, bless her, was to some extent to blame, having instructed me in her own straightforward old-fashioned ways and thus leaving me with a preference for those more traditional conjunctions.

At first I had refrained from asking about Lord Alderley, and how that relationship had fared. I could not, however, long contain my curiosity. Cecilia went a becoming shade of pink when I questioned her, and faltered over a few confused sentences before coming out with her story.

It appeared that the young rake had immediately engaged a suite of rooms for her and promised to visit her as regularly as possible between his other occupations. Shyly she had informed him, as she had informed me, that she was not yet ready to marry; whereupon he had blandly said that marriage had never been in his mind. There was some talk of his wedding a noble heiress early next year, but of course he would continue paying for Cecilia's upkeep. She had bridled at these offhanded suggestions, and after a week of wretchedness had walked out and gone to stay with her mother and new stepfather in the country. That, too, had been only a brief interlude: Mr Merivale began to take an apparently kindly interest in her, but Mrs Merivale, as she now was, made it clear that her daughter's presence was not welcome.

I could not but feel that there was more behind the tale, but when I tried to inquire further, Cecilia said with a steeliness which I would have thought foreign to her nature: 'And in your absence were you faithful to my memory?'

I decided it would be tactful not to pursue the matter. It was no time for regrets or reproaches. Our fortunes showed every sign of prospering. We soon found, however, that our original intention of accepting only the most respectable engagements would limit that prosperity. There was more to be earned at the clubs and salacious evenings than at subscription concerts, so we tried to achieve a tolerable balance between pure music and impure entertainment. At least such financial manoeuvring enabled us to buy our own little coach and a tolerable mare, and install a coachman above the stables at the back of the house.

Wherever we might be, Cecilia was inevitably the centre of attention, especially when indulging in her innocently suggestive little ditties. My occasional interludes of piano virtuosity were regarded as no more than a background accompaniment to an evening's debauchery. Nevertheless, handsomely remunerated, we were prepared to adapt to customers' requirements, until it became known in fashionable circles that no really high-class orgy would be complete without us. To add to the round of gaiety, the downfall of Napoleon Bonaparte set off, like an outburst of celebratory fireworks, a whole train of levees, banquets, balls and gala performances. Demands upon our services increased. Oh, the fugues and the fucking; the cunt and the counterpoint!

At last came the promised invitation from the Prince Regent himself, delivered by a boy in blue jacket and breeches, with a powdered wig which the afternoon's rain had rendered less than smart. We were not, however, summoned to Brighthelmstone by the sea, but to Carlton House. His Royal Highness had, regrettably, become so unpopular with the public that he dared not show himself in the streets, so had to stay indoors and invite people to come and visit him. In March of this *annus mirabilis* of 1814, he had been forced to entertain the ferocious Grand Duchess Catherine, sister of the Russian Tsar, at a grandiose dinner which got off to a poor start when she ordered that the band should be sent away, since music made her vomit. We were more fortunate. We were to perform before the Tsar himself, the King of Prussia, the cunning Austrian diplomat Count Metternich, and a host of exiled French royalties and minor princelings. There were also, as we discovered soon after our arrival, a number of richly apparelled Indian potentates, with the architecture of whose palaces the Prince Regent was said to be besotted.

I suggested to Cecilia that since this evening was to be such a remarkable change for us, we should also change our recent procedure, if only for this one occasion. She would not hear of it; but instead of going down on her knees to me, she waited until I was close to the bed, then laughed like a schoolgirl, playfully pushed me on to my back, and climbed over my face, kissing me all down my chest and belly until she reached her goal. I had only to reach up with my tongue, and was at once engaged by both her sets of palpitating, urgent lips. She tasted far sweeter than Mrs Robson, and her bush was like silk.

She was humming contentedly to herself as we set off for Carlton House, and did not cease until her breath was taken away by the sight of the extravagances which went far beyond common rumours of the Prince's profligacy.

I had never looked on such splendour, such riches, before. We were of course not allowed to stroll through the grounds or sup with the aristocratic guests under the florid vaulting of the Gothic conservatory; but while waiting to perform, and then during the course of the actual recital, it was possible to take in a hundred details of the lavish occasion. Before the Regent's own table there was set a huge bowl, from which a conduit carried a stream of water the length of the guests' main table, shimmering and leaping with live fish. After supping vigorously at the unlimited supplies of wine, a number of guests tried blearily to catch the slippery creatures, but usually failed. One who achieved his catch dangled it by its tail for a moment above the square cut of his neighbour's bodice, and then dropped it so smoothly that it slid effortlessly between her breasts and disappeared. The lady twitched once, screamed once, and stood up, trying to shake it free. After a moment an odd smile of appreciation plucked at the corners of her mouth, and she sat down again, ceasing for a while to concentrate on the food.

There were hot soups, roasts, cold meats, peaches, grapes and pineapples, all in silver tureens and bowls or arranged upon silver plates. Flunkeys moved swiftly and silently to and fro. Lesser mortals ate at small tables in the garden, and an orchestra played under a canopy like a crusader's tent. Flares of scarlet and topaz were interspersed between palm trees in tubs.

A tall, imposing major-domo came to tell us that the time for our contribution to the festivities was close.

As we waited to one side of the conservatory, I noticed a couple at the far side of the long table: a handsome young man with a dejected countenance, in the company of a woman a few years older than himself.

A discreet voice close to my left ear said: 'One of His Royal Highness's discarded mistresses. Lady Falmer.'

It was the major-domo, standing guard over us, who had provided this information. For all his lofty appearance it seemed that he was an inveterate gossip, and loved to display his superior knowledge to awestruck nonentities like ourselves. He went on to explain in an undertone that the young man was Count Rupert of Stoltenberg, a small principality near the borders of Bohemia. Since his wife had been unable to accompany him on his visit to England, the

Prince Regent had considerately provided a companion whose abilities, which he had personally tested, ought to comfort the young Count. It was rumoured that so far the relationship had not been a successful one.

Indeed, even as the major-domo ceased his informative whispering, the young man's attempt to caress Lady Falmer's hand was rudely repulsed, and she said in an unnecessarily loud voice: 'I may as well go back to my husband.'

I think this is one of the unkindest insults I have ever overheard in my entire career.

Our custodian indicated that it was time for us to perform, and led us forward. Conversation hardly abated until Cecilia began to sing. Then, gradually, the beauty of her voice insinuated itself through the babble, and as she soared to some of her loveliest high notes the other voices sank away into admiring silence.

From where I sat at the keyboard I could see the sullen face of Count Rupert begin to change. A remarkable light came into it, and after staring raptly at Cecilia as she executed an entrancing appoggiatura round a high A, he suddenly turned to his companion and murmured something. Lady Falmer look startled. He continued addressing her, and a new light came into her face also; though, as an expert by now on the matter, I would have been prepared to swear that it was not the light of artistic appreciation but of lust. Then, to my displeasure, the two of them slid away from the table and escaped from the conservatory into the darker end of the gardens outside. I would not have thought the Prince Regent would have approved of such discourtesy at his table, but when I managed to catch a glimpse of him by taking an accompanying phrase up to the treble end of the keyboard, I was under the impression that he was smirking.

The errant couple came back just before we embarked on our last rendition of the evening. The young Count resumed his rapt contemplation of Cecilia, though perhaps less intently than before; while Lady Falmer edged herself into a comfortable position in her chair, wincing slightly yet looking gratified and, as it were, well fed.

The Prince Regent rising from his place at the head of the table was a signal for the guests also to rise, and for many of them to saunter out for a stroll in the gardens. Cecilia and I were about to make a polite departure when our friend the major-domo reappeared, smiling upon us even more benevolently than before.

'His Royal Highness wishes a word with you.'

He led us the length of the conservatory and on into a small retiring-room within the main building. The Prince, sprawled on a couch which was none too large for him, was unlacing the stays of his corset and allowing his belly to sag comfortably forward, threatening to engulf his knees. He made no attempt to hide this as we entered, but smiled graciously at Cecilia, nodded civilly enough to me, and waved us towards two gilded chairs on neither of which had he himself assuredly ever ventured to sit.

At his side, standing in graceful relaxation by the end of the couch, was the young man we knew to be Count Rupert of Stoltenberg. As soon as Cecilia moved into the room he came forward, bowed low, and kissed her hand. Cecilia dropped both him and the Prince Regent a low curtsey; but fortunately did not pursue her usual course after this obeisance.

In a booming, boyishly cheerful voice the Prince said: 'My young friend Count Rupert here has been much smitten by your talents, m'dear.'

I felt a tremor of alarm.

'Indeed this is true.' The Count spoke with only the faintest trace of an accent. 'I have never known a voice have such an effect on me.'

'We saw, we saw,' chortled the Prince. 'Though we did not see the culmination, alas.'

Count Rupert's handsome features were made no less handsome by the flush of embarrassment which suffused his cheeks. He drew himself up and said very seriously, as if to counteract his host's coarse joviality: 'I would regard it as a privilege if you would accept the post of singer with my court orchestra.'

I had been right to feel apprehensive.

Cecilia silently consulted me, not knowing what to reply.

I said: 'It is a great honour, Your Grace, but at this juncture in her career I do not think it appropriate for my protégée to leave these shores for what one might call an enclosed engagement.'

'I don't think,' said the Prince coarsely, 'that my cousin Rupert is much concerned with your ideas of what's appropriate and what's not appropriate. He wishes to produce an heir to his lands, and this dear young lady shows every sign of making that possible.'

I was dumbfounded. While the preliminaries to implanting a child in Cecilia's exquisite body were such as to arouse the appetite of any full-blooded man, I could not believe that a nobleman of Count Rupert's lineage would contemplate a mere commoner as mother of his successor.

The Count became agitated, and his command of the English language slipped. 'Please, it is not... no, my royal cousin does not say it as it is... I mean... *ach*, this is not so, *ja*? I require but the music, the... how you say...?'

The Prince Regent appeared to be enjoying every moment of this. 'Putting it bluntly,' he snorted, 'my cousin finds difficulty in achieving any useful stature without the stimulus of music. He was not suggesting — nor was I, I assure you — that he required the services of a mistress. What he needs is a muse. An aria of such incomparable beauty every evening, and his ill-served Duchess may find herself suddenly fertilised and fruitful.'

Count Rupert blushed again, but looked steadily with a sincere yearning at Cecilia. I was torn by doubts. Could it truly be only the music that appealed to him? Once far away from her homeland, to what foreign practices might Cecilia not be subjected?

Again she turned to me, waving to include me in any decision which might be made. 'If my musical adviser agrees, it might be possible for us to spend a short period in Stoltenberg until such time as you —'

'There is, I fear, no question of my engaging anyone else,' said the Count politely but authoritatively. 'I have my own *konzertmeister*, and have no need of any further instrumentalists.'

'But I need Mr Rougiere.'

'What is so unique about Mr Rougiere?' asked the Prince Regent, eyeing me up and down and clearly remaining unimpressed.

Cecilia lowered her eyes. 'It is difficult to explain, Your Royal Highness.'

'I doubt,' said the Count, 'whether this gentleman can offer any services which my *konzertmeister* cannot fulfil with equal style and grace.'

I did not in the least care for the visions which this conjured up.

The Prince Regent became suddenly bored, as I had heard was his wont. There were other diversions awaiting him elsewhere in the building, and people of higher rank to be communed with. The whole situation between Cecilia and Count Rupert had tickled his crude sense of humour for some minutes. Now he was in a hurry to abandon it and move on. Creaking from one buttock to another, he waved imperiously and said: 'It is our wish that our cousin's request be granted. And I shall personally attend the christening of his heir, and I am sure that you' – he sketched a courtly nod in Cecilia's direction – 'will find something appropriate to sing at the ceremony.'

'I ask only,' said the Duke, 'that you be my little songbird.'

It was hardly possible to tell him outright that without my well-practised attentions his little songbird might well prove to be a crow rather than a nightingale. Without me on hand, could one be sure that the effect of her singing this evening would be repeated with such verve in new surroundings?

It was a grotesque situation. The young Count could not satisfy his wife unless first stimulated by the vibrations of a certain gifted voice. Equally, the quality of that voice could not be guaranteed without my first stimulating its producer. It was a chain which it might be fatal to break. The whole prospect was so disturbing that when we reached home I implored her: 'Do not go.'

'How can I not go, when it is a royal command?'

'Tell them we have too many engagements here for you to shut yourself away in a tiny principality such as – '

'But do you suppose we should continue to be offered those engagements if royal displeasure were voiced?'

I argued that there were many places where the Prince Regent was far from popular, and where his displeasure would be regarded as a recommendation. Unhappily the places where he still remained popular were just those venues which offered us the most profitable employment.

When we had both accepted the inevitable, I drew a deep breath and said:

'Let us be open with ourselves, just we two. Nobody can ever really come between us. So from now on let there be no jealousy. You agree? One should succumb honestly to any pleasure life has to offer, while still remaining faithful in principle to the highest of those pleasures. Better that than be wretched and filled with guilt.'

Cecilia looked dubious. 'I don't want to be anybody's plaything. And I don't wish to seek pleasure that is inferior to the best.'

'In music,' I said gently, 'a passing indulgence in minor composers such as Antonin Benda does not mean that one ceases to acknowledge the superiority of Mozart.'

Even if she were not persuaded, there was little now to be done about it. She would go with the Count; and I sensed that in spite of her reservations she was looking forward to new musical experiences in a faraway, romantic setting.

I wondered what disappointments might lie in store for her, and for Count Rupert. To be honest, I despicably hoped for disappointments rather than that she should find a helpmeet who would successfully ravish her in the cause of her ravishing voice.

And where, in her absence, should I find someone of the same calibre to train and inspire?

PART TWO
CECILIA'S DIARY

WEDNESDAY 6 JULY 1814

Mama insisted that from a very early age I should keep a diary. Somewhere she had heard that all young ladies of good breeding kept diaries. She also insisted that I show it to her at the end of each week. Ofttimes I had to rack my brains to find something polite and interesting to write for her benefit. I was sure she would not have approved of accurate descriptions of, for example, the two old men who regularly stood below the platform at Vauxhall to hear me sing, moving their hands within their pockets and tugging at themselves whenever I leaned forward or raised my hand delicately to my bosom.

Nor, when I was first introduced to Roger Rougiere – or, rather, when he first introduced himself into me – would she have liked to read my sensations recorded on paper. I was forced to write little daily entries about my musical progress while thinking constantly of that delicious dampness Mr Rougiere provoked between my legs, and the spasms and shudders which racked me so agreeably as he pumped that shaft of his with such perfect timing and vigour. Hitherto I had only guessed at such things, and my guesses had been far too restricted. Happily I had discovered at very short notice a taste and talent for such diversions, and could soon feel justifiable pride in my own skill. Even without my mother's prying eyes, I could not have expressed in mere words just how much I longed for the next ministration; though to preserve some shred of self-respect I soon made a point of confining these activities within a strictly musical context, so that they should never be allowed to become commonplace.

Also, perhaps because of the high standards my mother had imposed on me, I could not and cannot bring myself to indulge in certain coarse expressions, though there is often a lack of otherwise suitable words for what most interests me. I have always tried to preserve a proper vocabulary in my relations with both Mr Rougiere and Count Rupert, even in moments of greatest abandon.

Poor Mama. She would have been so proud of my association with Lord Alderley if I had maintained it while being discreet about its obligations; and was so angry with me for leaving it and fleeing to her for comfort. Doubtless she would be even more impressed by my present relationship with a blue-blooded Count; but she shall hear nothing of it.

She might be pleased to know that, far from home as I may be, I have been unable to shake off the habit of keeping a diary. But I doubt if she would be pleased by what I now choose to record. Away from her scrutiny I can jot down whatever appeals to me. Or what doesn't appeal to me. How would she feel if she were to read a comparison between the proportions and capabilities of Count Rupert's prick and that of Roger Rougiere, or of the dreams I have of Roger when Rupert has finished with me of an evening?

I have to admit to using the word 'prick', for after careful consideration I have reached the conclusion that any other term would be either dull or disgusting. I have come, in fact, to find it rather endearing – though in Rupert's case it is a matter for condescension rather than gloating.

For I must write down a further admission. In spite of his assurances that all he required was a songbird, the Count listened solely to my music for only a few weeks before suggesting that I might entertain him in other ways.

Relationships with his wife were not, after all, showing any great improvement. Perhaps my other talents might match those of my voice.

At first I was reluctant to comply. Then I remembered dear Roger's parting injunction. We would always remain true to each other in spirit, he and I; and the pawings of another man could be enjoyed or tolerated, just as I saw fit.

In truth, my modest talents are, in spite of my youth and inexperience, considerably in advance of the Count's. Blue-blooded he may be; red-blooded he certainly is not. He is proving a poor performer. For a while I was alarmed, wondering if the fault might be mine. There can be no doubt that my vocal capabilities have deteriorated, and the reason is plain. I miss the inspiration of Roger's warming ministrations before each recital, and so I do not sing at my best, and so the Count is perhaps not as inspired as he was when we first met. On one occasion I tried to persuade him to shaft me before an evening's music, but his member refused to rise to the occasion. Without the arousal of music he cannot perform. Yet without arousal beforehand, I cannot perform that music satisfactorily. I foresee trouble.

Last night I feared the worst. After I had sung a selection of arias from the pens of Signor Rossini and Herr von Weber, my noble employer seemed very downcast. The music had failed to touch him. Nor did my touching him have much effect. He lay on his silken sheet gazing at me longingly yet with no physical indication of hunger. The noble blood, of whatever hue, failed to race in the right direction. Even at its best his erection was a short, thin little thing, with a babyish pimple on the end instead of a great purple knob like my dear, distant Roger's. Tonight it slouched as insignificant and unchallenging as a little pink slug.

Who, I wondered dismally, might Roger be servicing tonight?

In an effort to dismiss such jealous fantasies from my mind and to give good value to the nobleman who had, after all, been treating me with the greatest courtesy and generosity, I set myself to breathe some fire into his loins. I made him wince with the grip of my fingers, then kneaded his blob of flesh in my palms. He writhed to and fro as I conscientiously scratched his cods (as I believe they are known in good society), going puce in the face as he tried to will himself into excitement. When I thought I felt some faint stirring, I sat upon him and tried to inhale the flaccid end into my lower lips, but it sagged away. Then I drew back and kneeled to apply my other lips, with no more success.

'I fear I have had an exhausting day,' the Count excused himself at last.

'Perhaps we should try Mozart on Saturday,' I suggested. 'An aria from *Le Nozze di Figaro*. And then next week the aria you like so much in *Don Giovanni*, and perhaps you will feel able to return to your wife in good fettle.'

He summoned up a wan smile, nibbled for a moment at my left nipple, and then dismissed me with a limp wave of the hand. It was not the only thing about him that was limp.

I was in no mood for sleep. If the Count had been unsatisfied tonight, then how much more dissatisfied was I! A vision of Roger again rose unbidden before me, and I thought of holding him as I had so often done with my hand until for both of us it was intolerable and there was such a desperate appetite for holding him in other ways. I felt my mouth shaping itself into a hungry O. But tonight there was nothing but a ghost to clutch or bite at.

I reached for my diary, since there was nothing else to occupy me.

Then there came a quiet tapping at my door. Had Count Rupert had a sudden resurgence of energy? I slipped my robe from my shoulders and hastened to open the door.

His wife, the Duchess Fulvia, stood outside. She looked me up and down in a long appraisal, while I sought for words. At last she said:

'May I come in? Or are you too tired for conversation, after your night's duties?'

Her tone of voice had alarming implications. I gulped, wondering what was in store for me. Although she always looked so icily self-possessed, it was said that she had a liking for beating her maids, and some girls did not appear for several days at a time, until their wounds had healed.

'Your Grace,' I stammered, 'I hope you don't. . . that is, you're not making some mistake. . .'

'Come, my dear Cecilia, let there be no pretences between us.' She spoke more slowly and less fluently than her husband, but she liked to pick her words over and be sure they conveyed exactly what she meant. 'I am not here to reproach you. Unless it be to suggest a certain lack of. . . how shall I say? . . . diligence.'

She came in quietly, and quietly closed the door.

She was a striking woman, dark-skinned and with hair as dark as a raven's wing. Her fingers were very long and slender. Her body, too, was slender, and some might have considered her too thin for perfection. I reached for my robe as I waited for her to explain further.

She said very gently: 'No, do not cover yourself, *meine Teure*. I suspected the rest of you would be as beautiful as your face. I see I was right.'

As she moved past me she touched my shoulder. It seemed a casual gesture, but her hand remained there for several seconds, and her lips parted slightly.

'Will you be seated, Your Grace?' I said awkwardly.

'You are Cecilia,' she said. 'And in this room with you I am Fulvia. The protocol is for elsewhere.'

Although there were two attractive gilded chairs in the room, she sat on the edge of the bed and patted the sheet to indicate that I should sit beside her.

'I am wondering,' she went on, 'whether you comfort my husband good this evening. Good. . . well enough, yes?'

'I fancy I did not sing as well as I might have done.'

'To tell the truth, I was of that opinion myself. But I speak of your private dancing afterwards. Do you not make the lively coupling?'

There was a shrewd question in her voice. Or a sort of doubt.

It was no use pretending not to understand. 'There was little liveliness this time,' I told her frankly. 'Perhaps the Count is tiring of me. No doubt that will please you.'

'On the contrary. Your coming here has been a great blessing. I have to confess, *liebling*, to a feeling of guilt. I somehow lack the ability to satisfy my husband. I do not possess your talents. And I confess that from the moment of our marriage I have been depressed by his. . . *ach*. . . *umherfühlken*. . . fumblings. I can not relax. I can not respond. I am at least partly to blame for his frequent impotence. You show me, please – how you handle him?'

'It's difficult to demonstrate,' I pointed out, 'when as a woman you lack some of the essential physical elements.'

'But I would like you to try.' It was little more than a whisper, followed by the whisper of her near-transparent muslin gown sliding to the floor.

She sank back on to the bed, looking hopefully up at me.

Her waist was tiny, and her hips narrow. Her breasts were very small, delicate mounds, with surprisingly large, very dark nipples like huge bruises in the centre. When I kissed them and bit them she flinched, but her gasp was one of appreciation rather than pain. Holding her was a new experience for me. Whenever I caressed my own body I found it soft and warm. By now I was more accustomed, though, to the hardness of male flesh and the rasp of male hair against me. The Duchess – Fulvia – was slim and very cool to the touch. She move sinuously in my arms, slow and supple as a serpent; and her tongue, like a serpent's, flicked out eagerly at me.

I turned her over and licked her back, and then forced her up to her knees and, gripping her between my thighs, demonstrated with my middle finger how her husband might care to enter her. Out of good manners I refrained from saying that it was a position requiring, for security, a longer prick than he possessed. On his pathetic attempts to perform the task with me, he all too frequently slipped out; unlike Roger, who could push me halfway across a room like a rutting dog.

It was Fulvia who then, all at once, took the initiative. She slid round, even more like a coiling and uncoiling snake, and her tongue dabbed its way down my belly and at last into me. To torment her I worked my head between her legs until it was well through and my lips were exploring her olive-skinned rump and the silky hairs of its cleft. I heard her trying to protest, only it was a matter not so much of hearing as of being tickled by a buzzing breath within me. At last, laughing, I drew back until my own tongue could seek its way into the moist warmth that was such a contrast to her cool skin and the oiliness of her black shrub of hair.

She tasted both sweet and spicy. We dabbed and sucked and murmured like two self-indulgent bees, until we were sated with the honey dribbling from our four pairs of lips.

When Fulvia was ready to leave she paused at the door and said; 'Thank you for your tuition, my dear Cecilia. Now, let me see – there is no concert tomorrow evening, I am right?'

'None until Saturday.'

'Then you must make it your task to ensure that my husband is satisfied on Saturday. If you should fail him again' – her lips were breathlessly parted once more – 'I shall bring my whip to you. Is that understood?'

A tremor ran through me like the harmonic of a violently plucked harp string. All I could say was: 'The Count might ask some awkward questions about the marks.'

'You would have to pleasure him on your back for a while, then, so that he observed nothing.'

'And that would hurt my back further.'

Fulvia nodded complacently. Her smile seemed to linger after she had closed the door and gone back to her room.

THURSDAY 7 JULY 1814

In spite of sleeping so well last night after my companionable session with the Countess, I found myself no less restless this morning. Fulvia had offered some unexpected flavours which I would be happy to taste again, but they were really no substitute for the solid meat I had come to crave. Oh, how guilty I feel for repulsing Roger so often in the past, on the pretext that I required him only to tune up my vocal chords. If he were here now I would seize him and demand a rest from music for a least a week, but no rest whatsoever for his thrusting and churning.

It was a warm day. I had no music to rehearse, nothing to do but stroll in the gardens and think.

Thinking of one thing only.

Count Rupert had stocked his grounds with statues rather than flowers. At the intersections of every avenue there were naked goddesses or large-bottomed nymphs stooping to pick up baskets or nosegays. Under one over-arching linden tree a little Cupid appeared to be shooting his arrow into the pendulous breast of a cowering maiden. There were two life-sized statues of naked men, each decked with a fig leaf, though there seemed to be no substantial swelling against the leaf from within. Perhaps the sculptor had used his noble patron as a model.

It was a graceful classical setting, but not one to suit my present needs.

In a remote corner of the estate I came across a statue which bore little resemblance to any of the others. It was of a mounted warrior in full armour, his lance tilting downwards as if to impale some enemy on the ground. Most probably it was one of Rupert's warlike ancestors, now rather scorned in our civilised times. Leaves cast a dappled shadow over the man and his horse, but the sun bore full down upon the tip of his lance. It might once have been sharp, but the stone had been blunted by age, and when I touched it I found it to be smooth and warm. And beautifully solid.

Its contours and size were too heartbreakingly reminiscent of someone far away. I stepped up on to the plinth. After a few moments of freeing myself from my petticoats and looping them aside, I eased myself on to the end of the lance. It did not move, did not swell and contract, retreat and plunge, but left me to set the tempo for myself. I clung with one hand to the stone stirrup nearest me, and impaled myself as far as I dared.

It was at the climax of satisfaction, spoiled only by the inability of the lance to pour any savoury juice into me, that a voice from under the trees said in heavily accented English: 'So that is what you need, *fräulein?*'

I refused to be distracted until I had finished my ecstasy. Then I lowered myself from the lance, readjusted my clothing, and turned to confront the Count's *konzertmeister*.

Wilhelm Grosz was a stocky man with long arms, which he loved to wave energetically to their full extent while directing the court orchestra. He was a passable violinist, with an admirable facility at sight-reading but few powers of interpretation. In short, he was a good artisan but not much of an artist. Nor had I ever liked his thick lips or the way he grimaced at me when signifying my entry after an orchestral introduction.

Now I was subjected to the full force of that gaze.

'I was spending an hour of leisure in the gardens,' I said lamely.

He grinned. 'If you need a companion in your leisure pursuits, I am at your service.'

'The Count would not approve.'

'The Count, it seems, does not entirely satisfy you.'

'If I were to report such impertinence to him – '

'But you will not, will you?'

He was coarse, insufferable, and his hands were covered in hair. But he had a certain rough masterfulness, which I had to admit he deployed quite constructively when leading the orchestra.

I was alarmed by my thoughts, and walked briskly away over the grass.

He caught me up with little trouble. Outside the little pavilion tucked away behind the orchard he growled: 'I keep you in good trim for our master, *nicht wahr*? Exercise very necessary. And I am better than stone. Hard, but not so hard.'

Wretchedly I was aware that I was already hungry again: the lance had been only a temporary sop.

We went into the pavilion.

It smelt damp, and the bench had been cracked at one end and would not take our weight. Grosz did not hesitate. As with a difficult symphonic passage, he tackled the problem head on. Though his head had little to do with it. Swiftly unfastening his belt and letting his trousers sink around his knees, he lifted me bodily in those long, powerful arms, and set me upon a ramrod as hard as that stone lance had been. But this rod was capable of movement. Pinning me to the wall and holding me steady with his hands under my buttocks, he drove in and out at a steady pace which I was sure was accompanied in his head by the music of a lolloping *ländler*. Yet there was more brute force than music in his approach. He had all the manner of a peasant rather than a musician, driving a tool into the yielding earth and dragging it back, thudding in, hauling back. There was no question of his trying to please me. He hammered my back against the wall until he was ready to discharge himself, grunting five times before loosing his grip on my bottom and leaving me to find my own balance once more.

But I had to admit to myself – though not to him – that even if he had not aimed to please, I was not entirely displeased.

'So,' said Grosz, fastening his belt again, 'I think we understand each other. We understand better now.'

I had a shameful feeling that we did, indeed, and that this would not be the last time I submitted to his mauling.

SUNDAY 17 JULY 1814

I have had to neglect my diary for this past week and more in order to rehearse a new cantata with which the Count wished to regale a visiting bishop. Last evening we offered a flawless rendition, and I could see Rupert's eyes ablaze with desire as my voice soared above the final chorale. He little knew how much he owed to his *konzertmeister*, who had taken me into his private quarters a mere half-hour before the performance and rushed us through a duet for our private parts. I was still aching from the experience when, unceremoniously bundling the bishop off the premises, the Duke offered his less bruising but reasonably successful attentions. I had hoped that he would turn his attentions to his wife, which had surely been the purpose of my being here; but it seemed he was in the mood for the physical appendages to my voice.

Count Rupert gallantly made time to congratulate me on my exquisite singing before coming at me. I raised my knee with just the right force to stimulate his cods, and in a moment he was squatting upon me and raving excitedly to himself in German, of which I knew just enough to deduce that he had now switched his congratulations to the quality of my *scheide*, which I assumed to be my vagina. The word sounded very harsh in German, though better than some versions in English, and he made up for it by resumption of his usual delicacy and charm as we parted. I fancy he was contentedly asleep within five or six minutes of leaving – unless, that is, his wife kept him awake with awkward questions.

Before I had finished brushing my hair there was a tap at the door. A shiver of something I did not care to identify ran down my spine. But surely the Duchess could not have come to whip me, when I had so thoroughly satisfied her husband?

Fulvia was smiling. But there was a wistfulness in her smile. 'I am almost disappointed,' she said, kissing my cheek and letting her lips rest there for a while. 'I had thought perhaps, for his sake and the sake of his inheritance. . . but no, that is selfish. Better that you make him happy. One day, perhaps. . . But you must tell me, my dear: what happened to raise you to such inspired heights?'

I hesitated. She might be appalled by the idea of my allowing a mere hireling like Grosz into the cranny reserved for the aristocratic member. I would lose her friendship, and perhaps a great deal more besides. But then a fine notion formed itself in my mind. Roger Rougiere might yet be *konzertmeister* at the court of Stoltenberg.

'Well?' probed Fulvia.

Instead of answering, I coaxed her into bed and we lay there chatting for ten minutes or so, playing drowsy games with our fingers and occasionally rubbing our knuckles affectionately against tufts of hair. Then I decided upon taking the risk.

'You are glad that I have found a way of restoring my voice to its true quality,' I began.

'Of course. The results were remarkable. *Glänzend*. And I still wish to know how it was accomplished.'

'You won't be angry with me?'

She kissed my shoulder. 'That I promise.'

So I told her. She went stiff for a moment, and I thought her promise would be broken. Then she said thoughtfully: 'The man is not to my taste. I have never thought highly of his musical skill. But what he lacks in musical ability himself, he draws it out in others. Or out of one other. You must use him as you see fit. Though it is a pity he has so little breeding.'

I said: 'It would undoubtedly be better if he could be replaced.'

'Replaced? By whom?'

I told her of Roger Rougiere. It was true that her husband had looked rather suspiciously on Roger and had refused to invite him to Stoltenberg. But what if the Count were given grounds for high-minded wrath upon catching me being debauched by the brutish Grosz? Surely the upright Englishman would be preferable to that?

Fulvia laughed delightedly. She wrapped her arms round me, and again I abandoned myself to the sleepy pleasure of her sinuous weaving and stroking.

'Yes,' she said. 'Oh, yes. It shall be so. You shall have your Roger, and my husband shall have his pleasure. But' – she struck my right buttock with sudden vicious force – 'you will reserve some time for me. Times like this one.'

'Of course,' I hastened to agree.

'Otherwise. . .'

'Otherwise?'

'Come, let us not suppose any "otherwise".'

Fulvia laughed again, her familiar cool laugh; but both her hands were now clenched on my bottom, and there was no tenderness in her grip.

I tried to distract her. 'When shall we start on Grosz?'

Slowly she slackened her hold, and we began to plot.

TUESDAY 2 AUGUST 1814

So it has been achieved. My fingers tremble as I write. For

although we have most slyly disposed of Herr Grosz, can I be sure that my Roger will come when called? Perhaps it is too presumptuous of me to suppose that he will. Abandoned for the second time, left behind in London, why should he drop whatever it is he may be doing simply because I have sent for him – or, rather, the Count has sent for him? He may by now have acquired another pupil with a well-rounded technique, another partner in music and much else. I cannot bear to think how far such a girl's instruction must have advanced in the time Roger and I have been apart. What positions on the staff may he be teaching her this very day, this very minute?

It was foolish not to ensure, before we arranged Grosz's dismissal, that Mr Rougiere would indeed be willing to replace him.

Yet was it not Roger himself who said that from now on there should be no doubts and jealousies between us? He came once before when I called. Why should he not come now?

The first part of the plan has gone without a hitch. It was set in motion by my singing very badly one evening in front of a distinguished group of the Count's guests, including two Westphalian barons on their way home from exile. Bonaparte has been banished to the island of Elba these many months ago, and all those he oppressed have been planning their lives without him. Conversation that evening was all of redrawing boundaries and reclaiming ancient rights, while keeping a watchful eye on Alexander of Russia. I doubt if the barons really wanted their talk interrupted by my singing, or even noticed that I was in poor voice. But certainly Count Rupert noticed.

Two nights later, when the guests had gone, he was in the mood for an intimate evening of music; just a few *lieder* accompanied by Grosz upon the spinet. I had deliberately avoided Grosz before the performance, and he was grumpy and suspicious, which made our efforts all the more ragged.

The Count glared at Grosz and looked at me plaintively. I could easily deduce that after the social exhaustion of the previous few days he had been in a mood to relax. But the disappointing recital had failed to arouse his passions in the direction of either his wife or myself.

Next morning Fulvia came to me to report that he had nevertheless attempted to impregnate her, but with pitiful results. He had thrashed about vainly for a while, then said it was the inadequacy of the music which had irritated him and rendered him unable to concentrate.

'What in heaven's name is happening to the girl? I did not engage her to produce such disagreeable sounds. Do you suppose she's ill? And as for Grosz –'

'Ah, yes, Grosz.' Fulvia seized the opportunity to raise a finely haughty eyebrow and fill her words with sombre insinuation.

'What about him?'

'It is my belief,' said Fulvia, 'that Grosz is mistreating the poor girl.'

'In what way?'

'That I cannot tell. Only, as a woman, I sense it.'

'I shall demand an explanation immediately.'

'No, no. It is only conjecture. If I am wrong, I would not wish him to be insulted by a false accusation. If I am right, he is such an insensitive brute that he will simply deny everything. The best course is to keep him under observation until we know precisely what is happening.'

This last Saturday the Countess suggested to her husband a musical evening built around some favourite pieces of her own. She asked for a *concerto grosso* from the orchestra, a few pianoforte pieces, and a song cycle from myself, with Grosz as accompanist. We had by then discussed what trap the *konzertmeister* might most easily be led into. He would conceitedly take as a matter of course my renewed need for his services before the concert, so where best for the Count to come upon us? A discovery in my own quarters might suggest a willingness on my part. For a while we both liked the idea of the Countess taking her husband for a stroll in the gardens and coming across Grosz humping over me in the shrubbery. But it would be difficult for me to persuade Grosz to expose himself in the open air: he preferred that shed we had used before, in a dark corner of the gardens to which only the most blatant contrivance would persuade the Count to let himself be led.

Then Fulvia smiled in that slow, calculating way she had, her lips opening only just enough to show her teeth closing, ready to bite.

She said: 'But of course. The dungeon!'

It was not a part of the premises of whose existence I had so far been aware. Now it was explained to me in grisly detail. In the days when the *schloss* had been essentially a defensive castle, before its late seventeenth-century conversion into a graceful residential mansion, one of Count Rupert's ancestors had installed a narrow vent from the subterranean dungeon up to his sitting room on the second floor. From there he could, simply by opening a small panel, listen appreciatively to the moans and shrieks of wretches being tortured and then left to starve in the foul depths. The dungeon had not been used for generations; but it was still there.

At first I did not understand what had to be done. When I did, I was none too comfortable at the prospect. But Fulvia was insistent. Having conceived the plan, she displayed an autocratic reluctance to have it criticised or amended in any way.

An hour before the concert I strolled along the south terrace in a light primrose muslin gown. It did not take long before Grosz appeared, signalling to me. I pretended not to notice, and went into the house by a side door. A tinder box and torch impregnated with pitch had been left where I could find them, though I put up a great pretence of being surprised by their presence. Having lit the torch, I proceeded into the gloom with a simulation of great curiosity. I could hear Grosz following me but made sure he did not catch up until I was at the foot of the flight of dank stone steps, outside the open door of the dungeon. Only a dismal smear of light filtered in through a slit on the turn of the stairwell, and my torch cast evil red splashes on the bottom step and across the dungeon floor.

'*Ach, so,*' grunted Grosz near my left ear. 'This . . . *ja, so?*'

Gleeful over what he supposed to be the vice of my hidden yearnings, he bundled me in, snatching the brand from me and thrusting it into a rusty link halfway up the wall. Then he snorted greedily as the light fell on gyves hanging from bolts in the walls.

Numbly I let him drag the muslin gown over my head. With that awful brute strength of his he lifted me bodily on to his shoulders, his head thrusting into my loins, and pinned my back against the slimy wall while he clamped the highest of the gyves around my wrists. I winced with the rasping pain of them as my weight sagged down; but did not want to make too much noise too early. He put my left ankle into a gyve at the foot of the wall, and was about to do the same for the right one when he noticed another iron claw further along. Straining my leg towards it, he succeeded in securing me with agonisingly splayed legs. Then he dragged his breeches off, not bothering with his shirt or jacket.

The sprawl of my legs was cruelly wide enough to give me pain if I stayed utterly still. Yet within a few moments of Grosz's coarse flesh and muscle swelling into me I could not help moving in response. My mind told me to be still and reserve my strength. My body betrayed me. Every thrust he made which drove my shoulders and bottom against the wall was a searing misery. Yet I was answering his brutality with a convulsive swaying from side to side, and pushing myself away from the wall in rhythm with his retreating and then returning shaft. A sob burst out of me. Then I cried out, and Grosz laughed uproariously, taking it for a cry of pleasure: which, to my shame, it was. But soon I knew that the time had come to summon help. I screamed; screamed again. Slavering, Grosz redoubled his efforts. I began to plead with him in a high shrill voice, then let myself go with another glissando of screams.

Now the agony was genuine. Ragged, rusty iron bit into my wrists and ankles. The spread of my legs was tearing me apart. Yet still, scream as I might, nobody came. I was possessed of utter terror. Had something gone wrong with the Countess's arrangements? Was there nobody listening in that room upstairs?

It seemed I was doomed to an eternity in this hell. Then, as I heard myself howling like a stricken animal which will soon be able to howl no longer, and as Grosz roared like a bull and discharged himself into me, footsteps clattered down the stairs and torches were raised to cast brighter light on the scene.

The Count let out a bellow of rage worthy of Grosz's own bellowings. His wife let out a faint sigh of horror, and said: 'So this is what the poor child has been suffering!'

Count Rupert seized Grosz by the shoulder and rushed him towards the stairs without allowing him time to reclaim his breeches. Over his shoulder he commanded: 'Free the child. Comfort her.'

Fulvia contemplated my sagging, bruised body. I thought she would at once move to release me from the hideous bondage. But she stood there a full, silent minute looking me up and down.

'Madam,' I gasped, 'you were so long coming. I didn't expect it to be so long.'

Her smile was reflective, almost amused. 'I had to listen to you for quite a while before my husband deigned to come into the room.'

'But he ought to have been there from the start. It was agreed . . .'

She put out a tentative hand, dabbed one fastidious finger into my sweat, and tasted it thoughtfully. Her eyes, too, were tasting me.

'It will be worth it, surely, to have your true love back?'

'Madam, I implore you, release me.'

She came very close and I thought she was about to reach up and free my wrists. Instead, she kissed my breasts where the clutch of Grosz's hands had left a harsh stinging memory. Her mouth slid down my belly, hesitated while she playfully tongued my navel, and then went on down. Her tongue had come out between her teeth, poised to enter, when she straightened up with a shiver of disdain. Clearly she had no wish to partake of anything Gosz might have deposited in there.

Still she was reluctant to free me until I made a pretence of crying out – very softly at first – and said: 'If your husband is back in that room, he may hear me and wonder why I am still down here.'

She released me with a bad grace, tried to make an affectionate joke of it, and led me back up the dank flight of steps.

Back in my room, Fulvia said she would arrange for this evening's performance to be postponed an hour or so while they revised the programme, allowing for the absence of a pianist and the need to ensure that the first violinist could handle the full leadership of the orchestra. Also he must devise a way of using some of the strings to provide me with an accompaniment in place of the keyboard harmonies. She would give me thirty minutes' notice of the actual starting time once these matters had been sorted out.

I expressed surprise that there should be any question of my singing this evening after what had happened.

Fulvia looked equally surprised. 'But you surely do not suppose we should alter our arrangements because of a mere personal incident involving a couple of our retainers? Besides' – she gave me a roguish smile from the door – 'I fancy my husband will have been stimulated by the sights below stairs, and while you are singing will be lost in a reverie while conjuring up fine flights of fancy.'

I washed myself, dabbed gently at the more tender spots and ugly abrasions, and paced around with time to spare. For a while I lay on my bed, unwilling yet to draw clothes over the stinging flesh, easing myself out of the squalor of what had happened and invoking the thought of Roger. He would come. He must come. He would be here, and all would be well again.

But this evening. . . If the Count was in receptive mood, how could I be sure of living up to his expectations? Grosz had fed me as he had done many a time before, but I had been concentrating mainly on keeping him going until the trap was sprung, and even when I had been unable to resist responding, there was as much disgust as exultation in me.

Was this to be another unworthy, uninspired performance?

There came a tap at the door, followed by something

unintelligible in a light, almost soprano voice which I took to be Fulvia's. I went to the door and opened it.

Outside was a pageboy in the Count's scarlet and yellow livery. He stared, held out a tray on which lay a note in what I recognised at once as Fulvia's handwriting: and went on staring up and down my body with a dawning realisation of things which had hitherto been a closed book to him.

I drew him in. The amazement and naïve longing in his eyes offered one of the most flattering, spontaneous tributes I have ever been paid.

Within half a minute I had divested him of his livery. The page had the most delicate skin, like a baby's. There was hardly a hair on his body, and one had a perfect view of his pretty pink prick and the sweetest little pink balls, so neatly encased in a scarcely wrinkled little pink bag.

The poor young innocent could not understand why that little organ of his was rising so gently and uncontrollably, but he was shy of it and instinctively cupped his hands across his crotch. I tugged them apart, drew him towards the edge of the bed, and took him on to my lap. For one so small, he showed promising signs of not needing to wait for enrolment in the Count's guard to sport a worthy weapon.

He put his arms round my neck as if seeking motherly comfort. But his prick was urging itself on impatiently – he knew not where. He prodded my thighs, made a vain thrust down into the bedding. And then I lay on my back and took him firmly in hand to guide him in. It was such a smooth, delightful plaything. He lay quite still within me, pushed himself up to risk a shy look into my face, and then slumped down again, motionless apart from that gradual swelling and pulsing inside me. And I could tell he was wondering: wondering what came next, what to do. . .

I tried to roll over so that I could lie upon him and instruct him in some essential motions, but even that slight shift caused him to pop out. He looked woeful, despairing. I lifted myself on to him and sat up so that unless he closed his eyes or looked shyly away he could see little else but my breasts. I swung them gently above him, and he did not look away but watched with young, bright, clear eyes. And then I took him in again, and moved gently up and down that short but firm length of his, and his eyes widened and his mouth opened in ever-increasing amazement.

What I most wanted for my throat's sake was the lubrication which I had always been too fastidious to accept from Grosz. I lifted myself off the boy, preparatory to the necessary readjustment of limbs and heads, and he proved himself a quick learner. Even as I was lowering my mouth to my task he anticipated me by pushing his pretty prick eagerly forward and clasping my head close to him. In a few seconds he was tickling my palate and finishing off with a hoot of boyish glee. It was so innocent, so cleansing, after the vulgarity of the unspeakable Grosz. I felt that I had acquired a pupil of my very own; and one who would become a master in his own right before he was much older.

Not with me, of course. I had started him. Let somebody else reap the benefit.

I sang very well that evening. Obviously too well, for the Countess came to see me next morning not in any congratulatory mood but with a reproachful frown.

'You were rather unrestrained, my dear. You provoked lack of restraint also. I am sore. My husband's behaviour was quite crude. Uncontrollable. Why did you sing so?'

'I. . . er. . . it was thinking about Mr Rougiere.'

She sniffed. 'When he is here, you must not go too far. You must in future continue to be good, of course – but not *excessively* good.'

I had a suspicion that if Roger were to come and join me there was a risk of my being superb.

And he must come. He must. I will write it down a dozen times, a score of times, on every page of this diary until he is here. He must come. . . he must. . .

MONDAY 5 SEPTEMBER 1814

He has come! At last, after delays and setbacks and uncertainties, my Roger Rougiere has come. He has come into Stoltenfeld and come in me – come over and over again, until he laughs and swears he is a dried-up husk; yet still I suffer a wonderful thirst.

The Countess, though disdainful of such ignominious craving for any one man, has behaved most considerately in the matter. When the date of Mr Rougiere's arrival was confirmed she arranged for her husband and herself to be invited on a brief visit to her uncle, the Margrave of Saxe-Hessen. 'I do not ask how you will spend the time,' she said with a sisterly caress of my arm, 'and I do not expect to be told too many repellent details. But I shall expect to see an improvement in the situation here. In every way I shall expect improvements.'

I am writing this while Roger goes to seek a dip in the stream running through the garden below my window: a little secret garden in which the Countess has promised we shall not be disturbed if we choose to spend any time out of doors. I confess that I have no immediate desire to leave this room. A few moments ago I went to the window, watching Roger splash the water over himself and clean around the stickiness we have created between us. I was vaguely tempted to join him, but could not summon up the energy to go downstairs; and now it occurs to me that this may be an excellent opportunity to jot a few details down in my diary before they slip my memory – small as that danger may be. So here I am, at an open page.

We have, up to this moment, spent eighteen hours and thirty-five minutes in this bed or in different situations around the room. I think I shall never forget the first impact of Roger's arrival. There was such adoration in his face; and he was so gratifyingly impatient to confirm that adoration with more solid evidence. In fact we were both so starved and impatient that our first encounter was too fast, too violent, too quickly consummated. He was like a soldier home from the wars, in a mood for rape rather than gentle courtship. Yet the fault was as much mine as his. We struck one another, bit, clutched and scratched madly, and finished on the floor like a savage dog and a bitch in ungovernable heat. Finished too soon.

But then there was time for reflection. Where we had

bitten, we kissed. Where he had struck me with his open palm and then with his clenched fist, he stroked. We coaxed the warmth slowly back, not wanting to rut so insensately again or so wantonly race to a conclusion.

I ran my nails very lightly up and down the inside of his thighs, each time brushing his cods with my knuckles. I knew to the instant when the potion began to brew in them again, and his prick was growing ready to transmit it. We clasped and turned, murmured silly meaningless sounds to each other, and out of a sated calm began to rise to fervour again. I twined round him like a creeper round a trunk. His prick like a storm-lashed branch tried to trap me and hold me steady. When he had penetrated me, and neither of us wished to hurry in spite of the intolerable heat burning within, I clutched him between my thighs and he told me things that were delirious and insane and intoxicating. Yet, though they were uttered such a short time ago, I cannot remember enough to write them down on this page.

There was the sheer, lovely laziness of the interludes. We talked idly about music and about what life in London was like today, and what my working conditions here were like; and then the burgeoning, the reawakening, the touching and warming and at last, once more, the wild threshing from one side of the bed to the other.

Not that we were so slothful as to lie abed all the time. Two hours ago we made love against the Gobelin tapestry on the wall, adjusting ourselves to the very heart of its pastoral scene. Roger took an aesthetic delight in pressing me exactly against the embroidered horn of a unicorn, which was mercifully not real – though Roger's horn could have been damaging enough if I had not been so eager and receptive to it and if it had not, unlike the sharp tip of the unicorn, been so evenly rounded into a smooth knob.

Now that he has gone into the garden for refreshment, I can dwell on such joys and scribble them down with the greatest pleasure, rather than fritter away the time simply lying on my back and conjuring up drowsy pictures of what may be attempted next time. But leaning over the bedside table in this fashion, with my knees hunched up to balance me as I write, I ought to have been aware that I present too easy a target. Before I have had a chance to be aware of it, Roger is back in the room, chilled and dripping with moisture; and gripping my waist with cold fingers he has aimed unerringly and is sunk into me, shaking my writing arm and a great deal more besides. My writing. . . this hand too unsteady. . . no, I must abandon my diary until. . .

He is dipping too vigorously.

Later. . .

TUESDAY 6 SEPTEMBER 1814

And now it is morning again, and there is silence. I try to write, but my back and shoulders are as sore as when Grosz tortured me. For I have in fact been tortured once more. Roger, also in pain, had gone back to his quarters to recuperate. And the Countess is doubtless in her boudoir. I wonder if she, too, keeps a diary? If so, I am sure it is more elegantly written and expressed than mine. But is she honest enough to express all that she feels?

We had not expected to see the Countess back so soon. It transpired in her later explanations that her husband, drinking heavily with her uncle, had become irritable and was fretting about the arrival of Roger in Stoltenfeld and asking awkward questions. To set his mind at rest the Countess had volunteered to come home and supervise the establishment, playing the part of duenna while he stayed and passed the time with the Margrave shooting hundreds of birds and beasts in daytime and drinking again deep into the hours of darkness. I thought it strange that so lacklustre a man should find pleasure in the energetic slaughter of the wildlife of field and forest, but it seems that this was a family tradition which even he took for granted and was capable of pursuing diligently.

The Countess came to my room unceremoniously, and for a few seconds we were unaware of her presence, being wrapped in an embrace which allowed little scope for consciousness of the outside world. Roger had lain down on his back and, with his hands on my hips from behind, had guided the mouth of my brimming flask on to his rejuvenated stopper. Gradually he raised his legs and I lowered my head until we each contemplated the other's arse. We were indeed happily contemplative, resting for a moment before pursuing the matter more vigorously, when I heard the click of the door opening, but ignored it because I thought merely that on his return Roger had not secured the handle properly. Then I observed, from an awkward sidelong turn of my head, that the Countess was present. Around the firmness of Roger's haunch I saw her there in riding habit, with a riding crop tapping her right leg, watching us with incredulous interest.

I tried to make some respectful acknowledgment in her direction but was hindered by Roger's legs. Suddenly conscious of our audience, he lowered them, and I was able to sit up and bob my head at Fulvia. At the same time I recognised that it was not merely Roger's legs which had come down. Perhaps enfeebled by some gentlemanly embarrassment in the presence of this unexpected intruder, his prick had shrunk within me and collapsed.

Fulvia said wonderingly: 'A most interesting position, this. It has the advantage that one need not look into the man's absurd face.'

Although Roger's face was at such moments a secondary consideration, I could not allow such a remark to pass without protest. 'Madam, I find no absurdity in – '

'Forgive me, *liebling*. I meant no offence to your. . . accompanist. I was thinking, I confess, of my husband. There is something so absurd about his grimaces when he finally achieves what he has been labouring over. If I did not have to look upon him, it might be more easily endurable.'

Impulsively and, I swear, quite without guile, I said: 'But madam, such an angle requires the services of a well-endowed member of reasonable length.'

It was not, I realised, the most tactful thing to say, and displayed more knowledge of her husband's anatomy than was perhaps polite in open conversation. But she did no more than purse her lips and scratch her calf with her riding crop.

'I would not be amiss to a personal demonstration,' she said. Without more ado she tossed the riding crop on to a chair and began to unbutton her jacket.

I was about to repeat, in a slightly different way, what I had already said about the prime necessity for such an exercise; or perhaps simply to gesture apologetically towards Roger's present incapacity. But when I glanced at him, I found that as he stared at the Countess's lithe body emerging from her shift his rod was rising in tribute. I felt furious at such a display of mental infidelity, and was tempted to spit on it to show how I despised him and it.

But of course I did not despise it. And had we not agreed there should be no jealousy, no reservations?

'It is a weakness, I confess,' said Fulvia in the most ingratiating way. 'I prefer a young woman's face before me rather than that of a man. That is not what is meant to be, hn? But our differences. . .' She sought gravely for a phrase which would satisfy her. 'Our temperamental differences,' she said with some pride, 'make for the interesting world, do they not?'

I was not sure whether this was a delicate hint, disguising her reluctance to suggest outright a creative idea which had just crossed her mind. We waited an interminable moment of indecision until Roger, most courteously ready to oblige or to relinquish his hold at the first word of protest, positioned himself behind her and very slowly drew her back on to him. With admirable smoothness he toppled back onto the bed, carrying Fulvia with him. She stared upwards until I came between her eyes and the ceiling. I put my hands on her hips from the front and steered her very slowly until she was in a position to sink precisely around Roger's mooring post. She must have been very tight and dry, for she blinked with pain for a moment, and gently I rocked her from side to side until she was able to settle down those last few inches and spread her legs backwards beside Roger's shoulders. Gradually she began to smile. Yet I could swear that it was not the sensations from below which produced this pleasure, but the way my hands were manipulating her.

Firmly impaled, she leaned forward, pulling me closer

until I found it necessary to spread my thighs across Roger's legs. Then Fulvia's face came close to mine, and her mouth opened, and within seconds our tongues were tasting and curling around each other. My hands moved over her shoulders and touched Roger playfully. But Fulvia, without an instant's hesitation, pulled them back and guided them on to the gentle little mounds of her breasts, while the middle finger of her own right hand began venturing down my belly and into the warmth so recently occupied by Roger.

So we played amicably enough for a few minutes, though I was not altogether pleased by the waywardness of Roger's hands. Every time I tried to draw them towards my own breasts they escaped, to be employed far too enthusiastically around Fulvia's legs and body, when it was clear to me, looking into her eyes, that she much preferred my own touch. There was only one way to give battle. I ceased attempting to reach Roger, and devoted myself to feathering Fulvia's nipples with my fingertips, jolting Roger's hands away, kissing her in the softness of her neck just as he was trying to bite her, and ravishing her mouth with my tongue.

Knowing him as I did, I knew what threatened when Roger's breathing began to quicken. As it reached a certain pitch I became desperate. Fulvia's finger had brought me to that same pitch, and I knew that if I had been placed where she was, both Roger and myself would reach our frenzy at the same moment. I could not bear that last hot gush of his to be wasted on someone else. I had to have it.

All self-restraint gone, I heaved the Countess bodily off her pivot, so that she sprawled away from us, on to the floor. I needed no helping hand from Roger to settle myself on that beloved prick, preparing to urge him into those last pulsations when he would no longer be able to hold back.

All at once there was a searing pain across my back. I cried out and instinctively twisted to one side, though without releasing my grip on Roger. The Countess had scrambled to her feet, seized her riding crop, and was raising it again. As the blow fell, Roger rolled protectively over on to me. I heard the terrible thwack of the crop against his bare back, and felt him leap and shudder through his entire body, right down to the tip buried within me.

'How dare you?' Fulvia's fury was a screaming whisper, all the more terrifying for being so hushed. 'What right have you. . . what presumption. . .'

The riding crop flailed again, scouring first across Roger and then scorching my left flank.

'Stand up. Stand, damn you.'

Fulvia whipped us off the bed and upright, dancing around us in a demented jig, striking Roger until he instinctively twisted away, thus offering her my shoulders and backside for her pleasure. We were still coupled, clinging desperately to each other. I did not dare release Roger, since from the feral gleam in her eye I felt convinced that she would lash at his prick with her crop, and I could not bear to think of such damage being inflicted on it.

Suddenly she was exhausted. Sweat dripping down her throat between her breasts, she tossed the crop aside and sank on to the chair.

'In future,' she hissed breathlessly, 'we will disengage when I say so. Not before.' And all at once she was laughing, and reaching her hands out to us as if we were the oldest and most cherished friends.

It will have to be later today, when we are sure she will not reappear, that Roger and I can come together again, kiss each other's weals, and resume what she so savagely interrupted.

WEDNESDAY 21 SEPTEMBER 1814

Nobody can deny that the musical quality of life in Stoltenberg has improved beyond measure these past two weeks. Our pattern of rehearsal, private overture – 'overture' meaning, as Roger slyly points out, an opening – and radiant performance is well established and productive. Indeed, there are moments when I wonder if there is not a danger of things becoming too predictable. Will there be a time when I take my ritual rogering for granted, and so grow numb and unresponsive, and sing less well?

It does not do to grow pessimistic so soon. For the moment all is as it should be.

That applies also to the Count and his lady. The whole purpose of my coming here from London seems to be fulfilling itself. After our evenings of music, Count Rupert devotes himself more and more assiduously to his wife. It is true that to some extent this was helped by the Countess Fulvia's coaxing him into abandoning his visits to me, though she did not tell him the main reason for this. What would he have made of walking into my room and finding Roger in my bed? And, come to think of it, how would Roger have reacted?

Again, let's not fret over problems that appear to have solved themselves.

A week ago Fulvia asked solicitously, though in no way apologetically, how my scars were healing, and then went on to commend the marital method we had taught her. She had offered the position to her husband and guided him in its niceties. He had been startled at first but then seemed quite captivated. And at least she herself, having endured his face for the larger part of the evening, could now turn her back on it and endure the congress quite philosophically. My singing may have contributed to his ardour, as indeed it is meant to do; but the approach in itself seems to provide its own stimulus. His fondness for it may have something to do with his devotion to dogs, whose copulations he can watch just as fondly as he can watch them tearing a hare or a deer to shreds.

As for Roger and myself, we have never yet had any reason for displeasure with any aspect of each other's body. We are rather surprised, really, how long it has taken the Count and his Countess to discover, or be taught, such a simple position to give them such simple satisfaction. It's not as if there were no sources of information close at hand. Whether introduced by himself to stir his waning powers, or whether inherited from a lustier ancestor, the young man's picture gallery and the paintings on the grand staircase and in a score of odd corners depict an admirable variety of human and heavenly couplings. One ceiling would be reminiscent of that deplorable London club were it not in some mysterious way so beautiful. Roger tells me that it is because it is a real work of art, painted by a genius. I am sure he is right. Yet the contents are pretty much the same. A plump woman, naked but for a wispy veil apparently disturbed by the wind and managing to hide nothing, spreads her legs to reveal a vast red tuft more like a spread of rough bracken than hair. Nymphs, cherubs and satyrs perform amazing feats all across the heavens, so that one is amazed they are capable of staying aloft with such ease. And in one corner of the firmament there is surely a coupling (or quadrupling) of classical Greeks looking commendably austere while tackling winsome youths from behind.

I am particularly fond of a large canvas of Leda and the Swan; though if the swan's relevant member is as thick and sinewy as its neck, the woman ought surely to look more rapturous and less diffident.

This last week the Count has demanded music at dinner every evening. It has been no great chore. In order to keep our appetites sharp and the music of sufficient vitality, Roger and I have been experimenting with some of the couplings symbolised or openly demonstrated in the paintings. There has been the sacrifice of the virgin on the stake, the dancing maiden juggling with balls above her head, and the conjunction of Mars and Venus in a clash of celestial weaponry. Any weariness which resulted from these games has been purely physical; and by the next evening we are invariably eager and fully equipped to seek new trials of strength.

SATURDAY 24 SEPTEMBER 1814

Only one slight embarrassment has threatened to mar our contented routine. Josef, the young page of whom I had made use in that moment of emergency some months ago, and whom I had taught a few basic principles, is proving somewhat of a nuisance. Clearly I had whetted his appetite, and now he is hungry for more. It is of course more than his job is worth for him to be seen impertinently approaching me of his own accord; but I have more than once observed him eyeing me from a distance, slinking behind hedges when I am strolling in the gardens, and giving me hopeful, suggestive little smiles.

A few days ago when I rode down from the *schloss* with Roger to watch the peasants dancing at a village wedding, and we got separated in the throng, I felt a playful little pinch on my bottom. I turned to find Josef beaming at me. He was no longer smart in his uniform, but like all the other local boys in woollen shirt and *lederhosen*. It is possible that one of his relatives was involved in the marriage and that the Count had given him a day off to attend the festivities. Whatever bawdy jokes might be passing from mouth to mouth, as they usually do on such nuptial occasions, he must have been fired by them and now was jerking his head in the direction of a cul-de-sac leading off the cobbled square.

Josef's dialect was thick, but I had by now acquired enough German to be able to pick out the gist of what he was saying. Even if I had not, there was no mistaking the meaning of his nods and grimaces, though whether his family had a cottage down the lane or whether he hoped merely for a quick exploit against the wall I could not be sure. Nor did I intend to find out. With what I hoped was a friendly but dismissive smile I edged away through the crowd.

He came after me, calling things which made many a head turn. Then Roger was beside me, taking my arm and leading me clear of the crush.

'What was all that about?'

Although there should be no shame or jealousy between us, I was somehow reluctant to admit to him that I had once been so desperate as to stoop – oh, so literally stoop – to employ the comforts of one so young. Fortunately Roger has not yet begun to master the local language, so accepted my assurance that the lad was one of the Count's pages who had been at the sour local wine rather too early in the day.

But when Josef was back in his livery and back at work,

he continued to appear at the corners of corridors or at a window, still staring and hoping.

Yesterday Roger and I went to the sunken garden to assess its possibilities for an alfresco concert. The autumn evenings have been warm and humid, and the Count now has a fancy for some music in the open air. Roger and I had decided that I would sing a few snatches in different parts of the sunken garden so that Roger could decide where the sound would be most effective.

It was a still, quite afternoon. A few bees droned over the flowerbeds, and the heady scent of late roses hung in the air. We walked slowly and soundlessly. This past week the drowsy warmth had made everyone move and talk more slowly, and often not bother to talk at all.

As we came to the top of the steps leading down through bushes to the sunken lawn, I caught a glimpse to my right of pink movement in the shadows of the covered pergola walk. Roger had noticed it at the same time. We stopped and remained utterly still save for a flicker of indulgent amusement round Roger's lips.

There in the shadows Josef, the little page, was fondling a blonde girl of some fourteen or fifteen summers whom I think I have seen in the linen room learning procedures from one of the Countess's maids. The two of them were naked: such a pretty, shadow-speckled pink in the shelter of the pergola. Josef was by no means a gallant swain: in order to protect his livery he had carefully folded his garments on top of the girl's, so that any grass or earth stains might mark her clothes and not his.

Nor, as we watched, was he showing himself very accomplished in his attentions to her slender, shy little body. He was touching her awkwardly, then waving his hands to no great purpose, then pushing himself against her, then muttering, while she could only shake her head and wonder what was supposed to happen. He wanted to be such a swaggering lover, airing his recently acquired knowledge, confident and overwhelming. Instead, he was going to bungle the whole thing.

It was so innocent, so charming. . . so pathetic.

I heard the disparaging intake of Roger's breath. This clumsiness obviously offended all his principles. Abruptly he seized my hand and dragged me towards the pergola.

The boy looked round, horrified. The girl clasped her arms nervously across her breasts, two quite admirable endowments for a child of her age, then desperately tried to combine this with spreading one hand over the golden shadow that stayed shimmering between her legs whichever way the sun might cast its other shadows.

Roger made reassuring noises and attempted a few words of German. As most of these came from Bach church cantatas, they were far from appropriate in present circumstances. The young couple still stared apprehensively.

Roger raised a hand like a priest about to bless them. Then he began to disrobe, motioning me to do the same. I guessed what was in his mind, and although I thought my pupil the page ought to have been able to manage without further demonstrations, I was ready for the girl's sake to ensure that the afternoon should not be a disappointing one.

We kept the lesson simple and fundamental. I merely lay on the ground while Roger stroked me, kissed me, and bit me gently, glancing round after each movement to make sure that our pupils were watching. I noticed that the girl's attention was directed most of the time, wonderingly, at Roger's staff as it braced itself for action. Josef took only one quick, despondent glance at it, and surreptitiously compared it with his own.

I spread my legs. Roger poised himself above me, taking his weight on his arms and keeping his bottom as high in the air as possible until the last minute, so that the other two could see how and where he was aiming. When at last I puckered myself round the end of him he still kept his movements very slow, allowing the young acolytes to watch the last inch of stem being gradually engulfed. When he began to pump, it was in a sequence of changing rhythms which could hardly have failed to entrance the audience, and which assuredly began to raise the temperature of the moisture within me.

Just when I feared there was a danger of his finishing in a

rush, Roger forced himself to withdraw, standing up and helping me to my feet.

'First lesson ended,' he said benevolently.

Josef's prick had been inspired by our demonstration to rise to those dimensions which I had earlier noted in him, though they appeared rather less admirable when set alongside Roger's, still rigid and rampant. Josef approached the girl with renewed enthusiasm, eager to start, though still nervous, far more nervous than he had been with me.

She sensed this, and it only added to her own nervousness. She pushed him away. He tried to force her down to the ground so that she would lie as I was lying, but his hands were so graceless that she wrenched to one side and put out a protective arm.

I got up and went to her, putting my own arm round her shoulders to calm her. She was very warm, and the corner of her throat was damp with a sweet-smelling sweat. I knew that she was already aching with desire for him, without truly understanding that ache and without knowing if he would be able to alleviate it. She wanted him yet did not know what she wanted. Instictively she felt she must fend him off, wait for him to prove himself, keep him away until in some way it was suddenly right. I remembered such feelings; remembered the first certainty and ecstasy of that first roger; and wanted her to experience the same fulfilment. The danger was that she would fend the boy off for too long: he would go cold and dismal, and they would both feel more ashamed about what hadn't happened than they ever would if it happened.

Josef came blundering towards her again. She sagged away from my arm and drew her knees up to her chin, wrapping her arms around them. Josef faltered, unsure how to get at her. It will take the lad a long time, I fear, to acquire the aptitude for sensing when a girl is ready, when she is uncertain, or when she is genuinely unreceptive.

I went behind the girl, reached over her shoulders, and laid my hands on her arms. Before she could react I rolled her gently back towards me on the curve of her sleek bottom, so that she was presenting her coral lips flagrantly to the lad. Again he was clumsy, going down on his knees and for a few seconds finding the angle too awkward a one. Then at last he was in, though only just, not expecting the virginal obstruction. Desperately he thrust forward. The girl cried out, but I knew the pain to be ecstasy and held her steady until, bathed in sweat, she began to shudder and try to push herself forward. Now all was as it should be. She had no further need of my comfort or encouragement: she was in a frenzy to drag more of him into her. Even with a youthful member with much yet to be developed, Josef could in this position achieve a penetration satisfying to both of them. Roger and I could feel well content with our charitable work.

The boy finished, as one might have predicted, too selfishly soon. When he scrambled up he looked proud of himself, though the drooping object between the petty globes of his pouch was by now nothing much to be proud of.

The girl unwrapped her arms and let her legs sprawl limply wherever they chose. She looked guilelessly at what remained of Josef and then at Roger. With growing self-confidence she reached out as if to test the sturdiness of that unfaltering shaft. To my annoyance, Roger did not look as if such homage would be beneath his dignity. Indeed, I began to suspect that it was the sight of her smooth young body, so close and attainable, and the flexibility of her covetous fingers, that was keeping Roger's erection in such fine trim.

All at once Josef moved with aggressive and unexpected speed. He got his hands beneath the girl's shoulders, dragged her to her feet, and urged her away towards their pile of clothes. So young and inexperienced, and already so jealous and possessive!

It was my moral duty to remove such temptation as that stripling girl from Roger's sight; and in any event I really could not much longer leave him in his present condition, unattended to and unsatisfied. I went down on my knees and withdrew his member from the girl's gaze, so deep into my mouth that there was nothing still visible for her to covet.

Absorbed in my task of absorbing Roger, my eyes were too close to his belly to see what the expressions of the others might be. But I heard a little gasp of excitement from Josef and a jubilant *Ja, ja, das ist...* Soon he would be boasting to her about his knowledge of this method, too, but not telling her where he had learnt it. She would be very stupid not to guess; but, being a girl, would never be stupid enough to give away her intuitions to a mere ignorant boy.

It is strange how much I could interpret from the quiver of Roger's sensitive rod within me. Stiff as he already was, he seemed to stiffen a fraction more. Did he detect something in the gauche young lad's tone of voice, and guess the reason? To distract his attention and avoid acrimonious discussion I clenched my teeth and scraped them to and fro along him more woundingly than I would normally have done. He flinched, but then vengefully drove into my throat as if to choke me. And then my throat was washed with his warmth, and I was happy.

Even though it had been meant only as a technical exercise to test the sound qualities of the surroundings, I sang quite splendidly in the sunken garden ten minutes later.

SATURDAY 1 OCTOBER 1814

I have no heart to write much today. But one thing I must set down, since I fear it may soon be of terrible importance. It is bad news, very bad news.

Lord Alderley has come visiting.

SUNDAY 2 OCTOBER 1814

I have to confess, though only to my diary, what I have never confessed to Roger. When he returned from Newcastle to rejoin me in London, he could not refrain from asking about my brief involvement with Lord Alderley. I, for my part, found it wise to refrain from going into too many details. It was not that I lied to him: simply that I omitted some things which it would have given him little joy to know. I have been learning that some things are best kept hidden from a man – not always one's body, but certain parts of one's mind. A man may think that because he has penetrated every physical cleft he must also be familiar with the recesses of the mind. It does no harm to let him think so; but it would be foolish to let it truly be so.

Wherefore I implied that Alderley had been a dismal failure, a silly whim of mine which I had immediately regretted, and that his arrogance in regarding me merely as a pet animal to be kept for his moments of idleness was such that my pride would not allow me to stay. I also implied that his physical capabilities were too puny to be worth mentioning ever again. Roger was all too smugly ready to accept this. As he rogered me in all the ways which I enjoyed as a variation from the throat lubrication which meant so much to me, I could sense his confidence that driving into me thus was enough to drive out the last pathetic droplets of the inadequate Alderley.

Which is true. Yet not all the truth.

I have not thought it politic to hint to Roger at the luxury with which Alderley at first surrounded me. In that elegant, dissipated manner of his he managed to convey that I must not set foot in his own house in St James's, but he spared no expense in setting me up in a suite of rooms behind Devonshire Street, accompanied by many a fine word and flattering gesture.

I was speedily to find that while his comportment was suave and his speech most eloquent and accomplished, his manners beneath the mannerisms were abominable.

In the first place, my installation in such lavishly appointed quarters was not merely to keep me at a good remove from the world in which his family and his affianced heiress lived. Nor was it that he was passionately in love with me and wanted to keep me to himself. He positively flaunted me in his box at the opera, and in private took great sport in showing me off to his dissolute friends. They would be brought in, often the worse for drink, to inspect me and comment upon my attributes. Once while he was using me showily and with a wealth of foul words, I realised halfway through the proceedings that a group of his cronies had let themselves into the room and were lolling against the wall, grinning and awarding points for his prowess in different directions.

His favourite entry into me was the same which he employed upon young urchins brought in from the gutter, though their ordeal did not last as long as mine. Pampered for a night, buggered by Alderley and by any of his guests who cared to avail themselves of the opportunity, they were then thrown out into the grey dawn. Alderley supposed he was flattering me when he once said, in his most languid drawl, that my bottom was almost as dainty as a boy's.

I was soon bitterly regretting my display that appalling evening which had so incensed Roger. His own conduct had been deplorable; but it had not left me with the sour aftertaste which every one of Alderley's actions and conceited sneers produced in me. I was lapped in comfort, but only so that I might be there whenever he deigned to want me, or wished to show me off as his fancy piece, his 'piece of nice game' kept in a private preserve.

It gave me no excitement to partake in diversions such as being shafted from behind while one of his street Arabs indulged him also from behind. Nor was I impressed by his offhanded suggestion that, should I feel neglected at the front, another of the young ruffians might attend to me from that direction.

The final insult was when he and five cronies arrived in the middle of the night from the gaming tables. He had decided that each and every one of them should be allowed to enjoy me as a kind of nightcap. Their last game of the evening, in fact, had been a matter of throwing dice to decide in which order they would take me.

While they drank in the sitting room, allowing me time to prepare myself for them in the agreed order, I hastily put on my outdoor clothes and gathered together such few belongings as I had brought with me. Sprawled around the room with glasses in their hands, they were quite unprepared for my march across the carpet towards the outer door.

I felt I could not go without some kind of leavetaking.

From the doorway I addressed myself to Lord Alderley. 'I thank you for your hospitality, but I fear I have little time for a man whose endowments are so puny that he needs a half-dozen friends to satisfy a woman on his behalf.'

Before they could make a move I was out in the street and hurrying to a corner where I was fortunate enough to find a hackney coach. Soon I was back in Roger's dear house.

Mrs Hiscock frowned reproach. I was sure she wanted to say, 'I hope that's taught you a lesson', but charitably she kept silent and somehow made me feel that I was welcome home.

Alderley came storming round to the house. His languid manner had for once deserted him. He cursed at me, insulted me, demanded that I return to him, and in the same breath said that I was a whore who would finish as a Mollisher in the gutters like the brats he so cheaply acquired and discarded.

The truth was that he hated to be deprived of anything he had once set his heart on – or, since his heart was so obviously missing, perhaps it should be described as anything that had given him an uncontrollable itch to possess. If boredom eventually took charge and he wished to discard yesterday's favourite, the initiative had to be his. It went against his self-esteem that anyone should voluntarily walk out on him.

Nevertheless I had done so. His aggressive appearance on our doorstep gained him nothing. Mrs Hiscock added her voice to mine, and we drowned out his most strident harangues. I believed I had seen the back of him, and was thankful for it.

Now it seems that I was wrong.

TUESDAY 4 OCTOBER 1814

When formally introduced to me by Count Rupert, Alderley summoned up one of his most courtly bows, but his eyes were glowing with a wickedness which made my heart miss several beats. No good could come of his presence here. But surely he had not journeyed all this way in pursuit of me?

In fact it turns out that Lord Alderley is here as an emissary of the British Government. Preliminary arrangements are in hand for the mounting of a huge European congress in Vienna, at which the Napoleonic empire will be manipulated back into its original separate parts, with certain readjustments over which the allies now wish to settle age-old arguments. It is all beyond me, but a lot of self-important men seem to enjoy making difficulties and then receiving promotion for appearing to solve them. Alderley conveys the impression that he is the major organiser of the whole conference, but Roger is of the opinion that the man is only one of a hundred subordinate messengers. His task is to gather information and opinions from the minor princelings of liberated Europe, sound them out especially about the possible establishment of a German Confederation, and then let his superiors make what pattern they will of the innumerable strands.

I have been told many of these details during the course of one of the long afternoon discussions between Count Rupert and Lord Alderley: told not by the two men, or by Roger, who had been directed to accompany their deliberations with unobtrusive music in an adjoining room, but by the Countess. Fulvia came into my bed yesterday, when the first real chills of autumn began to replace the long spell of warmth. She knew we would not be interrupted; and we both enjoyed the drowsy interlude, shut away from the outside world. We were lazy and in a mood for each other's company, sharing few words, in contrast to the solemn menfolk. It was here that Fulvia explained why Alderley was in Stoltenberg, and in return asked for my frank confession as to why I had looked so alarmed when he arrived.

I told her slightly more than I had told Roger, but only enough to ensure that she felt disgust towards the hypocritical fop. Then we lay companionably side by side, rousing ourselves only now and then to sketch a drowsy tracery over each other's flesh with meandering, unhurried hands. As the afternoon grew cooler, we did from time to time use tongues and fingers to poke the embers and start the fire glowing.

THURSDAY 6 OCTOBER 1814

Naturally Count Rupert has deemed it necessary to treat his guest to a display of the musical talent at his disposal, and Roger has been ordered to rehearse the orchestra and myself in a programme of Austrian music, which the Count recommends as a useful background for someone due to spend many months in Vienna, and a few English pieces in honour of the guest.

After Roger and I had evolved a programme and rehearsed the more ticklish passages, with two hours to spare before the actual recital we turned our attention to the usual procedures.

I was lovingly licking him up to the final eruption when the door of my room opened. For a moment or two I assumed it was Fulvia, who had more than once come to join us and been made welcome, once we had established that she had not brought her riding crop with her. But when I turned my head just enough to see past Roger's left haunch without relinquishing my hold, I saw that it was Lord Alderley.

He had doubtless assumed, with his usual arrogance, that the Count would not wish his guest to be deprived of any pleasure the *schloss* had to offer, and had swaggered his way to my room in gloatingly vengeful mood.

'So this,' he said, 'is the secret of your partnership!'

MONDAY 10 OCTOBER 1814

Now that evil swaggering swine is planning a spiteful revenge. Just as one might have expected. If it were not for the Countess's good offices, we would not even have guessed at the particular poison which Lord Alderley has been pouring into her husband's ears; and even so it may be too late to distil a convincing antidote.

He has contrived a most interesting story. Rather than denounce Roger and myself for fucking so fervently under our employer's roof, which he guessed might not be regarded as too heinous a crime, he has devised an accusation with sinister undertones which are bound to disturb a man of Count Rupert's susceptibilities. In addition, it shrewdly takes advantage of the Count's innate chivalry towards women by laying all blame upon the shoulders of Roger Rougiere – or, rather, upon the eyes of Roger Rougiere.

Alderley had reported his forebodings to his host with every show of regret and diffidence. He is good at carrying off such sorrowful honesty provided no one is present who has known him at all well. His story is that for a time I was under his care in London after he had rescued me from the evil influence of a mesmerist. For that is how he describes Roger. My natural talent has all along been misused and perverted by a charlatan. With little musical originality of his own, this man has exploited me by using the techniques of Dr Mesmer to bend me to his will. Alderley had taken me under his wing, hoping to effect a cure; but before that cure could be completed, the mesmerist had succeeded in luring me back into his clutches. It is a dark, terrifying story. Unfortunately its spurious details can all be tied in most convincingly with my own insistence that Roger Rougiere should be brought to Stoltenberg at the first available opportunity.

Hearing all this when matters had already progressed virtually beyond repair, the Countess suggested that her husband should challenge me directly and ask for my own interpretation. Alderley hastened to say that this would be useless: under the mesmerist's spell, I would say whatever the villain had implanted in my mind.

There has been a brief lull in which it has seemed that a way might be found out of such a deplorable situation. The Count, troubled and wavering, sent not for me but for Roger. Instead of immediately denouncing him, he asked in the most oblique way if Roger could use these mesmeric powers of his in the cause of his employer's own gratification. In short – though in fact it took him a long rather than a short time to reach what he had in mind – was Roger capable of putting a spell upon the Countess which would make it easier for her to succumb to certain ideas which her husband had so far found difficulty in fulfilling? And in

123

addition could Roger release him from certain mental impediments which added to those problems? In this preliminary inquiry he refused to go into details of what his fantasies and frustrations might be, but in an arch kind of way he let it be understood that he was not averse to Roger mesmerising me before a performance – to which the Count was now convinced could be attributed the remarkable effect my singing had had on him – provided that the gifted *konzertmeister* would cast similar spells upon the Countess and himself, details to be specified at times of the Count's choosing.

Roger explained as civilly as possible that he has no mesmeric powers whatsoever. My voice is my own.

Count Rupert refuses to believe him.

Wretchedly scribbling these sad words in my diary, I cannot decide whether Roger ought to be perfectly frank about his method of inspiring me before a concert. Perhaps the Count would forgive him and share a man-of-the-world laugh with him. Or perhaps not. Nor is it likely that the Count would contemplate a similar physical, non-mesmeric treatment of his wife by his *konzertmeister's* baton, even if the effects proved beneficial in just the way he had been hoping.

WEDNESDAY 12 OCTOBER 1814

Last night, hoping to distract me from my gloom, the Countess brought me an etching of an elaborate Indian carving. It was apparently copied from the palace of an Indian prince by a young French officer, and sold by him to pay his gambling debts. One of the Count's friends had then offered it in a wager which the Count had won. Perhaps it was the sight of such intricate inventiveness in copulation which had led him to make his enquiries about Roger's mesmeric powers.

Certainly one would need some mental or physical uplift to achieve the positions of the man and women on the carving. Fulvia and I greatly enjoyed our study of the intertwined legs, and the artistic moulding of voluptuous breasts against a manly chest, but were puzzled by the way in which this was accomplished, allowing for the complicated things going on behind the man's back. After some happy speculation we called on Roger for his opinion.

The position, according to an earnestly academic analysis passed on to the Count with his new winnings, 'requires great holiness and the assistance of two other ladies'. This, Roger was not slow to point out, meant the participation of three ladies in all. If we were planning to experiment with it, we must find another lady to join us. A maid. . . a serving girl? One of the Countess's attendants? It might be risky, especially at this juncture in our relationships with the Count.

Roger continued studying the etching for several minutes, turning it in different directions. Finally he shook his head.

'Even with the requisite ensemble, I feel it would be too constricting. See. . .' He pointed out various aspects of the very beautiful group. 'If the second lady's leg is looped over the man's shoulder thus. . . and the third lady's right foot is up the first lady's rectum. . . I think movement would be so impeded that the man would be unable fully to satisfy either his partner or himself.'

'It is a pretty tableau,' I was forced to agree, 'but any untoward movement would be fatal.'

The Countess sighed. It appeared that another of her husband's daydreams has gone the way of so many other frail fantasies. In truth, my own opinion is that Count Rupert derives more lasting pleasure from looking at ethereal figures in paintings and the texture of sculpted limbs than in actual consummation.

Of course Fulvia herself has, until recently, hardly been the most encouraging of wives to him, but I forebear to comment to her in this vein: we do need one ally in the *schloss*.

'So what is it we do?' She was, I realised, not talking now about her husband. And she was looking at me for an answer, not at Roger.

It was Roger who spoke, however. Like her, he was

looking at me. 'We may not be able to achieve that gymnastic position. But there are other ensembles. A closely knit trio will not come amiss. Why don't you act as the Countess's handmaiden for a brief spell?' In view of recent accusations, the word 'spell' made him chuckle ruefully.

Her handmaiden. I understood what he meant, and understood that he, too, saw the urgent need to gratify the Countess, if not the Count, and keep her as our ally.

I slowly undressed the lady, dwelling on the process as gently as any lover, any patient and adoring man. Into each movement I introduced the stroking of a hand, a light flutter of fingertips on a gradually bared shoulder, a pretended clumsiness with my knuckles into her groin. When I was lifting the last shred of muslin from her breasts, I matched my quickened breathing to her own.

As I finished I realised that during this process Roger had been soundlessly shedding his own clothes. I was tempted to suggest that his staff would prove more than adequate to carry the family standard but I restrained such levity.

Most respectfully Roger put his arm round the Countess's shoulders and persuaded her to take her ease on the couch while he helped me to disrobe. He did this rather more quickly and with fewer flourishes than I had bestowed on our patroness. I was not resentful. I understood that he wished her to feel that she had been given the extra attentiveness which was her due. When I was as naked as the two of them, he indicated that I, too, should take my ease – on my back on the rug. Gravely he took Fulvia's hand, and turned her over upon me, her thighs about my head and her tongue already beginning to dip greedily between my legs. I assumed that Roger was inviting me to enter her in symmetry, but before I could do so he had insinuated his body at right angles between us. He forced Fulvia's legs up and away from me and then turned her on to his slanting shaft. I felt a pang of envy for the fortunate woman: it must be such an exquisite sensation, having both mouths so hotly occupied, and with such different, contrasting rhythms.

They were in contrast for several minutes, her tongue and Roger's prick never quite synchronising. I could feel every convulsion of this syncopation through her, as if her mouth were echoing to a pounding, resonant ground bass, while down below a fast dance in a completely unrelated time signature was skipping gleefully. And it was all done as she would have wished, with her not having to look into the man's face.

As for me, I was less satisfactorily occupied. Roger's weight on me, Fulvia's added weight above him, was crushing me. Between my legs there was the comfort of Fulvia's tongue; but my own mouth was unoccupied. Perhaps it was as well, since breathing was already difficult enough; yet I felt a chill of neglect there.

Until Roger, with a dexterity at least as commendable as that in the Indian carving, suddenly slid tantalisingly away from between us, so that both Fulvia and I let out a moan of bereavement. In a few brief seconds he had swung dexterously about, thrust his still-throbbing and undischarged prick into my willing scabbard, pleasured me for a moment in passing, then spun Fulvia round and plunged into her mouth while I indulged her below. I was briefly alarmed, wondering if she would be repelled by this approach. But again I tasted her answering excitement, and now we all three fell into the same insistent rhythm.

When we were sated and had disentangled ourselves, I was touched that the Countess should look Roger full in the face and thank him most graciously for his services. But I was the one to whom she spoke.

'If I am to consider such a way of gratifying my husband, I need collaboration such as we have just had.'

I said: 'If the Count is not disconcerted by the presence of an extra party, I shall be glad to serve as that party.'

'You would allow him to insert. . .?'

'I think it would be more proper that that particular privilege should be yours, madam.'

'But if I were to indulge him so, *you* would. . .?'

'I shall willingly change roles and perform whichever of the two accompanying parts you prefer from this trio.'

The thought made her eyes sparkle. 'Then I suppose I can

endure the less interesting end. After all, it is unlikely to provide too massive a *bonne bouche*.'

FRIDAY 14 OCTOBER 1814

But things have not got that far. After writing as I did on Wednesday, I dared to hope that we might succeed in distracting the Count from brooding over the absurd tales of mesmerism. But he must have been pacing up and down, brooding, turning things over in his mind. Or else Lord Alderley has been continuing his denigration of Roger with cunning additions. Whatever the explanation, Roger has been bluntly informed that his employment here has been summarily terminated. There will be no scandal, provided he leaves the *schloss* at once.

I have tried to plead with the Count, but could snatch hardly more than a few minutes with him before the leering Alderley put in an appearance. And when I said that my singing would deteriorate the moment Roger Rougiere was no longer in charge, that warped sprig of nobility cried jubilantly:

'You see! Completely under his spell, poor child. It will take many weeks before the mesmeric plague has fled from her system. Then, I vow, you will hear her singing at her most angelic.'

I began to weep. 'If Mr Rougiere is to go, then I must go too. You must release me from my appointment here, and I will return to London with him.'

'Worse than I thought!' Alderley could scarce contain his glee. 'Do you not see? For her own sake she *must* be kept from him.'

So the Count has dismissed Roger. He thinks it very fine of himself to have ensured that the rest of his retainers know nothing of the circumstances. In such a setting it is supposedly not worthy of comment that one *konzertmeister* should so swiftly follow another into oblivion. It may be assumed that it has something to do with the quality of the music.

Mysteriously the Countess has just been to see me and tells me not to grieve. She has plans of her own.

Alderley may have cherished hopes of filling Roger's place, though not in any musical sense. I have no intention of letting him fill anything else. And Fulvia, well aware of what is in his mind, has acted most considerately. She cannot persuade her husband to listen to her on the matter of Roger; but has insisted that I move my quarters into her own suite in the west wing of the building. I have a sneaking feeling that she is rather pleased by the notion of having me at her beck and call, without Roger.

At least the Count ought not to be too displeased, when we share with him the benefits of the position to which Roger and I have introduced his lady.

Alderley's glare upon realising how he has been outmanoeuvred would be a great solace if it were not that there is no solace, nor ever can be, for Roger's absence. And I have no illusions about Alderley. He will bide his time and then find another way of pouncing: not because he loves me but because he cannot bear to be thwarted.

In the meantime he has found other diversions. Strolling in melancholy mood through the gardens but an hour since, I glimpsed him face down on the floor of the pavillion where I had once experienced the attentions of *konzertmeister* Grosz. It was only as I tiptoed past that I could see that between the English lord and the floor was a pageboy, also face down. He was wearing only the tight little jacket of his livery above a bottom which would have been bare had it not been so well covered and warmed by Lord Alderley.

Young Josef will certainly have acquired a varied repertoire long before he reaches maturity.

MONDAY 17 OCTOBER 1814

Events have taken on a turn of speed, as if a coach and four had bolted, which makes it difficult for me to write coherently. I must simply jot things down as they occur, and hope that in years to come I shall be able to look back and smile at my own uncertainties.

Lord Alderley has been summoned post haste to Vienna, where the Congress is under way and Viscount Castlereagh has need of his findings. The Count is also called to Vienna to join his cousins, second cousins, cousins twice removed and other less than lofty eminences in the debates which will doubtless go on for many a month.

This seemed to me a wonderful opportunity for resigning gracefully from the Count's service and returning to London in search of Roger. Count Rupert unfortunately has other plans. Or it might be truer to say that someone has implanted other ideas in his shallow but occasionally fertile mind. That someone must surely have been Lord Alderley. Whole households of the richer nobility are being transported to Vienna. Those of lesser fortune are taking smaller contingents of followers and advisers, together with mistresses and musicians in order to impress their fellow luminaries. Wives, it seems, are an optional adjunct. So Count Rupert leaves the Countess Fulvia as the only one he can trust to manage matters in Stoltenberg in his absence, as he did when visiting London. He proposes, however, to take me with him in order to show Prince Metternich and others that in spite of the smallness of the Stoltenberg principality he is a force to be reckoned with – an intellectual force, a patron of all that is good and creative in the finer arts of living.

I believe that this has come about through guileful suggestions from Alderley. God only knows what that man will devise for me, or against me, once we are plunged into the wild revelry of Vienna.

The Countess does not seem too distressed at the prospect of her husband's absence over several months. She is, however, much distressed by the thought of my own absence, though by now not from any fear of the Count preferring me as a mistress. She would not object to occasional indulgence on his part, since we understand each other so well by now; but we also understand that he is truly in love with my voice and only my voice. At least his pride in showing it off to his contemporaries is managed in much more civilised fashion than Alderley's when showing me off to his foul friends. Yet I will swear it is the scheming Alderley who has provoked in him this latest whim.

I vow that whatever ills befall me I will in no circumstances ever again open my legs, lips or any other cleavage of my flesh to Alderley. If hunger and thirst grow too desperate, I shall use my fingertips, my memory and my imagination to conjure up a vision of Roger.

We have only twenty-four hours in which to prepare our departure. The Count has commanded as large a retinue from his menfolk as he can afford to pay for in the expensive houses of the Austrian capital, where rents are now at a dizzying premium. Hearing that wives are not to be part of this entourage, the married ladies of our little Court are devastated. Their husbands maintain a stiff upper lip, deplore the necessity of obeying Count Rupert's orders, and talk stoically of their duty to follow their lord and master. In fact there is a covert murmuring of anticipation as they consider what the capital of the Austrian Empire may have to offer.

I can only trust that Lord Alderley finds similar diversions; or, indeed, any diversions which he may choose, so long as they do not include me. It may be that demands made on him by his superiors will leave him little time for pleasure; and that if he does seek such pleasure, he may by some good grace be sent home in disgrace and with a dose of the clap.

Still I find it hard to comprehend that I shall be wrenched away from this quiet little principality and thrown into the hurly-burly of a capital city. London's pleasures and perils I know and can cope with. Vienna's will be a challenge which I would prefer to face in the company of someone I can trust.

But where is he now?

TUESDAY 18 OCTOBER 1814

We are packed and ready to depart. The Count has made his wife a polite farewell. And the Countess Fulvia arranged a farewell for me which was totally unexpected. Now I understand her secretive little smiles and her assurances that I must not be too distressed.

The Count had commanded a final concert yestereve before leaving his home territory. With a sparkling, knowing smile, the Countess suggested in the late afternoon that a ride round the familiar gardens would be soothing for both of us. I half anticipated that somewhere in the depths of the woods she would insist on tethering our mounts and uncovering our mounds of Venus. To my surprise she led me without halting to the outskirts of the estate and to an abandoned gamekeeper's cottage. And there, framed in the doorway, was Roger.

She has installed him in this old, half-forgotten building to save him from having to return to England. It had been her intention, before we heard of the summons from Vienna, to ensure that before each recital in the *schloss* I should be able to ride to the cottage and be ridden by Roger. Now there had to be a ceremony which was both preparation for the concert and a farewell to Roger.

Fulvia was thoughtful enough to leave us together for our first encounter after so many barren days. We had greedily made the beast with two backs, the dog and bitch, and the sweet tasting of the divine *soixante-neuf*, when she interrupted and imperiously demanded that after all she had done for us she should also be appropriately done. We showed her our gratitude in the ways which most pleased her, and I said a tearful farewell to Roger.

That evening I excelled myself, in spite of being close to tears. The Count nodded appreciatively at Alderley.

'She is recovering from that mesmeric influence, as you predicted.'

But Alderley, looking at my face and at the Countess's, was all too obviously taunted by suspicion. I am glad that there is so little time left for him in Stoltenberg to follow up those suspicions.

When night fell I spent a grateful hour in Fulvia's bed. One might have expected Count Rupert to pay her a courteous farewell visit, but he is the kind of man who, at the end of a furlough from military duties or being commanded to report for such duties, prefers a sound sleep to the exhaustion of amorous wakefulness. When I was sure that the Countess was satisfied and that she, too, was asleep, I made my way to the cottage once more. Here I forever abandoned all pretence that I require Roger's meat and muscle simply in order to feed my musical appetite. I told him things I never expected to tell any man; uttered words I had for long been too diffident even to contemplate; and sprawled my body in a happy display so that he might choose whichever way he most wished to serve me. For, however much he might think that he was using me for his pleasure, he was in reality the servant and I was the one commanding his services. I shamelessly told him so, and told him many more things. I swallowed his prick as deeply as I could draw it down, and murmured round it. When he shafted me in the easiest, simplest way, staring down into my eyes until his own eyes filmed over like a cat's and his mouth was slack and uncontrollable, I said lovingly, 'Fuck me' and 'Roger me' and 'Oh, my fucking darling Roger', and the words made the most beautiful lyrics to the most beautiful music. I knew I was forever in love with him. Even if I had hated him I would still have craved his prick, but it was lovelier when there was love. And it was sweet to tease, to show him who was the dominating one: to tease him by pulling away and making him beg to get back in, tormenting him by holding his stopper in my hand to prove that I was the one who called the tune, set the tempo of the music.

And in the end, it was neither him nor me but just us, the two of us, two become one.

And I said: 'I love you.'

It was a terrible, irrevocable thing to say.

In the dawn I knew I must leave and be smart and clean and well attired when the Count announced the time for us to set off. Still I could not tear myself away. I kissed him again, and bit him again, and carried the smell of him in my nostrils. And we found it was possible to wrap ourselves round each other for a last time, and he shafted me tenderly rather than fiercely, and afterwards I sucked him dry and then mopped him with my hair.

As I went down the path I caught a flutter of movement close to the wide window of the cottage. I made a move towards it, but the trees and bushes engulfed the wisp of fabric, the swirl of a dress. I was quite sure it had been the figure of that girl we had met with Josef in the garden, and into whom we had directed the clumsy page. She must have been watching Roger and myself through the window.

I had not much cared for her covetous expression before, staring at Roger and reaching greedily out at him. I like the thought of it even less now, together with the thought of being far away.

Roger and I have agreed on the futility of jealousy, have we not? While we are apart we must satisfy our appetites if they grow too intense, and deal with situations as they present themselves. In the end, in all basic things, we trust each other and know what is lasting and what is transient.

So there must be no gnawing suspicion and no jealousy.

Yet still I cannot but regret the kind-hearted instruction which Roger and I gave that girl and Josef the page. How long before she steals back to that secluded cottage: how long before he sets about teaching her all the things he has shared with me?

PART THREE

DUETS AND VARIATIONS AT THE ORGAN

Chapter 1

In which Roger Rougiere fills in many a lonely hour and is invited to fill many a deserted wife

So I am left without Cecilia. In spite of recent diversions I wonder if there is any real purpose in remaining here in Stoltenberg. I am in the position of a pet hound, no longer a favourite of the family, condescendingly provided with a kennel far from the house and fed regularly, but no more. During the first week my food was brought down from the *schloss* kitchens every morning by some servant who left it covered with a cloth in a basket on the step of the cottage. I did not see the servant, who had probably been given strict instructions by the Countess not to pry and not to ask questions. And so the dog skulks in his kennel, fed yet famished, without a bitch to play with. Why linger on here? Why not return of my own free will to London?

A few mornings ago I awoke early from a dream of Cecilia so vivid that I was saved only by a matter of seconds from wasting my seed in the blankets. I could not go back to sleep. Dared not. I dressed and went out into the chill of the late October dawn. A faint frost clung hazily to the branches of the trees. My breath was a silvery smoke drifting ahead of me and around my cheeks. The cold forced me to walk briskly, and after twenty minutes I was glad to come full circle back to the cottage.

A girl was just settling a basket down on the doorstep and conscientiously tucking the edges of the cloth around its contents. Her ample skirt shrouded her down to the ankles, but failed to disguise the ample contours of her bottom. I stopped in my tracks and contemplated her for a moment, wondering whether the grace of her movements would be betrayed by an ugly, pockmarked face.

She turned to move away, and was staring straight at me. It was the girl whom Cecilia and I had assisted in her clumsy conjunction with the Count's inept little pageboy. She offered me a smile which was meant to be deferential and demure; but spoiled it by licking her lips with one faint, swift flick of the tongue. When I returned her smile I found myself thinking not of those lips but of the pink virginal pout she had offered the lad's pink little prick. Not that she could be called virginal any longer, of course: though I doubted if she had been much stretched by his efforts, even if he had persevered with further bouts at which Cecilia and I had not been present.

I passed close to her and opened the door. It had been cold in the woods, but now the chill was ebbing fast. I went into the cottage, leaving the door open but saying nothing. I thought of Cecilia and longed to be faithful. But I had left those thoughts too late. As I passed her the girl had given off that irresistibly sweet, dewy yet dirty smell of youth. Still I said nothing. But she picked up the basket and carried it in, and waited for me to close the door. Then she licked her lips again, slowly and deliberately this time, put the basket of food on the table, and pointed at my breeches to make it clear what food it was she craved.

It was too soon after Cecilia's departure for me to contemplate such a liaison. The girl was too young and inexperienced, and it would all be quite wrong. Anyway she was not to be trusted. There was no telling what she might reveal to the Countess or to anyone else ready to listen.

She was taking off her clothes. I could not simply stand there and remain fully clothed, on my dignity, insultingly rejecting her. I tossed my garments into the corner. As I did so, she sank to the floor and with breathtaking suppleness raised her legs and wrapped her ankles round her neck. It was much as she had been when the pageboy bumbled his way into her. She might almost have been practising the position, remembering and perfecting it. Her smile was triumphant and beautiful. Even more beautiful was the pink yawn of those other lips, waiting to be widened. I withdrew my objections and inserted my approval.

She was as luscious as a very ripe, dripping peach. It was most flattering, the way she first winced and then hummed with joy at the slow then quickening thrust of my member. Unlike her mistress, the Countess, she was by no means reluctant to look in a man's face. Indeed, between those supple legs she stared at me with eyes which widened with every spasm of her clutching lips. It was as if she wished to miss nothing, except to learn something extra from the expression in my face as much as from the grip of my fingers and the grip she now had on me. When she rolled a fraction backwards, just sufficiently to pull my prick downwards in a tightness which ought to have been displeasing but was not, my balls swung so freely that they slapped loudly against her buttocks.

Her name was Grethe. That was about all I was able to understand from her on that first encounter in the cottage. We exchanged even fewer words on the second meeting, next morning. I had not gone out for a walk this time and had not troubled to dress. She made no pretence of putting the basket on the doorstep or timidly rapping on the door, but marched boldly in and closed the door herself. I helped her to undress, which did not take long. In spite of the morning chill she had not burdened herself with excess garments. I was about to draw her closer, realising that she was a sufficiently tall girl for us to stand unsupported and move freely back and forth, with our backs and buttocks exposed to be stroked, struck and kneaded in handfuls, when she murmured something guttural and went down on her knees.

Of course. I remembered the avid gleam in her eyes as she watched Cecilia finally freeing me at the end of our little lesson. Now the greed in those eyes was as nothing compared to the greed in her mouth. She gulped, gagged for a moment, and then drew my ferrule in to the very back of her throat. And still she gulped in, as if to choke herself. She was clumsy, without guiles and without skill. She butted her head into my navel, and clung desperately with her arms as far round my bottom as she could get them. She knew nothing yet of the possible use in such a posture of the fingers in and around one's arse, or of the inflammatory scorch of nails into the cods from behind. She would soon become boring unless someone devoted time and patience to her education. But for the moment her sheet avidity was enough to set me on fire, and when I could hold myself in no longer it felt like molten lava passing through me and into her.

When she had gone I felt regretful. I was betraying Cecilia. Of course we had promised each other to feel no jealousy and to behave according to our needs; but I felt that this had been too sudden and too crude.

The self-reproaches faded long before evening, and were non-existent next morning. As soon as Grethe arrived I set about teaching her the pleasures of slowness and self-control, the combination of twining and supporting, and the technique of teasing with dabbing contacts and withdrawals. But she was too impetuous. Immediately after the throes of one orgasm she craved another. And I must admit that within such a short time of starting her career as a grown woman she was remarkably fortunate in the swift and uninhibited succession of her orgasms.

It was after the last of these, when I had closed our morning devotions with a conventional delivery at the front, that I heard the faint clip-clop of horses' hoofs through the trees. Hastily I flung Grethe's clothes at her, and peered out of the creaking back door to make sure she could cover the gap between here and the wood without being observed from the far side. I just had time to return indoors, throw on a few clothes, and make a show of taking my day's food out of the basket, when there was a peremptory tap at the front door.

It was the Countess Fulvia.

I was stricken with panic. In spite of her distaste for the attentions of a man *tout seul*, was the Countess beginning to miss her husband – or, more likely, was she missing the combined devotions of Cecilia and myself? Perhaps at this very moment she was anticipating sitting upon me, presenting her back while she stared austerely ahead at the roughcast wall of the cottage bedroom. I would have been happy to oblige; but needed time to brew up more juice after my recent injection of Grethe.

The Countess looked around the room and sniffed. Someone so well-bred might have a discriminating sense of smell, receptive to the aroma which Gethe had left on the air. But after a moment she simply said:

'You are satisfied with your diet, Herr Rougiere?'

'It is adequate, thank you.'

'There are some things you miss, though?'

'I. . . er. . .'

'I think it is time we resume some of our old customs, yes?'

Here it came. Frantically I tried to urge some life into my limp member. If I had truly been a mesmerist, it might have been possible. But, as I had made plain to the Count, I was no mesmerist.

'I shall be honoured,' I said.

'It must be lonely every day. . . without your music.'

Was she about to offer to have a spinet sent down from the *schloss*, or was she talking in sly metaphors about what she really wanted?

She said: 'I think we should resume the evening recitals of which my husband is so fond.'

'The orchestra has been disbanded in the Count's absence,' I pointed out. I was still probing for her true intentions. 'Do you mean that I should play for you in private?'

'I mean that you play for my ladies and myself at dinner.'

'But I have been dismissed from the Court. Banished.'

'Who knows this? There was no scandal. You went home to England, yes? And now you are back, only to find the Count has departed. So – how do you say it in the English? – your fingers are at a loose end, I think?'

'You could say that, yes.'

'Then you will come to the music room this afternoon.' It was not a suggestion but a command. 'You will practise. And then you play for us at dinner tonight.'

And so, having washed and made myself as spruce as every *konzertmeister* should be, I walked up in the grey afternoon to the *schloss*, vowing that if this were now to become a regular routine I would ask for a horse to enable me to make the double journey with less effort.

As I went along the gallery towards the music room I caught a glimpse of Grethe carrying an armful of linen into a room on the corner. She looked startled at the sight of me; but I took care not to make any grimace or gesture of recognition.

It was an agreeable afternoon, practising many pieces which I had not played for what seemed a lifetime. I am indeed an incomplete person away from the keyboard for too long. During those few hours I thought of nothing but the music itself; and was still thinking about it when I went that evening to the pianoforte at the end of the banqueting room.

Although there was no orchestra, the room was noisier than it had ever been when the Count and his menfolk were present. He had never cared for excessive chattering by his retainers' wives, especially when there was music to be heard. Nor had he been in the habit of indulging in conversational gallantries with any particular lady, or ever expected those retainers to be complaisant about sharing their wives with him. The fact that he would have been unable to cope with such exertions was of course never mentioned. Now, freed from the constraints of his presence, the womenfolk were singing and shrieking away like a concourse of parrots. Their bare arms waved, their heads turned this way and that, sparkling with reflections from jewelled combs and a-flutter with bird-of-paradise plumes. Fans waved or stabbed to emphasize a point. My afternoon's practice had been superfluous: every note and chord of the pianoforte was drowned out by their clamour. I might as well not have been there at all; though every now and then one lady or another might become aware of my presence, and two of them did briefly seem distracted from the conversation by thoughts not unrelated to my physical appearance.

For my own delectation I played the middle movement of the Mozart A minor Sonata. It required a great deal of concentration, being assailed throughout by vocal outbursts in different keys. Approaching the concluding bars, I looked up in a trance of adoration for what the composer had achieved, only to find my remote gaze being intercepted by a statuesque lady with strong bare shoulders which rose in creamy extravagance above a net drapery gown. Unlike everybody else about that turbulent table she seemed to be trying to hear what I was playing. At least, she was concentrating very hard on my arm movements and looking at my face as if to divine all the notes by some sort of thought transference.

When the ladies clattered to their feet after dinner and moved into the card room, this one showed herself to be a full six feet tall, with other proportions to match. The lace over her breasts rose and fell in rhythm to the magnificence of her breathing. I had not seen her among the Countess's retinue before, which was surprising when one considered how she towered above the others.

Countess Fulvia had ordained that the card room door should be left open and I should continue playing in the banqueting room while the servants cleared away. I thought there was even less likelihood of my being heard from that distance, but was content to contemplate a further programme of my own choice.

While I sipped the glass of wine I had been given during the company's move from one room to the other, two ladies smiled condescendingly and congratulated me on my beautiful touch. As they swept on their way, I sensed another presence, near my left shoulder. Her own shoulder was even more magnificent at such close quarters.

Her English was slow and ponderous but very clear. And decisive. I do not know the Germans words for 'if' or 'perhaps', but I am convinced they do not exist in the vocabulary of Helga von Hauptfeld – for such is her name. If she had been a man she would certainly have clicked her heels as she enunciated the words. Her husband was, so far as I could interpret the incredibly long compound word, a major in the Prussian army. He had led a gallant charge which proved crucial in the defeat of Napoleon at Leipzig. 'A strong man,' she assured me. Obviously she was very proud of him and of her own Prussian ancestry. 'A strong man,' she said with relish. She struck her bosom resoundingly with her right hand, and let it lie there in a declamatory gesture. 'I need a strong man.'

She asked outright for the whereabouts of my quarters in the *schloss*, and thundered on: 'I trust you are well cared for? A small place, this. I am used to larger. But they find you the comfortable place? You let me see?'

I temporised by saying that I was not yet entirely resettled, having but recently returned from England.

'You will play well at your next recital,' she announced. 'It will be soon.'

It was not a question but a statement of fact.

I continued on my personal selection of Haydn and Hümmel until the Countess came in, closing the intervening door, and told me I might leave. She was in fine fettle. Her cheeks glowed and her eyes were full of laughter. Clearly the conversation had been of stimulating quality, and she could look forward to retiring shortly without the chore of satisfying her husband's music-inspired passion.

With a twinkle which must have owed something to alcohol and something to verbal exhilaration she said: 'I have been asked the precise location of your quarters, which for some reason are supposed to be in the east wing. I suspect there will be the sleepwalking tonight. I was considering offering you your old accommodation, but for the moment I suggest you remain in the cottage until you decide what is your wish.'

'I decide?'

'Rest, and think,' she laughed. 'Decide what happens when that huntress finds you. Because she will find you, that is certain.' She gave me a quizzical look. 'If she proves to your taste, and I decide she is one I trust, perhaps we play our trios again?'

'With a contrabass instead of a cello?' I said.

We laughed conspiratorially, agreeing that Helga's

dimensions would threaten to overbalance the whole precarious equilibrium.

Just before leaving, the Countess said: 'I arrange that your food tomorrow comes with one of the footmen.' Before I could protest, she went on: 'It is best for you, I think. Too much exercise, not good.'

I went back to my cottage in two minds about all this. It was not so much the fact that the Countess knew or guessed everything about Grethe as that I preferred to make my own decisions as to my current consort. If the mighty Helga did in fact track me down, the consequences should still be my choice. And if she did not come, was I to be summarily deprived of any diversion whatsoever?

Helga von Hauptfeld found me the afternoon of the next day. To preserve her dignity – by which she set great store – she made it appear that this was a chance encounter. She had been out riding and happened to come across the cottage, with myself nearby gathering sticks for a fire. From her high colour and the horse's heavy panting I surmised that in reality she had spent a considerable time combing the estate and was growing impatient.

She swung down from her mount and tethered it to the rail beside the cottage.

'Yes. It is cold.' The way she declared this would have made the sun fearful of showing itself in public at any time later that day. 'A fire. Is good.'

She opened the door and waved me in. I had been intending to light a fire in any case, but was not happy at being commanded to do so. Still, here she was, and I might as well see what transpired.

When there was a cheering blaze in the grate, she took off her black beaver riding hat and hung it carefully behind the door. I heard the bolt shoot into place. 'Is good,' she barked again. 'Now we ride, yes?'

When I look puzzled she gave me a playful slap of her vast hand which almost hurled me on to the leaping flames. As I regained my balance she pointed to a line of hooks and eyes down her dark green tunic. There was a faint touch of Grethe about her. When it came to expressing their desires, both the serving girl and the Prussian aristocrat had a directness which brooked no misunderstanding. Grethe had virtually ordered me to undo my own fastenings; Helga was ordering me to undo hers. She hissed and grunted encouragement as I freed her from the tunic and then from her tightly laced under-dress. Each removal allowed her flesh to relax outwards. Stripped at last of all save a large cabuchon ring, she made a really superb sight. Yet those magnificent proportions might perhaps have been more appropriate to a statue than to a human being. Sculpted stone would have been equally impressive and considerably less tremulous than those awe-inspiring ridges and hillocks of flesh.

But she had not come here simply for me to make aesthetic judgments. I shed my clothes, and she inspected me in frank detail. Finally she deigned to nod. 'It is enough.' Without more ado she went down on all fours, her great hands and feet set firmly on the rug before the fire. 'We ride,' she said again. This time it was an urgent, imperious command.

We rode.

She wanted no caresses, no slow lead-up to consummation. From the moment we started it had all the frenzy of a hunt or a race which simply had to be won. She bucked and swung, reared up and crashed down to the rug again, shook her vast arse to and fro, and began to sweat all down her back. Whinnying like a horse, she seemed bent on throwing me off. And at last, rearing up on her hind legs, she succeeded in doing so. The whinny became a wild laugh. Before she could triumph too noisily, I pushed her down again and remounted, this time clinging to her shoulders as one would cling to those of a crazed runaway without harness. My own feet were well off the ground now. She had wished to be ridden, and she was being ridden. I dug my fingers deeper into her shoulders, and kneed her flanks until she was straining wildly to attain the goal she had set herself. When it came for both of us, she let out one last whinny and went absolutely still as if to concentrate solely on the stallion shaft within her. Her breath rasped, her sides were streaming, her whole frame shuddered in a final convulsion. And slowly she sagged forward and collapsed as if pole-axed in a knacker's yard.

There could have been no more than ten seconds of this sated tranquillity. Then she got to her feet and waved imperiously at her clothes. I fetched them one by one and helped her to dress.

'Good,' she said condescendingly.

'Do you ride daily?' I asked with some apprehension.

'I call when the mount needs exercise. You will be here.'

When I unbolted the door and held it open for her to leave, I ventured: 'You are staying with the Countess for long?'

'Until my husband comes for me.'

'Your husband will come here?'

'When he is ready. He has much work to complete.'

'And you don't think he. . . I mean, if he found out. . .' I glanced back into the room.

'Ach, he will kill you,' she said cheerfully. 'He is a strong man. You are strong, too. But not so strong. Also he has a strong temper.'

That was a pleasant prospect to sleep on.

The next morning my food was again brought by Grethe, who let herself in as before and began to disrobe before I was even halfway across the room. I did not want to admit that I was privy to the Countess's rearrangement of duties, but I asked vaguely: 'The footman. . . ?'

'He . . . ' She struggled for words, then mimed someone falling over. Then she tapped her leg and bent it as awkwardly as she could manage, and made a grimace of extreme pain.

'He fell over?'

'*Ja.*'

She beamed, and went on miming with her leg.

'And broke his leg?' I guessed.

Her nod was vigorous and exultant. I wondered whether the poor wretch had fallen, or whether he had been tripped.

Because I had not been expecting her, I had devised no new variations to extend her education, and she seemed to have dreamed none of her own, so we spent a fairly straightforward half-hour, twining rather than riding.

When Grethe had gone, I found myself wistfully wondering how my Cecilia might be comporting herself. I felt no jealousy regarding the Count, for already I knew how little competition he offered as a performer. In taking Cecilia with him to Vienna he was genuinely thinking of her as a musician rather than as a bedmate. There was, of course, a possibility that that impudent little page might be pursuing his researches, just as his Grethe was doing with me, and possibly learning just as fast as she. It was no matter for jealousy.

But there might be worse things to contemplate. I was sure Cecilia would find ways of fighting off the repulsive Lord Alderley. But surely, in fashionable Vienna in the throes of such an inrush of great men and rich rogues, there would be many of them less repulsive than Alderley? Too many, I feared.

I tried to shake off my nagging worries and prepare myself for a further onslaught from Helga which I suspected would not be long delayed.

Chapter 2

In which Cecilia speedily discovers many a congress in Vienna

Such splendour I have seen only once in my life, and that at the Prince Regent's reception. But while that had been one special occasion, here there are such occasions every day and every night. I marvel that the city can cope with such an invasion of royalty, aristocracy, gentry and spongers. And as for the music. . . ah, if only Roger were here to benefit both himself and me! Everywhere there are concerts, music at receptions, music in the gardens, the never-ending sequences of polonaises and above all the daring waltz, which was still viewed with suspicion in England when we left, though a great favourite at Almack's and such venues.

It is said that among the sovereigns and statesmen who have arrived here, many without any formal invitation, there are the crowned heads of five dynasties, over two hundred princes, dukes, margraves, counts and suchlike, turning Vienna into a kind of high-bred Vauxhall. Though one might observe that their behaviour, regrettably, does not always remain high bred. Some of the princelings from the minor Courts are so dazzled by the beauty of the city and even more so by the beauty of its resident beauties that they squander half their inheritance in the space of a few besotted nights. Those who have been misguided enough to bring their wives with them squander the same amount on appallingly expensive clothes because the wives refuse to go into reception rooms or ballrooms unless they can compete with the hundreds of others flaunting their feathers and finery. Contemplating the scrawny arms and shrivelled throats of many of them, one can only wince at what they must look like when that finery is doffed.

Some burghers and citizens grumble that the country's Exchequer cannot long sustain the extravagance of all the official and semi-official functions. Princess Metternich's lavish balls are said to be devised mainly to distract delegates' attention from the fact that there is really no point in their being here, and little point in the Congress at all. The sly French negotiator, Talleyrand, has secured for himself the entire Kaunitz Palace and given his twenty-one-year-old niece *carte blanche* as hostess. Monarchs and ministers meet for most of their discussions not in council chambers but in the boudoirs of Princess Esterhazy and other great ladies. It is rumoured that certain of these gentlemen do not always leave when their colleagues have left.

And in some of the smaller parties given by the lower echelons of Viennese society, I sing.

Count Rupert has discovered that neither he nor his opinions carry any weight whatsoever in the political dealings here. He could as well have stayed at home in Stoltenberg. But of course nobody has dared to stay at home at this moment in history: not dared, and not wanted to be left out of anything. Each petty potentate strives to draw attention to himself by some specialty, some gesture, some attribute which his fellows do not possess. And here I can say with all due modesty that I am serving my master well.

My voice first attracted attention at a Thursday *soirée* given by Princess Trautmansdorf. Count Rupert had been invited only through the influence of this wife's uncle, the Margrave of Saxe-Hessen, and seized the opportunity of making his mark by suggesting that he would be greatly honoured if allowed to provide a musical interlude. The Princess, already satisfied with her own clavier player, seemed uninterested by this suggestion, but finally gave in. Now came the question: should I rely entirely on the intrinsic quality of my voice to carry the afternoon or, to ensure that I was remarked upon and could look forward to further acclaim in Vienna, should I seek that invaluable preface which had warmed my performances so often in the past?

And if so, where was I to find a Roger substitute?

There was only one thing for it as such short notice. I must seek out Josef, the page. His prick was puny on the palate, but the juice had been sweet in my throat and I was sure a renewal of the dosage could prove beneficial.

It did so prove. I had some trouble in finding him and was beginning to despair when at last I was led to him in a wine tavern near the *Rathaus*. He was well steeped in some local concoction, and at first I felt that he would not be capable of adequate provision. There was so little time to lose that I dragged him round to the stables at the rear, flung him on a bed of straw which had fortunately been renewed not too long ago, and undid his breeches for him. He gave me a bleary grin of recognition and willingness, but for some minutes that was all he could provide. I worked feverishly on him with my lips, teeth and tongue until he began to show signs of life down below, if not in his befuddled face. It was degrading to have to work so hard on such unpromising material; but when his pink prong stiffened I began to feel quite tender sentiments towards it, and bent over to drink from it before he fell hopelessly asleep. Avoiding the danger of losing most of the result as it threatened to dribble back out of my mouth, I kept my lips tightly clenched and finally threw my head back and gargled refreshingly.

I sang most sweetly afterwards, and within a matter of days the Count found himself invited to other receptions and *soirées* which would otherwise not have been offered to him. It was understood that for such functions he would always bring his songbird with him.

And in the small, select audience at one of them was, as I might have foreseen, Lord Alderley.

It was fortunate that he should have chosen that evening to make advances to a somewhat ungainly but blue-blooded girl from Carinthia, and so had neither the time nor opportunity to concentrate his venom upon me. Yet he could not resist one brief approach, accompanied by the most winning smile which would have fooled anyone watching. His eyes glinted more evilly than ever under the sparkle of the crystal chandeliers.

'So your career blossoms, my dear.'

'I sing as I have always done. If it pleases the listener, I am pleased.'

'With what inspiration nowadays?'

'The works of the great composers, as ever.'

His smile did not falter, but in an undertone he said equably: 'Lying slut. Who is servicing you here in Vienna?' Before I could fashion a reply, a couple of his acquaintances drifted near, and he went on addressing me in the warmest, most admiring tone. 'There are times when it seems that the whole political future of Europe depends upon who succumbs most willingly to your high trills.' As the couple smiled at him and at me and went on their way, he added: 'And also upon those bright and alert enough after the night's congress to cope with morning sessions of the Congress.'

Which was a shameful imputation, since I had spent my nights alone since arriving in the capital.

Worse: did he guess how much I hated spending my nights alone? If he did, I swore yet again that he of all men should never again be my companion.

The weather was cold yet bright. I found it refreshing to walk below the ramparts of the Inner City of a morning, watching young bloods shielding their eyes against daylight after the excesses of the previous night and older men displaying their wealth and the splendours of their equipages. At precisely ten o'clock each forenoon an English nobleman drove his own four-in-hand through the Prater with its carpet of rustling autumn leaves, scorning borrowed animals: the Emperor Francis of Austria was said to have provided fourteen hundred horses from his Imperial stables for use of his city's guests, but there was no doubt that Lord Corbridge had brought his own.

One Friday morning this gentleman, resplendently

attired in brass-buttoned plum coat and cream breeches, with a perfectly knotted Osbaldeston neckcloth below his imperious chin, reined in and beckoned me to approach. I gave him a very correct curtsey and waited to discover what might be coursing through his mind, or through other parts of his anatomy.

'I believe, young lady,' he said in a deep, courteous voice, 'I had the pleasure of hearing you sing in the Countess Zichy's salon two nights ago.'

'That could be so, my lord.'

'Delightful. Not much of a one for music, I confess. But you were charming.'

I bobbed him another respectful curtsey.

He sprang down from his carriage. He must have been in his early sixties, but was very agile. When he looked me up and down he might well have been assessing a piece of horseflesh. But although his gaze was undoubtedly lecherous, he contrived to make it also flattering.

'You are satisfied in Count Rupert's service?'

'Indeed yes, sir.'

'You would not consider changing your patron for a higher salary... and certain comforts? As well as the familiarity of your own English language and surroundings?'

'The Count and his Countess have always treated me most generously,' I said. 'I would not wish to desert them so long as they wish to retain my services.'

'Commendable of you, young lady.' He doffed his squat felt hat, replaced it, climbed back into his carriage, and looked down speculatively at me. 'So long as *they* wish it, ha?'

I could not fathom this, and as he drove away I turned my attention to some sprightly antics of a young pair of acrobats until their movements became so wantonly suggestive that they were led away by two uniformed members of the Imperial police.

In the middle of the following week I was invited to sing at a levee of the Princess Fürstenberg, and at the last minute found myself escorted there by Count Rupert's chamberlain rather than the Count himself. This was a remarkable occurrence. The Count had done so well for himself as my patron, accepting the praise lavished upon me as his personal due. What could he possibly have found to do that was more important than this?

I was soon to learn. He was absent the following evening also, and when he reappeared in the small dwelling which he had taken for the duration of the Congress it was clear that something catastrophic had happened. His eyes were dull, his shirt and stock hung loose and dishevelled, and his cheeks were suffused with drink. As he went through the entrance hall he looked miserably ahead and avoided my gaze; but at the end of an hour sent for me.

He had washed and shaved, adjusted his dress and donned his best powdered wig; but still he looked blotched and disconsolate.

He said: 'I have to tell you, Fraülein Laidlaw, that I. . . I fear I must. . . dispense with your services.'

I could not take this in. It made no sense to me. My bemused silence made him look even more hangdog.

'It has been agreed,' he said laboriously, 'that you will enter the service of my good friend Lord Corbridge.'

'But I have no wish to enter Lord Corbridge's service.'

My own wishes seemed too irrelevant to be worthy of comment. 'As an Englishman he will take the good care of you. I am sure you will find it. . .' The Count struggled, and dug up a word from his limited vocabulary: 'Congenial.'

He surely owed me more than this. I said: 'You have tired of my singing, sir?'

I swear there were tears in his eyes. 'No, oh no. I shall never forget. . . I only wish. . .'

'You don't *need* to forget. You retain my services, and I sing for you as I have always sung. Why should I go and sing for someone else? Do I even know that he has musical tastes?' From what I recalled of that brief morning conversation of ours, I had reason to think otherwise.

'It is a matter of honour.'

'Honour?' It seemed a strange word in the circumstances.

'A debt of honour,' mumbled the Count.

And then it all came out. I had been the pledge at the

gaming table. Count Rupert had bet, and lost. I had been gambled away, and later today would be collected by Lord Corbridge. At least the victor had had the courtesy not to come for his winnings in the small hours of the morning.

Lord Corbridge in fact retained his courteous disposition, though making no pretences about his reasons for indulging in such a devious scheme for laying his hands on me. Within an hour of my being shown to my boudoir in a tall, narrow dwelling near the Kartnertor Theatre, he came to me and politely asked me to undress.

I said: 'My lord, I was not a willing party to your games. If you have any consideration for a young lady without friends in a country not her own, you will allow me to leave and return to England.'

'But you are not without friends,' he said earnestly. 'You have many friends and admirers in Vienna. I trust you will include me among them.'

'I'll consider you a friend when you release me from this unacceptable obligation.'

He studied me for a moment. He was a grizzled but handsome man, with wrinkles round his eyes as if he had spent too long staring into an alien sun. His mouth was very firm, yet not stubborn. I felt that he was a man who would very quickly make up his mind and then stick by his decisions; but that he would not have reached those decisions purely on uncritical impulse.

'Did you ask your previous patron also to release you? Would he not have been prepared to help you return to England and deprive me of my prize?'

It was a shrewd question. I had in fact contemplated flinging myself on Count Rupert's mercy and begging him to send me away. But I had been unsure of the consequences to him.

I said: 'No, My Lord, I did not ask the Count for assistance. I felt that this would put him too dangerously in your debt, and there was no knowing what restitution you might claim for his failure to honour his gambling pledge.'

'And that genuinely worried you?'

'The Count has been a generous employer. I would not wish him to suffer.'

He really had the most engaging smile. 'You are admirable, Miss Laidlaw. A truly admirable lady.' He was a straightforward, soldierly man, quite without guile, and could not disguise an expression of regret as he went on: 'Very well. If you wish to leave, you are free to go. I would not wish to hold such a gel against her will. Fine gel, upon my word.'

I gasped. 'You mean this?'

'Upon my honour, you shall have every assistance you require for the homeward journey.'

All at once I found myself growing agreeably interested in him. He was notably offering me my freedom from an engagement into which I had not personally entered, and it was difficult not to look on him with respect. I almost began to regret that our acquaintance should not have been extended. I was at a loss for words.

My own uncertainty must have been as clear to him as his regret was to me. He cleared his throat and said gruffly: 'I suppose it would be an unwarrantable imposition to ask if you might not consider staying a week or two? Just two weeks, let us say, and then you can decide whether to continue enjoying the resources of this city in my company, or whether you still wish to go back to London.'

He was aching for my response, but kept his mouth as firm as ever. His back, too, was stiff: ramrod stiff. I found myself deplorably curious about what other ramrod he might be capable of thrusting into a breach already seriously imperilled.

I said: 'It is a bargain, my lord. Two weeks.'

He beamed. And without more ado, as direct as one might have expected, he said: 'Splendid. Undress, then. Down to the buff, hey?' He chuckled. It was a buoyant, manly chuckle, very warm and genuine.

He contrived to be very formal and correct even when settling me into the conventional position he required on the bed. He nodded admiration as I put my arms back and my breasts tightened, and then climbed upon me and immediately apologised as his knee jarred mine. When he came into me I would not have been surprised if he had uttered some formal introduction before setting about his steady, disciplined rummage.

Lord Corbridge did not boast a very long prick, but it was a tough, meaty one which produced the most agreeable friction against my clitoris. I let out a spontaneous moan of pleasure, which brought Corbridge suddenly to a stop. He pushed himself up on his hands to look into my face, and his expression was one of serious reproach. I could only assume that no woman he had known hitherto had wished, or been allowed, to express pleasure in being shafted. After he had resumed his dogged pounding I kept the rest of my sensations obediently silent. Only towards the end did Corbridge himself lose control and begin to snort what sounded like muffled war-cries.

The first week was pleasant and undemanding. Since he knew I was fond of music, my protector took me to the ballet, though I observed that by the middle of the programme he had great difficulty in keeping his eyes open. I rode with him through the chestnut avenues of the Prater and practised a stiff little bow to acquaintances who stared up in envy. At night he was the stiff one, and we rode without spectators. Once we galloped out to inspect vineyards on the slopes above the city, once joined a hunting party, and once attended a succession of *tableaux vivants* specially devised by Prince Metternich. It was being increasingly said that the Austrian Chancellor was more interested in Court entertainments than in meeting ambassadors and thrashing out the future of Europe.

'And,' said Corbridge severely, 'he's known to be extremely loose and giddy with women.'

I endeavoured to look suitably shocked.

Then it was Corbridge's turn to be even more shocked. I had been invited to sing at a grandiose levee of the Princess Thurn-und-Taxis, and was somewhat concerned that I was out of practice and lacking in the wherewithal for warming up. So two hours before we were due at the function, I went in my flimsiest silk robe to His Lordship's quarters, listened at his door to make sure his valet was not in attendance, and entered with the suggestion that we have a brief turn upon his bed before selecting our attire.

'Down to the buff, hey?' I tried to mimic his chuckle.

He was taken aback. I realised that again I had transgressed. No lady was allowed to come of her own accord to his chamber. And assuredly no lady initiated a healthy humping. Only a gentleman was allowed such desires, and allowed to set the time and place. Nevertheless I could plainly see, from the fact that while waiting for his valet he had not dreamed of donning even the most fundamental items of underwear, that he was heating up in spite of himself.

I was desperate. Sure that he could not help but succumb in that state, I went down on my knees in front of that stubby, muscular thumb of a cock and took a greedy mouthful to hasten its swelling.

He pulled himself away, outraged. I almost toppled forward, my mouth open and empty.

'Dammit,' he spluttered. 'Where did you learn such abominations?'

'I felt that such a variation might please you.'

'Another of these Continental infamies. Thought better of young Stoltenberg.'

I could not take my gaze off his supplier of physick. I yearned for that invigorating drench while watching its conduit shrink before my very eyes.

'Get up,' he ordered. 'Go and dress. And we will say no more about it.'

He was true to his word. The subject was not mentioned again. Also he was true to his promise of the previous week. The night before the end of the period agreed between us, he came to my boudoir and nodded his polite yet implacable signal that I should undress. He touched my nipples almost reverently, and then completed his standard pleasant but unexciting ritual, allowing himself a regretful sigh as he poured what might be his final draught.

The following morning we went again through the Prater. He was particularly attentive, making sure I was wrapped up against the late October chill, asking if I was comfortable and if I needed anything. And then he asked the question for which I had been apprehensively waiting.

'Miss Laidlaw, do you wish to return to England or would you consider renewing our little contract?'

I had foolishly postponed any decision even within my own mind. It had been too comfortable, too easy to drift along these last pampered days. All my needs were catered for; and if Corbridge's performances in bed did not inflame me, at least they provided pleasant warmth where I enjoyed it. Why should I surrender all this for a future of uncertainty?

Still unsure, I turned away and stared out over a carpet of fallen leaves. In the middle of the golden morning I espied Count Rupert with a small entourage of nonentities, and gave him a wave which I hoped combined respect with genuine affection. His eyes followed our progress wistfully.

It occurred to me that he must have had to write to his wife to explain what had happened. Or was he postponing the evil moment when the truth would have to be told? Or concocting some dazzling untruth?

Countess Fulvia would be far from pleased.

Lord Corbridge interrupted my train of thought. 'Well, m'dear? Do you stay, or do you wish to go?'

At that moment a man strode towards us. He gave Lord Corbridge an insultingly perfunctory nod, and then grinned at me in even more insulting derision. I suspected he had been drinking all night; and could guess at other things he had been doing. Whatever Lord Alderley might have to say, one could be sure that the mere sound of his voice would tarnish and contaminate the gold of the morning.

Chapter 3

In which Roger says farewell to his lusty steed but vows, mounted or unmounted, to turn knight errant

Helga had galloped to a standstill and pawed the rug. She was demanding a rub-down, her latest addition to our equine cavortings. I gratified this desire while she nuzzled my arm, and concluded with a friendly pat on her nose. She snorted and made a pretence of kicking me, but I was used to this by now and knew precisely when to dodge.

What I was not prepared for was her announcement, as she stood up and reached for her garments: 'My husband arrives one week from today.'

'Oh. You. . . er. . . you must be pleased.'

'But of course. Perhaps he is not so pleased, though.'

'You don't mean you're going to tell him. . .'

'There are no secrets between us,' she said proudly.

'But if you admit you sought me out, surely he'll –'

'Ach, no.' She drew herself up to her full height, which was considerable, and indicated that I should lace up her black half-boots. Far above my head she boomed: 'I do not do the seeking. No man of breeding can wish to hide behind my skirts. No gentleman would pretend that he did not make the first move.'

So one had to be a gentleman and take the consequences. The woman was always the weakling, the man the brute. Yet surely, even to the most unimaginative husband, the idea of anyone having the strength to rape Helga von Hauptfeld was manifestly ridiculous.

'I have heard it said' – she stepped back as I finished the lacing and now was purring rather than peremptory – 'that you are a disciple of Dr Mesmer.'

'Completely untrue,' I protested.

'Yet so I have heard it whispered. My husband disapproves of all such charlatans. But perhaps now he will believe in some of these forces. It must be that you mesmerise me. I yield to you, yes? It must be so.' Fully clothed again, she stopped in the doorway. 'But I think we still have several rides before he comes? Before it is too late.'

I thought otherwise. It seemed to me that it was high time to leave Stoltenfeld.

I spent most of the day brooding over the situation without reaching any useful conclusion. To return to London and take up my career again, renewing old acquaintanceships and seeking out new outlets for my music, seemed the most sensible plan. Or perhaps I should seek the hospitality which I felt could soon be guaranteed again in Newcastle. But that would take me farther and farther away from Cecilia. Even those bold-eyed Northumbrian girls could not in the long term compensate for that. I considered asking the Countess for her husband's address in Vienna and writing to implore Cecilia to return to London and join me there. Or would that come better once I was back in London myself? In either event, the Count might be displeased and forbid his protégée to quit his service so arbitrarily.

Quite apart from the imminent threat of a vengeful Major von Hauptfeld descending upon the cottage, I felt little inclination to stay in Stoltenfeld any longer. The routine had grown tedious. Yet still I was incapable of making a clear, rational decision.

That evening Countess Fulvia rode through the woods to my humble dwelling. I thought as she approached that she might be summoning me for an impromptu musical evening, but one sight of her face dispelled any such idea. I had never seen her so furious, even when she had turned upon Cecilia and myself and lashed us in a rage which, to be honest, she had thoroughly enjoyed. Now something had happened which she was certainly not enjoying.

Without any conventional preamble she said: 'I bring very serious news, Herr Rougiere.'

'The Count has had an accident?'

'To his mind, it appears.'

I had no idea how to interpret this, or how to make some non-committal reply.

She went on: 'He has given our Cecilia away.'

'How can he give her away?'

'He writes me an interminable letter about diplomacy, and the code of honour between nations and the code of honour between gentlemen. What all the words amount to, my friend, is the fact that he has staked Cecilia at the gaming tables . . . and lost her.'

'To whom?'

'Some Englishman.'

Her command of English began to falter in her rage, and much of her story was in a kind of bilingual gibberish. But I gathered that Cecilia had been taken into the household of a wealthy Lord Corbridge where, the Count assured his beloved lady wife, she would feel very much at home in noble English company.

'And Cecilia?' I demanded. 'What about *her* wishes in the matter?'

'They are of no concern.'

It was difficult to tell whether she was expressing genuine contempt for the men concerned in this shabby transaction or whether, in her autocratic way, she tended to agree with at least that aspect of it.

There was no further doubt in my mind. 'You must release me from my position here.'

She smiled wryly. 'You propose to snatch your Cecilia from the arms of this English milord?'

'Somehow or other, yes.'

'I think you are safer here.'

I had a vision of von Hauptfeld, complete with sabre and duelling pistols, and thought not. My weapon had not been despised by his wife, but I felt I had no other weapon which would be a match for his armoury. Though really that was irrelevant. Cecilia was what counted. Count Rupert had betrayed our trust in him. 'I must go to Vienna,' I said.

The Countess was calming down. After a brief spell of reflection she said: 'I think I owe it, yes. To you and to Cecilia. You may have a horse. I will give you my husband's address in Vienna.' For an apprehensive moment I wondered if she was about to commission me to seize her husband in a dark alley and break an arm or two. Instead she went on: 'You may leave the horse in his stables. He will recognise it, and its presence will perplex him.'

'I could leave a message with a groom – '

'No. It perplexes him. That is good, I think.'

I looked about the room. I had few belongings to pack, but would have to cut those few down if I was to ride on horseback all the way to Vienna. And when I arrived, where would I find accommodation: to whom would I turn?

The Countess said: 'Ah, of course. You will need money. I hear it is very expensive there now. We say, yes, that you take a final salary from Stoltenberg? You have worked well here. I am sure,' she concluded frostily, 'that my husband will not argue when he returns.'

So I thanked the Countess for all her kindnesses, tolerantly forgetting the scars on my back which had long since healed, and made my preparations to set off. Grethe, bringing me a breakfast basket whose unusually generous proportions puzzled her, burst into tears when I conveyed to her that this was to sustain me on a long journey. She cried the whole time I was rogering her against the table, and even when we concluded with her mouth locked in a fond farewell about my shaft she was still hiccuping and blubbering around it.

So yet again I set off to Cecilia's rescue. One could only pray that this time she had not fallen into the clutches of another libertine such as Alderley.

Accommodation was indeed hard to find in that tumultuous city. But if one had sufficient funds, no questions were asked. Few people other than ambassadors and influential minor royalty had been actually invited to Vienna: most came just because it was the hub of post-Bonapartist machinations, and there was an exhilarating social life, interwoven with opportunities for self-advancement and quick profit. The money provided by the Countess would not last very long, but it would enable me to establish a base.

Having found an overpriced lodging not too far from the banks of the Danube I made my first task the search for Count Rupert's establishment, which proved not too difficult. Rather than risk a chance encounter with anyone who might recognise me, I tethered my horse to an outer post of the stableyard and then set out to familiarise myself with the city. After an hour I found that the journey from Stoltenberg had tired me more than I had anticipated, and when I returned to my lodging I abandoned all hope of inspecting the night life of the city until some later date. I put my head on the pillow, and slept immediately.

When I awoke it was a chill, misty morning. After such a night of uninterrupted slumber I was wide awake.

I went out and walked through the clinging haze which drifted from the river into streets and patches of park and garden. Within a short time I was lost, which in a foreign city like this was hardly surprising. I was not greatly concerned, but strolled at my leisure, admiring a fine building here, a noble terrace there, and glimpses of the cathedral down many a wide or narrow street.

Absorbed in these fresh sights, I turned a corner beside a wide stretch of greensward shaded by lime trees, and bumped heavily into a man striding off the grass on to the pavement.

He said: 'What the deuce. . .'

In the same instant I said: 'I do beg your pardon, sir.'

His grouchiness was gone instantly, plucked away into the mist. 'You are English, sir?'

'I am indeed.'

'Blessed providence!' He caught my arm and began dragging me back the way he had come, over the grass. 'You will serve, sir. His Lordship will be well satisfied.'

'I'm sorry, but I don't follow.' I tried in fact to dig my heels into the damp turf and literally not follow.

'We will detain you but a few moments, sir. My employer is about to fight a duel, and has been shamefully let down by one of his chosen seconds. It appears that this erstwhile friend has allowed himself to be swayed early this very morning to cry off. It is not seemly, says some little functionary in our delegation, to take even the most minor role in such barbarous practices.'

'I have no experience of the niceties of such things,' I demurred.

'There is no need. It is simply that custom demands two seconds for each gentleman. I know the necessary formalities, and will probably require no more than token assistance from you.'

It was not a prospect I relished, yet I felt a certain grisly curiosity. If this was to be my real introduction to Viennese life, it was undoubtedly a dramatic one. When my accoster saw that I was willing to partake, he let go of my arm and led the way briskly towards six hazy figures in the centre of the small park.

As we went, I asked: 'Over what is this duel being fought?'

'Over a lady,' he said, 'as usual.'

'The winner to claim her as reward?'

'That will depend on the outcome.' Instead of urging me on, he now held me back for a moment. 'Our opponent has been called out because he impugned the honour of a lady under my master's protection. Should my master be killed this morning, he does not wish the lady to fall into the hands of this blackguard. That is another good reason why there should be two of us at his side. Should the worst happen, the lady must be carried off without delay.'

This was taking on even more troublesome aspects. I was tempted to turn tail and dash off into the swirling mist. But on a field of combat such as this I sensed it would be regarded as contemptible cowardice.

We approached the group. A small man standing to one side with a leather bag at his feet was clearly the doctor surgeon *de rigueur* on such occasions. A tall, bolt upright man who turned towards me as I approached must be the challenger. The other man . . .

In spite of the wisps of greyness which blurred the whole scene, my first quick glance told me the identity of the one so accurately described by my companion as a blackguard. It was none other than Lord Alderley. I averted my head and pulled my collar up about my ears. Fortunately the tingling chill had prompted Alderley's two seconds to do the same, so this caused no comment.

I was introduced to the dignified gentleman who required my services. The name of Lord Corbridge struck almost as harsh a discord in my mind as had that of Alderley. This was the rogue who had snatched Cecilia from Count Rupert. And if he won this duel, doubtless he would dismiss me with a seigneurial wave of the hand and ride off with her again.

All along I had been aware of a seventh figure set apart from the others – a veiled woman seated in an open two-wheeled carriage a few yards away. Carefully not looking at her or letting her glimpse my face, I knew full well who this had to be. I sensed her in every fibre of my body. But whichever of them won this absurd contest, he would be unlikely to hand my Cecilia back to me.

The duellists took up their positions. One of Alderley's seconds recited the rules, and my fellow second concurred while I nodded my head knowingly. Alderley and Corbridge stood back to back, their right hands holding pistols pointing upwards. At the command from my companion, they began their ten steady paces forward, and then turned.

I will swear that Alderley swung round before quite completing that last pace. He spun on his heel and fired; and Lord Corbridge stood very erect and still for an interminable moment, before crumpling to the damp ground.

Alderley blew a wisp of smoke from the end of his pistol, blandly waiting for the doctor to come forward and make his examination. There could be little doubt. Lord Corbridge was dead.

My fellow second was at my elbow. 'Now!' he whispered. 'I must see to the formalities with the doctor and Lord Alderley. Drive the lady away at once. Fast! Take her back to Lord Corbridge's establishment – in the little square of the pelican fountain off the Herrengasse – and wait for me there. You will both be safe, and I'll see that you're well rewarded.'

Alderley was all too blatantly preparing to approach the veiled lady and inflict whatever mockery suited him. Before he could set one foot in front of the other in that direction, I ran towards the curricle, leapt up, and with little skill but reasonable control set the two horses trotting and then galloping across the grass. Alderley let out a yell of rage. Behind me, Cecilia let out a cry of fear.

Whilst I cried out in joyful reassurance: 'It's time we made music again!'

'No. . . it cannot be. . . Roger?'

'Roger,' I yelled to the skies and to a startled elderly gentleman on horseback, out for his morning constitutional.

'How is it possible?'

'I will tell you my story,' I said over my shoulder, 'and you can tell me your story. After we have exhausted another topic.'

'We shall never exhaust that.' Then, sadly, she added: 'I grieve for poor Lord Corbridge.'

I drove in silence for a while, giving her time to sort out the confusion of her thoughts, until I realised I had no idea whither I was heading.

'Where is Lord Corbridge's mansion? You'll have to direct me.'

She remained silent as if in grief, then said: 'I do not wish to return there. It had been agreed that I should soon leave anyway, and I would not want to be found there by Alderley. Where are *you* staying?'

I told her the address, but stressed that it was unlikely to compare favourably with the luxury in which she had been living. She said: 'We are not too far from there. I suggest you leave the carriage at the crossroads, and we will walk the rest of the way.'

It seemed to me that I had been abandoning other people's horseflesh somewhat freely of late, this time to be accompanied by the vehicle. Nevertheless I accepted the suggestion and, taking Cecilia's hand, led her through a maze of back streets and alleys which ought surely to throw any pursuer of the scent. Or perhaps it would be truer to say that she led me, since her knowledge of Vienna had clearly become extensive.

When we were shut away in my unambitious little room, I said: 'At least here we shall be safe. There are so many people, nobody can tell where this one or that one is. The city is full, as I discovered when seeking a lodging. Utterly full.'

'But I am empty,' she said. 'I have been empty for so long.'

Her veil still shadowed her face. I lifted it gently, and kissed her. But I could not resist a probing question. 'You mean to tell me the dashing Lord Corbridge won you merely as an ornament?'

She looked demurely down. 'Lord Corbridge treated me as a virile man should. But he was of no great stature. A gentleman of high quality but lower quantity.'

'No enjoyment in it?'

I knew of old the pinkness in her cheeks, the little curl of her lips as she tried to concoct a swift little tale. But like Helga von Hauptfeld and her husband, she could not bring herself to lie to me. Or was there, hidden in it, some minor lie, some cunning reservation, such as Helga would have used with her self-justifying hints of mesmerism?

She said: 'There was mild pleasure. I won't deny it. But he could reach to the end neither of my mouth nor my cunt. My fancy was not tickled where I most needed it.'

It might not be the whole truth, but she looked so beautiful that I could not bring myself to embark on any further inquisition. We looked at each other, and went on looking. It might be that convention demanded she should observe a short period of mourning for her protector, which was poor news for the tension that was building between my legs. Then when she smiled I knew that her period of mourning was already over.

She began shedding her fur-trimmed mantle and the cambrick frock beneath. As she emerged from lifting a silk petticoat over her head, straining her incomparable breasts upwards and unavoidably sending a tremor through the fronds about her quim, she said archly:

'Have you developed any new dances or variations in my absence?'

The riding jaunts with Helga could hardly have been classified as new in their approach, though when indulging in similar positions with this adorable filly pacing before me now I had never contemplated flogging her along with such force as the older mare had demanded. As for Grethe, she had proved fetchingly supple and capable of unwonted gyrations with her legs, but there was little inventiveness in her movements. I thought kindly of her; shivered momentarily at the thought of Helga; and turned my attention back to Cecilia, whose mouth was trembling with desire and who was dragging my hands towards her.

I wanted to touch her everywhere at once: to grip her shoulders, brush her nipples with my palm, prize open her cunt with my middle finger, and clasp her buttocks in my hands to steady her ready for the entry. But I could not touch one sweetness of her flesh without abandoning another. Nor did she want to be steadied and pinned down yet: she had a fancy to indulge in her own tormenting little games, twitching her haunches from one side to the other, opening her knees and then clamping them shut, making quick grabs at my cods and squeezing them in affection which became agony, until I could endure no more and flung her bodily on to the bed. She laughed, spread herself at last for the feast I had been starved of, and we fucked without a care as only true, forever unconstrained lovers can fuck. In the middle of the night we drowsily reached for each other, and fucked as only friends know how, without haste or excessive demands. And then in the morning she awoke me with a simple 'Roger', which might have been my name or a demand or both; and I was wonderstruck by what she could inspire in me and what she could still suck out of me.

* * *

We troubled ourselves little with the outside world for a full three days. Then we had to agree that if we were not to face penury we must either seek musical engagements here or return speedily to London and pick up old threads. Since the centre of musical activity for all Europe was during these months in Vienna, and there was still a dearth of qualified performers, it seemed more sensible to remain here and amass profits for as long as the Congress should last.

But Cecilia could not be plunged straight back into the high society of the capital. Lord Corbridge's death had aroused a certain amount of comment, though the name of his opponent in that fatal duel was not noised abroad, and would have done Alderley little damage if it had been. As to the singer under Corbridge's protection, she was missed in many of the better salons, but it was assumed that she would promptly have sought another patron. If he were of sufficient standing, she might be allowed to reappear in his company in due course. I was not, I feared, of such stature.

We had little difficulty in finding employment in the more mundane wine taverns on the slopes of the Vienna Woods. When we had been heard there a number of times in a number of bars (both vinous and musical), invitations came for performances closer to the heart of the city. There were perils in this; but we determined to face them when they arose, and not to cower in third-rate venues forever.

And so, inevitably, we came face to face once more with Lord Alderley, in the salon of a minor Marquise.

His expression when he saw me was quite a study in hatred and incredulity mixed in equal proportions. 'So *this* is what . . . ' He paused, then with the most unconvincing self-righteousness thundered: '*You* were poor Corbridge's assassin. You connived with this whore to – '

'No, sir,' said Cecilia at my side, before I could launch myself at the repellent creature's throat. 'That dishonour falls on you. I was there to witness it. And so was Mr Rougiere – as one of Lord Corbridge's seconds.'

'Ah. That explains many things.' Alderley did not seem too disconcerted by this revelation but, seeing my clenched fist, backed hastily away before he could become involved in another duel which would have begun and ended with few formalities. As he moved off he said menacingly to Cecilia: 'Our little charade is not yet finished, that I promise you.'

Faces which were apparently known well to Cecilia began to appear on our scene. Ladies spoke patronisingly to her, completely ignoring my presence. But they were amiable enough in their own grotesque way, and we received a couple more invitations to some of the higher echelons of society. Or, let me still endeavour to write only the exact truth: Cecilia was invited 'with her accompanist.'

Learning as I had done so many of the ways of this world, I refused to take umbrage. We played and sang, we were paid, and Cecilia's voice had never been better. That unvarying pre-performance ritual of ours might have become boring, yet never did so. She had only to go down on her knees for me to be engulfed – not just by her mouth but by ecstatic paroxysms throughout my whole body. I guiltily wondered if she could ever possibly experience the same joy which she so richly gave to me.

Then came a most unexpected summons. We were commanded to attend upon Viscount Castlereagh. Not upon some minor functionary arranging an entertainment, but upon the British Foreign Secretary himself.

Could such a remote, awe-inspiring figure have designs upon Cecilia?

We bought new clothes for the occasion, and decided that expenditure on the hire of a smart equipage would be worth our while. I was rather surprised when we arrived in the Minoritenplatz below his twenty-two-room apartment to find no other coaches arriving, and no fashionable throng swirling in towards the grand staircase.

As we went hesitantly towards the door, two men in the uniform of the Austrian imperial police intercepted me, one of them snapping something out in a sing-song dialect I did not understand.

Behind me, Alderley's well-remembered voice said: 'They are telling you that you're under arrest.'

Chapter 4

In which Cecilia draws secrets from men's minds and sustenance from their fountains

He stood before me once more, hateful and gloating. We were in a small ante-room with only two chairs and a small circular table. With an exaggerated bow he had directed me towards one of the chairs, but I refused to sit down.

'This is an outrage,' I said. 'We have been dragged here under false pretences. If this is really Lord Castlereagh's house –'

'Oh, it is indeed Lord Castlereagh's house, make no mistake about that.'

'Then where is he? And why am I here?'

'You are here,' said Alderley with a slimy relish, 'to help your country.'

'And what have you done with Mr Rougiere?'

'You will see him again . . . when you agree to help your country.'

Before I could say another word, the door opened and a footman in blue tunic and white knee breeches stood in the opening. 'His Lordship will see you now.'

The man walked a good ten paces ahead of us along passages and galleries hung with mirrors and paintings: very dull portraits of middle-aged and elderly men with beards, interspersed occasionally with ladies displaying pursed lips and bosoms like pavilion awnings. Keeping step with me, Alderley muttered:

'Do not make a fool of yourself, Cecilia. A great opportunity is being offered to you. Accept what His Lordship suggests, and you will do well. You may even feel grateful to me in the end.'

Whatever part he might have played in these mysterious doings, I doubted whether his motives could have been such as to call for my gratitude. Some perverse humiliation must surely be in store.

We were ushered into a large room with a whole range of high windows looking down to the bright, bustling street. From the far side of a long table with ornately carved and gilded legs, Lord Castlereagh rose to greet me. He was incredibly tall, in good proportion with the windows, though his own vast, long legs seemed less sturdy than those of the table. His long face would have been handsome if it had not been set in a mask of what looked like perpetual boredom. Even when he spoke to me in a measured, oddly shy voice I felt that he might inadvertently yawn.

I settled as comfortably as possible on a rather small gilded chair. Alderley sat to one side from which I could sense him eyeing me in complacent fashion.

Castlereagh said: 'Miss Laidlaw, it is everyone's patriotic duty in these perplexing times to serve his or her country wholeheartedly and without question.'

'I am sure it is, My Lord,' I said. 'But before we go any further, may I ask what has happened to my companion, Mr Roger Rougiere? Until I can be assured – '

'I did say, young lady, that patriotic service should be without question.'

I sat even more stiffly upright, folded my hands in my lap, and inwardly vowed that I would say nothing until there had been an explanation of the way in which Roger had been hurried away upon our arrival. The Foreign Secretary stared austerely at me, then allowed himself the faintest enquiring turn of the head towards Alderley.

Alderley said smoothly: 'Mr Rougiere is being well attended to, my lord, as agreed. The Austrian police have proved most co-operative. Though they do not know the full circumstances, of course, and will take no further action either way until notified. Either way,' he repeated with some relish.

Castlereagh turned his attention back to me. 'I believe,' he said with a disdainful twitch of his bony nose, 'that Mr Rougiere may play a supporting role in the operations we shall be asking you to undertake. These are, to be frank, not undertakings in which I would normally consider engaging a charming person such as yourself. But Lord Alderley has assured me that you possess certain – ah – attributes which would lend themselves admirably to our purposes, and that from his personal knowledge of your character he – um – believes you would not be averse to playing the necessary part with conviction.'

If there was any yawning to be done, I felt it would soon be my turn. Although Lord Castlereagh was clearly one for disquisitions as long as his legs, and loftily reluctant to be interrupted by other mere mortals, I was impatient to know what he was talking about.

'My lord,' I ventured, 'I believe my musical talents are well recognised in this city. When commissioned, I am reliable in attendance and performance. Perhaps you will tell me the nature of the part you are suggesting, and the terms of the engagement.'

It was difficult to imagine those remote features ever being touched by real embarrassment, but I felt in him a reluctance to come out directly with whatever it was.

When Castlereagh did begin to speak again, it seemed at first just a continuation of vague generalities, with which I could see no personal connection for myself. He spoke with austere disapproval of the machinations of other nations' representatives at the Congress. Under a pretence of being allies anxious only for a peaceable settlement of international disputes, all the kings and princes, ambassadors and foreign secretaries, were in fact scheming against one another. There was the problem of Poland; of the Netherlands; of what on earth the Tsar of Russia was up to; what influences were being brought to bear upon Spain and upon Portugal. And as for the Italian states . . .

I tried to follow all this, with little success, until his

lordship slowly changed tack. Now he was describing the deplorable methods used by Baron Hager, director of the Austrian *Oberste Polizei* and *Censur Hofstelle*. This secret police chief had spies everywhere, digging into waste-paper baskets, listening to gossip at receptions, and reporting the results in minute detail to the Emperor Francis. Hall porters at national delegations were bullied into providing tittle-tattle of every kind. Two housemaids within this very building had only yesterday been discovered trying to open a box of Lord Castlereagh's private papers. Such procedures were so rife that Prince Metternich had even suggested, in the most approving terms, that an entire secret police force should be incorporated in the plans for a German Confederation.

In what way, I dazedly wondered, was I supposed to help in stopping this?

Then at last the truth emerged.

I was not expected to stop spying by Baron Hager or anyone else. 'Reluctantly,' said Castlereagh, as if some particularly displeasing aroma had just been wafted under his nose, 'I feel we must operate our own system of . . . hm . . . investigation.'

I waited for him to go on. Instead, implying that the actual details were all too sordid for him, he waved a weary hand in Alderley's direction.

Alderley enjoyed every moment of this task. This was the humiliation he had planned for me. Although he wasted no time in getting to the point, he still managed to dwell on certain words and implications. Putting it as starkly as I may – which Lord Castlereagh had found himself unable to do – the scheme was that I should use my wide range of musical contacts and the venues in which I appeared to seduce plenipotentiaries, delegation secretaries, or even the lowliest clerk if there was a chance of unearthing some secret of value to our own negotiators. Many men had in the past tried to lure me away from the recital salons and into their beds, with little success. Now I was being commanded not to spurn them but to coax them on.

I did not deign to answer Alderley, but addressed Lord

Castlereagh direct. 'You are in effect ordering me to become a prostitute.'

'My dear young lady, in spite of what I have to admit are extremely distasteful circumstances, I personally would set my face against ever considering your patriotic actions in such a – '

'A prostitute,' I repeated, 'and a scheming, common one at that.'

Alderley said: 'By no means common, Cecilia. A very uncommon one, I should say.'

I rose from my chair. 'I will take no part in this.'

'You'll enjoy the challenge,' said Alderley.

If there was to be a challenge, I was the one to issue it. I marched towards Castlereagh behind his table. 'With your permission, my lord, Mr Rougiere and I will leave now, and I will do you the favour of forgetting everything which has been said here today . . . '

Behind me, Alderley purred: 'If you leave, it will be alone. His lordship here will not be in a position to tell the Austrian police that there has been a mistake on the part of one of his underlings and that Mr Rougiere must be released.'

I stared into Castlereagh's face, and saw that behind the disdain and the reluctance to be involved in such squalid matters there was the implacability of one basically indifferent to anyone's concerns but those which occupied him at any given period. He endured my gaze for a few seconds, then said remotely:

'Thousands of British soldiers have laid down their lives for their country during these past years of war. Can it be asking too much of you to lay down your body? After all, unlike them you will have the good fortune to remain alive.'

'And live to fuck another day,' said Alderley in an undertone which I am sure did not reach the Foreign Secretary.

Roger stormed: 'You should have left me there. You have no right to let yourself be defiled. Nor to expect me to encourage it. No, I'll take no part in it.'

It was an echo of my own words. But I knew we would

have to play the game their way until we found some means of escaping. And if we did somehow contrive to flee to England, how immune could we count ourselves there if the Foreign Secretary chose to use his minions against us?

It was clear that I would have to lie back and think unselfishly of Britain.

There was only one way to tackle such a distasteful job. Where mild enjoyment was possible, I should not scorn to enjoy it. Nature has shaped us to take pleasure from certain bodily sensations, and even if some partners are preferable to others, it is ungrateful of us and perhaps even bad for our health not to accept such treatment as can be shown to soothe our itches. My mother had been as assiduous in reading uplifting books to me as she later became in encouraging my keeping of a diary in my best handwriting. I remember one solemn passage about it being hard to kick against the pricks. It must, I now supposed, be better to succumb and humbly accept such gratification as the pricks might offer. At the same time I must reassure Roger that all such experiences were meaningless and that he need feel no mortification on my behalf.

So we set about a different musical career in various cellars and taverns known to . . . well, to those in the know. Not that there was any basic difference between their clientele and the guests at the unending receptions. Everywhere it was becoming necessary to behave more outrageously every evening in order to retain the attentions of the overfed, overwined and bleary aristocratic mob. It became the practice for Roger to stay at the pianoforte while I meandered like some Magyar violinist between the tables, selecting my target and concentrating on him. I would approach the man, ogle him, sing straight at him, and lean over so that my low-cut bodice would give him a glimpse of one shadowy cleft which would only make him crave a lower cleft. If he had a lady companion, she might be disposed to object. I made a point of not looking at such ladies or of trying either to taunt or console them. It was up to the man to overcome that particular problem, if he wished to.

It was flattering to me, though it said little for their constancy, that so many men did wish to deal with the problem.

What most distressed me was the fact that my victims – for how else could I regard them? – were selected and notified to me by Lord Alderley. I often felt guilty to be making insincere conversation with a man who believed that my willingness to allow his staff to throb itself to extinction within me was a wiltingly feminine tribute to his manhood. Would that manhood have flagged if he had known I was seeking only what he might tell me about his country's attitude to Great Britain's policy on the slave trade?

Then there was the case of Don Pedro, in the service of King Ferdinand of Spain, who offered me a pampered position in his well-appointed household after I had proved to him that I could screw myself down on his august cock and then screw slowly round and round so that he had views of my back and bottom alternating with my breasts dancing over him. With these demands I did not feel defiled. His sobbing adoration as his geyser spouted upwards into me was a tribute, not an insult. But I did feel stained when I asked him supposedly casual questions about his monarch's plots to impose obscure Bourbon relatives upon a number of Italian principalities.

One shabby little creature, too drunk to realise that he had failed to satisfy me, mumbled in smelly slumber that if the English – the word British was hardly ever used – had any sense, they would threaten war against Russia in order to get more sensible negotiations over the matter of Poland. When I had passed this on to Alderley, I was commended and then ordered two nights later to sing at a grand reception where the Tsar's top adviser on Polish affairs, Prince Adam Czertoryski, would be plied with sufficient wine to make him an easy prey. I was tempted to inform Alderley that I could command any man I chose without recourse to the befuddlement of liquor; but he would have wantonly misinterpreted that in too many ways and reported the worst back to Castlereagh.

Prince Adam in fact provided nothing. It takes a great deal to make a Polish nobleman pass out completely, but the imbeciles had achieved it long before I leaned over his table to finish my final alluring notes. Alderley was displeased, but could scarcely lay the blame at my feet or anywhere else upon me. I was glad to imagine Lord Castlereagh being even more displeased and Alderley bearing the brunt of the blame.

Other victims were more forthcoming, though it was interesting to observe that the feebler their coming in bed, the more boastfully they came out with tales of their importance elsewhere. One little Brandenburger who could not squeeze out even a trickle for my benefit excused himself on the grounds that he had been up all the previous night conferring with ministers of state upon a possible coalition of Russia and Prussia in order to slice up Poland. On top of this, to bolster his own importance he assured me that the Austrians had solved the English secret cyphers and knew every contrary move being made by Talleyrand and Castlereagh. Castlereagh was horrified by my discovery in this instance, but also grateful, and set his lackeys about the business of contriving new codes.

How could these foolish matters be of such importance to grown men? My contempt for all of them made it easier to go through with my tasks.

But, the inquisitive reader may ask, did not this repetitive poking into my body destroy any idea of pleasure with anybody else . . . with Mr Rougiere? I am surprised, myself, but happy to say that it did not. Somehow there was a clear distinction between the two activities. I might be weary after a long tussle with an incompetent, near-impotent Dutchman, or sore from the attentions of an all too competent Portuguese grandee, yet the moment I was with Roger I was eager to strip my clothes away again and see what flesh could do to set fire to flesh. I kissed him, enclosed him, drank him. I thrust my head into his belly or down into a pillow while he rutted with his lovely horn deep inside me. With other men I coldly played a part. With Roger there were no pretences. We were in harmony, mutually sensing exactly when to be tender and when to unsheathe our nails. To me the most poetic word in the English language will always be 'rogering'.

One evening early in the New Year, in one of the better-class restaurants behind the Prater, I was instructed by Alderley to concentrate my attentions on a Turkish diplomat who was engaged in some strange manoeuvres with Russian negotiators. On my way to this delegate's table, singing an old Bohemian folk song which had become a favourite in our repertoire, I passed close to another table from which a hand suddenly rose in greeting. Count Rupert of Stoltenberg beckoned me closer.

This might be contrary to Alderley's orders, but I welcomed the respite. When I had finished the song and the applause had died away, I sat for a few moments at the Count's table and accepted a glass of wine.

He said: 'Dear *Fraülein* Laidlaw, I have a favour to ask of you.'

I might well have refused out of hand, after his very unfavourable treatment of me in that gambling matter. But he looked rather lost and pathetic, so I waited for him to go on.

'My wife, the Countess Fulvià,' he said, 'desires a portrait of you. I would like to make a gift of it to her.'

'A portrait, sir? I fear I have had no portrait painted.'

'But there shall be one. I am prepared to commission the artist Isabey to do what my wife requires – a classical pose of you in a sylvan setting. I am told the man is very accomplished.'

I thought of Countess Fulvia, and our hours together. How could I refuse?

The painter Isabey was one of the busiest tradesmen in all Vienna. He might object to my describing him as a tradesman, but the speed at which he rushed out portraits of politicians, diplomats, and soldiers in full dress uniform surely made him that rather than a true artist. Within a few months he had completed over fifty paintings, some of large, solemn-looking groups, and was prone to spend his substantial fees in the Café Jüngling near his studio.

He greeted me with genuine enthusiasm. Painting the faces of corrupt old men trying to look statesmanlike was beginning to bore him.

'It is so long since I painted a nude,' he confided.

He was impatient for me to take my clothes off. I felt that this was in no degree touched by lascivious motives, but simply that he had set himself a target of so many pictures a week and there was no time for delay.

Nevertheless he produced a most complimentary smile when I stood before him naked. 'Exquisite. Such an opportunity. I am honoured, mam'selle.'

He painted swiftly and impetuously, yet with consummate flair. At the end of the first session I was amazed by the sight of myself emerging like some shining goddess from a background still no more than a thin spattering of colour. Isabey had created a long shaft of light across the whole composition which guided the viewer's attention directly to the golden blaze of my pubic hair. Pictures and statues of classical female figures were usually quite smooth and bare in that region. I did not think, however, that Fulvia would be too disapproving.

'Next time,' he said, 'we relate you to the plants, I think.'

The sylvan surroundings which Fulvia had specified were partly drawn from Isabey's mind, but on that next sitting he also provided a number of large plants which he proceeded to arrange loosely around my shoulders and hips. A few of the thicker tendrils moved faintly as I breathed or moved involuntarily. Absorbed in his work, the painter did not appear to notice that the fronds were tickling me. One in particular seemed to have a life of its own. Its weight was such that, dangling from my left shoulder, it swayed and twisted and drifted mischievously between my legs. Moving as inconspicuously as possible, I managed after several vain attempts to grip it in my crotch. But, desperate as I was to wrap myself round the thick, rubbery end of it, I lacked the power to inhale through those lips.

All at once Isabey, studying me with his brush hesitant in his hand, became aware of my plight. He coughed out a bawdy laugh, laid his brush down, and came to my rescue.

Gently and appreciatively he directed the blunt, slithering stalk into my quim and chuckled at the sigh of relief I let out.

'Please,' he said. 'Your face. Your expression, yes? You keep it, please.'

He hurried back to his easel and began to make feverish alterations to the picture.

As he was finishing, Count Rupert came unannounced into the studio. He stood at Isabey's elbow, watching those last dabs and flicks of the brush; and then stared past the canvas at me. I endeavoured not to move or let my expression change.

The Count murmured something to the painter. It must have been complimentary, since Isabey answered with a respectful bow of his head. The two of them stared at me rather than at the canvas. The Count murmured something else, and appeared to pass a handful of coins to the painter; whereupon Isabey wiped his brush on a rag, smiled a crooked smile of complicity, and sauntered off in what I had little doubt was the direction of the Café Jüngling.

I had not expected this. The gleam in the Count's eye was something I had hitherto seen only when I had finished singing. He came towards me in that courteous, diffident way of his, and stood a few inches from me.

'I understand why my wife wishes the portrait of you,' he said.

His eyes grew more intense. For a few moments he studied me as if he and not Isabey were the painter, calculating what dab of green would be needed here and what shading needed there. 'If you will permit. . .' His right hand reached for the tendril snaking within me, pulled it free, and replaced it with the middle finger of his right hand as if to test what sort of welcome he might expect. 'A plant does not feel,' he murmured, 'does not deserve . . .'

As I have said, I had not expected this. But in spite of the Lord Corbridge episode, which I am sure the Count must have regretted a hundred times, I remained fond of him: sorry for him yet affectionate and mildly admiring. If the classical study with its pagan woodland overtones had stimulated him in an unexpected way, then I was not undisposed to please him.

He was politely waiting, still unwilling to assert himself. I freed myself from the other writhing foliage, took his hand – the hand with the damp middle finger which I extracted from myself – and led him behind the stack of canvases tilted one against the other in the corner of the studio. Behind them was another layer of paintings, and a couple of plaster models of animals which I suspected Isabey used as quick reference for auxiliary features in his paintings. One was of a dog with its back legs splayed, eager to respond to some scent or sound.

I was gently pleased that I should be appealing to the Count in this way. He would be a welcome guest. I wondered if I might have to assist him, kneading him up to a reasonable hardness; but I need not have worried. He was well poised to aim, and impatient to enter.

Remembering his tastes, and having intercepted his sidelong glance at the model dog, I lowered myself slowly, face down, on a heap of sacking which would be used to wrap round pictures when Isabey wished to prepare them for collection. The sacking was rough on my knees, and behind the shelter of the stacked-up canvases a cool draught came up between my thighs. Then it was replaced by Count Rupert.

The artist's painting had truly had a remarkable effect on him. He was thoroughly satisfying. I unashamedly enjoyed the tilt of his lance and its exultant thrust. I was glad that I should have aroused such passion in him. Or was it just Isabey's interpretation that had aroused the passion? Whatever the explanation, he was in excellent form, sinking his teeth in my neck and slapping my haunches and pushing so hard into me that my knees grew sore on the sacking.

When he had finished we lay there for a while, his exhausted body heavy on my back. In front of me as I raised my head was a canvas stacked against three or four others, like tombstones propped against a churchyard wall. I took in the features without paying much attention, being still attentive to Count Rupert's well-being and waiting for his ebbing prick to plop finally out. Then, as I relinquished him, the lineaments of the painting became sharper and more immediate.

It was a large dramatic study in oils of Laocoön. In the middle of the snaking coils was the face of someone I knew. Three naked male figures writhed over one another, and the more one looked into the detail the more one found strange convolutions and conjunctions. One man's cods were in the mouth of another; a cock was either withdrawing from or about to stopper a rectum; one of the snakes was apparently being used for a more lively purpose than the plant frond which I had employed earlier; and the face of the central figure was tormented by ecstasy. As I recognised it, I also felt that I could identify the features of the young man making such a feast of his balls, despite the awkward angle at which he had been painted. I had seen him at several receptions, though in more decorous mood.

The central body was that of Lord Alderley. I found the accompanying snakes very much in keeping with his character. His most joyful participant in the tangle was the military councillor to the Tsar Alexander's delegation in Vienna. Mistrust of Russian motives was growing daily, most markedly among the British representatives, as I had already gleaned from Lord Castlereagh's instructions to me. Yet here was Alderley cavorting obscenely with one of the most dangerous of our supposed allies. Had he been set to do this by Castlereagh's orders, just as I had been set similar tasks? I doubted it. Such a relationship should have been kept tightly confidential, not self-indulgently recorded in paint.

We heard Isabey puffing back up the stairs, producing a tactful volume of noise. When he crashed back cheerfully into his studio, the Count was fully clad and I was toying with the end of a strand of creeper.

I said: 'I wish to take that picture away – the one of Laocoön.'

He was winded. 'Please, I do not think . . . no, it is not for sale. Not yours to take.'

'I know Lord Alderley,' I said. 'I shall be visiting the British residency later today. I shall take great pleasure in delivering it personally.'

'He collect it himself. It had better be soon. He has not yet paid me.'

'I am confident you will be paid,' I said with a fine show of assurance, though I had no idea who might eventually pay, or how much.

He wanted to argue, but the Count, though not understanding my motives, rallied gallantly to my cause. The autocratic gaze he bent upon Isabey made it clear that my wishes were to be obeyed.

'It will go to Lord Alderley?' the painter implored. 'It was an unusual commission. A special commission. I do not wish that – '

'It will go where it belongs,' I reassured him. 'I will personally see to that.'

I did in fact ensure that it went straight in to Lord Castlereagh's office. Now it would be revealed whether Alderley had been engaged in official duties, and was in fact trapping the Russian military councillor rather than being trapped by him.

Next morning we heard that Lord Alderley had been summarily returned to London, and there was a murmur, quickly suppressed, of possible treason charges. I hoped I could be kept informed of the outcome.

The matter might have given rise to more gossip and speculation, which were numbered among the Congress's main pastimes, had it not been for something which overshadowed every other concern and seemed to threaten the whole purpose of the Congress.

On the 6th of March the exiled Napoleon Bonaparte escaped from Elba. Five days later he was on French soil.

Chapter 5

A sound of revelry by night and sound rogerings at all hours of the day and night

The night before the battle on the plains of Waterloo, it was considered the duty of every woman who loved her country (whichever country that happened to be) to love any man who might lose his life in the morning. This left an insignificant male civilian like myself with little company until the fervour should pass and the battle be won. As a professional musician, Roger Rougiere was of no consequence compared with the professional soldier. It surprised me that the Duke of Wellington, such a martinet in so many ways, did not insist on his troops conserving their energies. Indeed, contemplating the orgy of tirelessly gaping cunts, like the beaks of nestlings voracious for whatever could be thrust in, I thought it might be more patriotic for the ladies to offer themselves to the enemy and thereby tire *them* out before the fray.

Cecilia and I had travelled to Brussels in the wake of the Iron Duke and other key figures. Wellington had for a time replaced Castlereagh as British representative in Vienna, and at once abandoned the espionage methods which had been forced upon Cecilia. They were far too underhanded for his straightforward tastes. We were allowed to resume a purely musical career. But Vienna itself was tiring of its Congress and interminable bickerings, and once Napoleon was on the march again the military representatives and princelings left hurriedly. Some were intent on raising their troops against the renewed threat. Other aristocrats who had been indulging themselves at the gaming tables and seducing ladies at the fashionable receptions went pale with fear when news came through that Napoleon was once more established in Paris, and scuttled back to their dens. Instead of calculating the odds at the tables, they devoted themselves now to weighing up the pros and cons of supporting Napoleon and saving their properties, or denouncing him and saving their properties.

We heard that Wellington had taken command of armies in the Low Countries and established his headquarters in Brussels. The social life there was less flamboyant and abandoned than in Vienna; but Brussels was for the time being, nevertheless, the centre of such things.

To our surprise, Count Rupert appeared with a small force of ill-equipped men from Stoltenberg. He announced that he would prefer to serve alongside the Duke of Wellington and his Englishmen rather than with Blücher and his Prussians. And in his entourage was the Countess, who had declared that at such a moment in history she wished to be at her husband's side.

I never doubted her sincerity, but at the same time I did observe that her face became truly radiant only when she set eyes on Cecilia once more.

'A painting,' she said, 'is a poor substitute. Though it is a fine painting and I am grateful to my husband for bringing it to me.'

That work of art had obviously made a lasting impression. One late afternoon I came into our quarters unexpectedly, to find Cecilia naked, with the Countess lovingly draping flowers and tendrils of creeper over her shoulders, letting her fingers linger at every move. I was about to apologise and withdraw, but both ladies turned their delightful heads towards me, one so dark and one so fair, and the Countess suggested that I might care to stay.

At first I took this as a hint that I would shortly be called on to partake of the pleasures in which they were indulging. I soon discovered that this was not the case. I was invited only to be a spectator. This was not so much to tantalise my own bodily desires, but to give an added spice to their own gratification. They became actresses, loving their role but needing to startle an audience. Languor turned into vigorous inventiveness. And every now and then, wrapped around and in and over each other, their faces turned appealingly towards me to see if I was concentrating on all the finer nuances.

It made, to be honest, a beautiful sight. There are fewer more exquisite visions in the world than the bodies of two graceful women entwining, interlacing, sliding over each other like dolphins at play. A breast appears and disappears behind a gleaming shoulder. Moist mouths appear at both ends and are momentarily, lovingly covered, to emerge moister than ever. Fingers cajole, plucking skittishly at a dark tuft of hair, then a golden one. The two triangles begin to glisten. A leisurely smile becomes a sudden grimace of ecstasy. Only an out-and-out boor could fail to appreciate the loveliness of it simply for its own sake.

Even when, in spite of his best endeavours, he has to discipline a hardness that could quickly shatter the mood.

That night Cecilia apologised most sweetly for the torments she knew they had inflicted on me, and promised to make up for it in any way I chose. She did so with a deplorable chuckle in her throat. I soon silenced that throat in the most forceful way I knew, and then took her at her word and chose three different angles of attack before finally filling her with all the love I could summon.

Yet I admit I retain to this day a memory of the two women in that exquisite embrace. It could not be immortalised in paint or in stone: without the slow, sensuous movements of hip, thigh, breasts, head and hands, the drifts of dishevelled hair across shoulders and knees, it would be meaningless.

It was the last lovely interlude before the utterly different clash of male, murderous bodies.

Word came that Napoleon, at the head of his army, had defeated Blücher and his Prussians at Ligny on the 16th of June and was turning vengefully towards Wellington's forces, which had checked Marshal Ney at Quatre-Bras. Wellington with his motley collection of British, Dutch, and smaller German contingents hastily notified Blücher that they must join up at the fields of Waterloo, ten miles south of Brussels, where he would be waiting for the Bonapartist thrust.

And so, on the night of the 17th of June, there came the extravagance of a grand ball and a number of lesser functions. Cecilia and I played and sang for those of the troops still in the city who were capable of listening. The cream of fighting men were already on their way south. What remained were bloodthirsty old warriors who could rant on without fear of being involved in any real fighting, and some even more warlike women who liked the idea of blood – provided they did not themselves get spattered with it. After a few nostalgic ballads about our home country, we were advised to adhere to bright, martial airs with a strong marching rhythm.

I noticed that Count Rupert's little pageboy had somehow managed to avoid accompanying his master to the front. These last few weeks he had exerted himself looking after the serving maids while their mistresses were busy being gallant soldiers' mistresses for a brief spell. Now he was turning his attentions to more highly born ladies temporarily – or it could be permanently – deprived of their menfolk.

The next day we had nothing to do but wait apprehensively for news to come back from Waterloo.

It was a victory, though a damned close-run thing. We had lost more than twenty thousand men. Among the dead, to our grief, was Count Rupert of Stoltenberg, who had been hit by a stray bullet while riding to urge the dilatory Blücher to hurry to the battlefield.

Men still begrimed and caked with blood came limping back or marching triumphantly back. Some washed off the stains of battle in the Senne or the Willebroek canal; and were joined there by women who claimed to have inspired them on their way to battle and now required the fruits of victory.

Cecilia and I delayed a few days before venturing to express our respects to the widowed Countess Fulvia. I suggested that Cecilia should go first, knowing the bond between them, and I followed after a discreet two hours. I had anticipated joining the ladies, adding my commiserations to Cecilia's, and then escorting Cecilia away. When I arrived, however, Cecilia came out to say that the Countess wished to see me alone, as she had several confidential things to say to me. I was mildly surprised, unable to imagine what confidences she might impart to me that she would be reluctant to impart to Cecilia. Nevertheless I went gravely in.

Now I was more than mildly surprised. Expecting to find the Countess in mourning attire, I came upon her removing her last shred of clothing. She turned to greet me with a dignity which was enhanced rather than impaired by her nakedness.

Perhaps she and Cecilia had indulged in a last affectionate embrace. Yet she ought then to have been resuming her garments, not discarding them.

She stood a few feet away from me, spreading her arms as if to insist that I looked full at her, missing nothing. There was none of the coquettishness which she had displayed while tussling so recently in front of me with Cecilia. In her expression was something quite different – something which I suddenly recognised as desperation.

'It is a tragedy,' she said.

'The loss of Count Rupert is a tragic day for all of us,' I agreed.

'A tragedy,' she said, 'that there will now be no true heir to Stoltenfeld.'

She hated having to confide the details to me, but was too proud to evade the issue. Characteristically, her husband had not made love to her during the whole time of his mustering troops and attending Wellington's councils of war. That, I recalled, was how he had always been. Now it was too late. The estates would all go to a worthless cousin. At best the widow would be permitted to live in a small dower house on the fringes of the estate. She told me this with dignified pathos, in no way self-conscious about the picture of sleek, slender womanhood she was presenting to me.

And suddenly, fool that I was, I understood.

'It is essential that you try to have an heir,' I said.

'I have had no fortune so far.'

'A last attempt?'

'It might be that at the last moment' – she was looking steadily at me – 'my husband, full of noble manhood before the battle, succeeded in impregnating me. People would be glad to believe that. It would be splendid for Stoltenberg if it were so.'

I disrobed. I expected her then to turn away so that she did not need to look into the face of the man who serviced her. Instead, she leaned back against the silk-covered arm of the chaise longue and spread her legs, wriggling most enticingly as she adjusted to the padded corners of the arm.

'I think this makes it easier for the deep penetration, yes? And that is best?'

I looked at the pleasure she was presenting to me. Even that pink yawn managed to be an aristocratic yawn.

'Yes,' I said, 'that is best.'

As I approached and went into her as smoothly as I would have walked into a room whose door had been held welcomingly open to me, I half expected her to close her eyes. But those liquid dark eyes were as wide and watchful as Grethe's had ever been; and more beautiful, almost too beautiful.

She said: 'I think it would not be right, not to look into the face of the man who fathers my child.'

I rocked her to and fro, sometimes far enough over to lift her heels from the ground, and all the time she smiled and clung to my back with soft but firm fingers. It was absurd to feel so respectful and yet at the same time be so hot and hard.

Abruptly she braced herself and refused to be moved even a fraction of an inch.

'You are too polite,' she said.

'I thought you would not wish – '

'I wish a child. I think we do not make a child so gently.'

It was a debatable point, but this was no time for debate. If she believed in fierceness to meet her ends, she should have my end at its fiercest. I pretended that I was trying to screw right through her and into the sofa arm, and now her fingers proved to have nails, and my right shoulder felt her teeth. But she pulled her head back again and, in a paroxysm such as I had never known other than with Cecilia, shook and thrashed from side to side. At the culmination of her last spasm she cried in a strained, hoarse whisper: 'Yes, it must be. He is here! I *know* it!'

There was little point in telling her not to be too optimistic. As she mopped herself up afterwards, she kept shooting bright little glances at me, smiling gratitude, reaching out in the most comradely way to touch me and thank me again and again.

Cecilia was curious about the length of time I had been closeted with the Countess. I was about to tell her frankly what had happened, but was stopped by some inexplicable twinge of gallantry. I simply said that the widow was anxious to talk to old friends with whom she felt no inhibitions, as Cecilia herself must surely have noticed. Or perhaps the two of them had been too occupied with other concerns for the Countess to have had time to unburden herself of all her woes. Cecilia went faintly pink and changed the subject. I congratulated myself on this flash of inspiration.

For several nights there was, not surprisingly, even more exuberant revelry in Brussels than there had been on the night before Waterloo. Fear of death was gone; sheer exhilaration at being still alive made for interminable celebrations, drinking, singing and dancing. Cecilia's services were much in demand. It made little difference whether she sang at her best or just in reasonably good form, with such jubilant audiences. Nevertheless we had our own standards, and I liked to prepare her with the usual ritual.

The evening after our separate encounters with Countess Fulvia, it struck me that Cecilia was tackling my shaft with rather less commitment than usual. It was as if she were absentmindedly licking the fat from the skin of a local *wurst* while thinking of something else. After I had supplied her lubrication, she still seemed reflective rather than fulfilled, and mused: 'Do you think that Fulvia would welcome an intimate meeting as a sort of farewell present?'

'I think that would hardly be proper.'

'Proper? Her ladyship did not consider it beneath her dignity in the not too distant past.'

I thought of the Countess's face as I left her, and of her hope for a son. Intuitively I knew that she would not welcome any further invasion of her body, even with Cecilia caressing and exploring.

'It's not the time,' I said. 'We've said our farewells. Let's leave it at that.'

Cecilia remained puzzled, but was touched by what she construed as unusual but praiseworthy delicacy on my part. We left for England without seeing the dear lady again. Yet I had a premonition that someday, somehow, our paths would cross once more.

Cecilia's fame had gone ahead of us. Wounded officers, invalided home in advance of other returning troops, spoke of her voice and of the inspiration she had provided to the country's fighting men. Others, I learned, made colourful, suggestive remarks. I am prepared to believe that in the pre-battle heat she had nobly satisfied certain gentlemen, but only those whom she discerned to be truly gentlemen. The lascivious daydreams of others doubtless sustained them in the hours before the conflict. One had to be magnanimous. And assuredly none of it had done Cecilia any harm. Her cheeks were as young and girlish as ever, her voice as pure and undefiled as ever. We had both been through some trying experiences abroad, and now we were back home.

Together we made a triumphant reappearance at Vauxhall Gardens. During a sequence of tableaux telling the whole story of British exploits from Trafalgar to Waterloo, Cecilia sang patriotic songs, and the evening ended with marching and countermarching by boys in gaudy and somewhat inaccurate uniforms. I felt that a more appropriate pageant could have been produced by cordoning off a section of the gardens and throwing a hundred naked girls in, with torches positioned to show what really occupied the victorious troops rather than marching and flag-waving. The authorities would doubtless have regarded this as too cynical a view.

We were soon offered a handsome contract for regular performances at Vauxhall. Things went splendidly for the first few weeks, but then Cecilia's voice seemed to deteriorate. On three successive occasions she complained of dizziness while singing, and then one morning was so sick that I decided she should lie abed for the day while I went in search of a substitute and rehearsed the orchestra in a modified programme.

It was a mellow August morning, and the gardens looked far more natural, less artificial, than under the misleading hues of the evening lanterns. Workmen were sweeping the paths and collecting the occasional empty tankard from the flowerbeds. Horses trudged towards the small bars, steak rooms and ham kitchens with their heavy loads of beer casks. A somnolent drunk was eased out of the shrubbery, blinking groggily into the daylight. Birds scavenged for scraps of dropped food near the bandstands before the cleaners could reach them and sweep it up.

'Good morning, sir. You're about early.'

The young lady who accosted me was so smartly attired in a fawn walking dress trimmed with swansdown, with her hands tucked into a fashionable sealskin muff in spite of the warmth of the day, that at first I did not recognise her. Then the little curl of the lip and the gleam in her eye brought it all back to me. Instinctively I looked down; but the ankle-length muslin of her dress concealed the long white legs I remembered with such appreciation.

I raised my hat. 'Polly.'

'You have been away from these parts for a long time.'

'And you still spend all your time here?'

She smiled. It was still the same frank, inviting smile. 'By no means, sir. My – ah – gentleman prefers me to stay at home if he cannot accompany me here himself.'

It was hard to blame the fellow. Since he must clearly be the one who had provided the expensive garments, it was understandable that he should not wish other men to remove them at frequent intervals.

'But he is not accompanying you here at this time of day?' I ventured, looking around.

'On the contrary, sir. He is here. But much occupied at the moment.'

Since the only men occupied with anything at this hour were the sweepers, cleaners and delivery men, I could not even begin to speculate what her gentleman friend's occupation might be.

Polly rubbed her muff against her stomach. It must be a new addition to her wardrobe: she was looking down at it with girlish pleasure, as if unsure that it might not be snatched away.

'My friend is a businessman from the provinces,' she said, with a half-apologetic note in her unmistakably London voice. 'He has put up the money – investment, he calls it – to replace the old cascade and install a grotto beneath it.'

Now I understood. Going through one of its periodic crises, Vauxhall was raising money from a number of men who foresaw handsome profits in the end. One of them had provided his own plans for a grotto, now almost completed, though I confess I had never troubled to look inside.

'He spends a great deal of time in London supervising the work?' I suggested.

She lowered her eyes, smiling more impishly than ever. 'He finds it necessary to travel to and fro,' she said, 'and of course there are long periods when he has to concentrate on his other interests. When he is here, I am one of his interests.'

'And when he is not here?'

'It can be lonely,' she said archly. 'Just my apartment, and my thoughts.'

'But very rewarding during his spells of residence?'

She giggled. She really had the most appealing giggle. 'I make sure it's rewarding. I make him pay every time.'

'You mean. . .'

'Well, I mean, I've got the apartment now, and food and things to wear. But I like to charge him a proper rate every time he. . . well, we. . .' Her hands seemed to be twitching strangely within the muff. Suddenly she burst out: 'You know, it wouldn't seem natural to do it without getting paid each time. Even if it's only a crown, which is what I usually get from him.'

'Even though he provides all those other things?' I marvelled.

'It's good for him,' she said. 'He takes money so seriously.' Again she was giggling. 'D'you know, sometimes he gets so careful. . . so worried about his finances. . . he adds figures up on sheets of paper and then decides he can't afford me for three nights.'

'What a waste,' I said involuntarily.

Her eyes sparkled with pleasure. 'I do give my money's worth, wouldn't you say?'

I assured her that to the best of my recollection she indeed gave very fine value. And then, willing myself to bid her a polite farewell and walk on, I felt myself weakening – weakening in one sense, though growing uncomfortably stronger in another.

I took out a guinea, as if absentmindedly, and turned it over on my right palm.

Polly's face went very grave for a moment. I thought I had offended her and that, honest girl as she had always been, she disapproved of attempted trespass on her protector's territory. Then she took the guinea from me and contemplated it.

'And what will you demand for *this*?'

'No demands,' I assured her. 'A shared pleasure is more to my taste.'

She led me to a palisade of pollarded trees behind which was the entrance to the new grotto which her businessman was financing. At first it was dark inside, but then my eyes became accustomed to the faint green light cunningly directed through glass panes in an imitation cave roof. It glowed on banks of moss tilting towards a dark, still pool. At the end a fountain poured gently from a satyr's stone mouth, making a soothing, splashing sound. The pool looked cleaner and sweeter than the Thames. When open to the public it would be equipped, Polly told me as she withdrew her hands from the muff and shed her clothes, with a number of scantily clad water nymphs. None of them would, presumably, be as scantily clad as Polly now was.

Her slim body slid into the water, her long legs twisting more ravishingly than the tail of any mermaid. I heard her gasp at the cold, and then she thrust her legs down and stood up, facing me and waiting. Her tits rested just on the water level, and even in that light I could see them darkening with the chill. I plunged in towards her, gasping in my turn as my shaft was lapped in an icy embrace. I reached her, put my arms around her, and felt the cold water splashing over her shoulders. Below the surface I explored, probing for her, and made her laugh a protest. She began to move backwards, half swimming, half stumbling, until we came under the froth of the waterfall. Faintly glinting lines of water streamed down her face and between her breasts. As I thrust her back and back, until I felt there would be nothing to support her, she closed her eyes against the downpour. Then her shoulders met the mossy slope, and she was steady, gasping as she opened her mouth and swallowed water, and then gasping again as she opened below the water and swallowed me.

She was so sweet and refreshing, was Polly. I quit her with regret, and helped her to the bank with a laughing but sincere display of gallantry which I think she deserved.

She did her best to dry her hair, and finished by cramming it as inconspicuously as possible under her sealskin hat. At the exit from the grotto, she stopped for a moment and said demurely:

'I think the fee was too generous. If you wish to make an assignation one day... or one evening... I think I should provide you with more for your money.'

From our first encounter she had been so meticulous. But already I was feeling guilty. Physically fulfilled, but guilty. Poor Cecilia ill at home, while I was disporting myself with a chance acquaintance!

I felt even more guilty when I got home that night, after a rather mediocre performance by both the orchestra and myself. As I entered the bedroom to ask solicitously after the dear girl's health, she sat up, pale but filled with a dewy happiness.

'My dear Roger, I am *enceinte*.' She flung her arms round my neck. 'I am carrying your child.'

Chapter 6

Last leaves from Cecilia's diary

WEDNESDAY 9 AUGUST 1815

Roger has again asked me, most honourably, to marry him. This time I feel I cannot refuse. My child must bear his name, even though I suspect it ought to carry a much nobler one. In view of all the diversions I have had, I have been unsure how Roger would accept my assurance that he is the father. In the end I risked saying bluntly:

'I *know* when it happened. The very moment when it happened, that night just before we left Vienna for Brussels. There had been no other men at that time – just you and I. And it was then that we made a child. Women do have a deep-seated intuition for such a moment.'

I was faintly ashamed at playing so selfishly on his masculine naïvety, though I half believe the story myself – insofar as I had experienced just that intuition when Count Rupert shot his seed into me. I confess I am surprised that Roger has accepted it so readily, as though the concept of a woman's instinctive knowledge is one which is not new to him. He nodded so smugly and approvingly. Yet where else could he have heard such things? Dear Roger. He must be so anxious to believe it is true that he believes it without any doubt.

He must never be told that the father was almost certainly

the late Count Rupert of Stoltenberg. Nor, sadly, can my son ever know – for I can feel within me that it will be a son. Alas for poor Fulvia, and alas for what the Count would have wished. The true heir will forever be banished, unknowingly, from his inheritance; and I will not spoil his life or Roger's by confessing the truth. Roger and I will have other children, and we shall all be as one.

THURSDAY 17 AUGUST 1815

Today we have had a most remarkable missive from the Countess Fulvia. It appears that she, too, is *enceinte*. Clearly the Count, knowing that death might face him on the morrow, had a fine last flush of manhood and spread his seed vigorously. It can only be hazy speculation at best, but I do wonder which of the two was planted first – the one in Fulvia, or the one in me? Almost certainly mine, since it took place in Vienna, and the Countess did not rejoin her husband until the days in Brussels. My son is assuredly the true heir.

But no claim can ever be made, no word ever said.

In her letter the Countess invites us to Carlsbad, where she proposes to take the waters and rest. She summons us to join her, and I am sure she will redouble the invitation once she learns that I, too, am with child. We will have much to talk about – save the one thing which it would be most interesting to talk about.

And Roger, dear Roger, will from now on be faithful to me. That I will ensure. We are a respectable married couple now, and I will share him with nobody. Nor shall I stray, since I intend all later children, after this first blue-blooded one, to be his.

I am impatient to bear the child and set about making the next one.

Still, as every woman knows, there are things it is better not to tell one's husband. They are happier without certain knowledge of things which can be kept amiably uncertain.

CODA BY ROGER ROUGIERE

There are things it's better not to tell one's wife. Dearest Cecilia has shown me the invitation from the Countess Fulvia, the birth of whose son is eagerly awaited in Stoltenberg. For a son it must surely be. And I know whose son it surely is, but dare never tell the truth. The Countess will bring him up without ever allowing his true father to confess. Yet I now fancy that her reason for inviting us to spend time with her in Carlsbad is so that she may again verify the lineaments of the man who impregnated her. I shall be delighted to see the noble lady again; but she will be the first to understand that I am now a married man with responsibilities which I take seriously. It may give her a moment or two of civilised amusement to realise that in her presence there stands the father of both her child and that of her adored Cecilia. It is a matter for a man to be proud of; especially if both should prove to be boys.

I am now faithful. I shall continue to be faithful.

It speaks well for my resolve that last week I encountered sweet fucking Polly and was able to resist temptations which were offered. The meeting came in a late afternoon in Vauxhall, when I was on my way to inspect a more generous distribution of music-desks for which I had long been pleading in the main pavilion. I was ambling down the broad walk towards the ornamental façade when she hove into view, accoutred in a bright emerald habit with pseudo-military trimmings and green half-boots. Linking arms with her was a plump, red-faced man of indeterminate age – determinable, if at all, on the wrong side of fifty – who was glaring at any male passerby who dared to glance at his companion, yet glaring even more if they ignored her. This must be her protector, financier of the new features of Vauxhall.

Polly looked at me, unsure of whether or not to acknowledge me. I suffered similar doubts. But her escort was in no doubt whatsoever. He stared at me, went red with embarrassment, and then boomed full out to cover his awkwardness.

'So this is where you make the music now, me lad?'

It was my old acquaintance Mr Armstrong from Newcastle upon Tyne. I wondered what his frilly-cunted wife would say if she knew what sweetmeats he kept for himself in London; and wondered, in a purely abstract way, how much of his beloved cash I might squeeze out of him in return for my silence if I were so minded. I was sure that I interpreted in his eyes a fear of just that magnitude.

But I simply said: 'My dear Mr Armstrong. What a pleasure to see you again after all this time.'

Polly looked startled, and not altogether pleased. Doubtless she had things to wonder about, too: such as, what notes and reminiscences might we not exchange if we sat drinking together when she was elsewhere?

'Eeh, lad, like you say, this is a right pleasure. How are you fettling, then?'

'Canny,' I said, remembering some of his local jargon.

He slapped me on the shoulder and drew Polly closer. He introduced us, grinning and winking at me to boast of what he had acquired. After Polly and I had exchanged a few meaningless pleasantries, he invited me to accompany him to inspect work on the grotto and the new cascade. Polly, he intimated, could go for a twenty-minute stroll, after which he would collect her and take her for tea and an enjoyable evening. He winked and leered grotesquely as he uttered the word 'enjoyable'.

My moment of temptation came as we entered the grotto and he laboriously explained all its features. I thought it unlikely that he had personally indulged in the facilities it offered, or indeed that he would be capable of pursuing his plaything through icy cold water and pinning her to the slope beneath the waterfall. Nevertheless I listened respectfully, laughed at a few of his coarse jokes, and said that yes, I had often thought of returning to Newcastle and availing myself of the diversions he had offered.

As we came out into the daylight he said thoughtfully: 'Seen my little lass before, have you?'

I was tempted to prevaricate, but he was shrewd enough

to have picked up that fleeting glance between Polly and myself. As bluffly as possible I said:

'A few times, I'm sure. Not recently, but I think she used to come and listen to our recitals in the musicians' gallery.'

'Ay, that'd be it. Very keen on good music, my Polly. Got a great ear for a tune.'

And a great cunt for a beat, I thought reverently and silently.

He too was silent for a time. I thought he might be calculating the cost of some new feature for Vauxhall, or something to do with his shipbuilding enterprise on the Tyne. Instead he said, with surprising diffidence:

'You like the lass?'

'Charming, so far as I could see,' I said warily.

'I have to be away up north a lot, you know.'

'I remember how busy you used to be up there.'

He snorted, then looked unsure whether it was a joke or not. 'Look, lad, we got on all right together, right?'

'Admirably.'

'I can trust you.'

'I like to think you could, if circumstances made it necessary.'

'Ay, well. It's like this. My Polly could get a bit lonely when I'm away. Wouldn't get up to anything dishonourable, mind you. I'm not saying that. Wouldn't ever say that about her. But I was wondering . . . maybe . . . if there was someone I could trust . . .'

I had an inkling that I was about to be invited to become a chaperon, which was not really my metier. Nor did I think it would be quite suited to Polly's temperament.

Armstrong blundered on. 'The place is there, Polly's there. If you were to make sure there wasn't anybody else while I was away . . . I mean, if you was to keep an eye on her and . . . I mean, lad, if *you* felt like keeping her cosy every now and then, I wouldn't object. We know one another, don't we?' His nudge in the ribs was enough to inflict a nasty injury on the nearest available bone. 'But just you, and nobody else. Everything's provided. Wouldn't cost you.'

Except the odd crown or guinea, I thought.

'Well, lad? I can't offer it fairer than that. And if you ever think of coming back to Newcastle, then I'll promise to set you up with something very special.'

It speaks well for my integrity that I refused him. I thought of the shape of pretty Polly, and of her movements, and of what she tasted like and felt like, and of what she could offer in return for what I had so much enjoyed giving her. And still I said no.

We parted good friends, though Mr Armstrong looked puzzled, as well he might. What sensible full-blooded man could turn down an offer like that? I did hope he would not now begin to have doubts about Polly's worth and misread my reluctance as disparagement.

I am a married man. A happily married, faithful husband. I will never again play disloyal games with any other woman. Cecilia and I will accept the Countess's invitation to stay with her in Carlsbad. The ladies will take the waters and take care of their health as the babies swell within them. And I shall take the air in the gardens; play music wherever the chance offers; stroll along the Bohemian boulevards studying the surrounding hilltops; and will lift my hat to all the fashionable ladies taking the waters and indulging themselves in those fantasies which, I am told, afflict all imaginative women who take spartan cures at spas. . .

Nexus

THE BEST IN EROTIC READING – BY POST

The Nexus Library of Erotica – over a hundred volumes – is available from many booksellers and newsagents. If you have any difficulty obtaining the books you require, you can order them by post. Photocopy the list below, or tear the list out of the book; then tick the titles you want and fill in the form at the end of the list. Titles marked 1992 are not yet available: please do not try to order them – just look out for them in the shops!

EDWARDIAN, VICTORIAN & OLDER EROTICA

ADVENTURES OF A SCHOOLBOY	Anonymous	£3.99	
THE AUTOBIOGRAPHY OF A FLEA	Anonymous	£2.99	
BEATRICE	Anonymous	£3.99	
THE BOUDOIR	Anonymous	£3.99	
THE DIARY OF A CHAMBERMAID	Mirabeau	£2.99	
THE LIFTED CURTAIN	Mirabeau	£3.50	
EVELINE	Anonymous	£2.99	
MORE EVELINE	Anonymous	£3.99	
FESTIVAL OF VENUS	Anonymous	£4.50	1992
'FRANK' & I	Anonymous	£2.99	
GARDENS OF DESIRE	Roger Rougiere	£4.50	1992
OH, WICKED COUNTRY	Anonymous	£3.50	
LASCIVIOUS SCENES	Anonymous	£4.50	1992
THE LASCIVIOUS MONK	Anonymous	£2.99	
LAURA MIDDLETON	Anonymous	£3.99	
A MAN WITH A MAID 1	Anonymous	£3.50	
A MAN WITH A MAID 2	Anonymous	£3.50	
A MAN WITH A MAID 3	Anonymous	£3.50	
MAUDIE	Anonymous	£2.99	
THE MEMOIRS OF DOLLY MORTON	Anonymous	£3.99	

A NIGHT IN A MOORISH HAREM	Anonymous	£3.99	
PARISIAN FROLICS	Anonymous	£2.99	
PLEASURE BOUND	Anonymous	£3.99	
THE PLEASURES OF LOLOTTE	Andrea de Nerciat	£3.99	
THE PRIMA DONNA	Anonymous	£2.99	
RANDIANA	Anonymous	£4.50	
REGINE	E.K.	£2.99	
THE ROMANCE OF LUST 1	Anonymous	£3.99	
THE ROMANCE OF LUST 2	Anonymous	£2.99	
ROSA FIELDING	Anonymous	£2.99	
SUBURBAN SOULS 1	Anonymous	£2.99	
SUBURBAN SOULS 2	Anonymous	£2.50	
THREE TIMES A WOMAN	Anonymous	£2.99	
THE TWO SISTERS	Anonymous	£3.99	
VIOLETTE	Anonymous	£2.99	

"THE JAZZ AGE"

ALTAR OF VENUS	Anonymous	£2.99	
THE SECRET GARDEN ROOM	Georgette de la Tour	£3.50	
BEHIND THE BEADED CURTAIN	Georgette de la Tour	£3.50	
BLANCHE	Anonymous	£3.99	
BLUE ANGEL NIGHTS	Margarete von Falkensee	£2.99	
BLUE ANGEL DAYS	Margarete von Falkensee	£3.99	
BLUE ANGEL SECRETS	Margarete von Falkensee	£2.99	
CAROUSEL	Anonymous	£3.99	
CONFESSIONS OF AN ENGLISH MAID	Anonymous	£3.99	
FLOSSIE	Anonymous	£2.50	
SABINE	Anonymous	£3.99	
PLAISIR D'AMOUR	Anne-Marie Villefranche	£2.99	
FOLIES D'AMOUR	Anne-Marie Villefranche	£2.99	
JOIE D'AMOUR	Anne-Marie Villefranche	£3.99	
MYSTERE D'AMOUR	Anne-Marie Villefranche	£3.99	
SECRETS D'AMOUR	Anne-Marie Villefranche	£3.50	
SOUVENIR D'AMOUR	Anne-Marie Villefranche	£3.99	
SPIES IN SILK	Piers Falconer	£4.50	1992

CONTEMPORARY EROTICA

AMAZONS	Erin Caine	£3.99	1992
COCKTAILS	Stanley Carten	£3.99	
CITY OF ONE-NIGHT STANDS	Stanley Carten	£4.50	1992
CONTOURS OF DARKNESS	Marco Vassi	£3.50	
THE GENTLE DEGENERATES	Marco Vassi	£3.99	

Title	Author	Price	Year
MIND BLOWER	Marco Vassi	£3.50	
THE SALINE SOLUTION	Marco Vassi	£2.99	
DARK FANTASIES	Nigel Anthony	£3.99	
THE DAYS AND NIGHTS OF MIGUMI	P.M.	£3.99	
THE LATIN LOVER	P.M.	£3.99	
THE DEVIL'S ADVOCATE	Anonymous	£3.99	
DIPLOMATIC SECRETS	Antoine Lelouche	£3.50	
DIPLOMATIC PLEASURES	Antoine Lelouche	£3.50	
DIPLOMATIC DIVERSIONS	Antoine Lelouche	£3.99	1992
ENGINE OF DESIRE	Alexis Arven	£3.99	
DIRTY WORK	Alexis Arven	£3.99	
DREAMS OF FAIR WOMEN	Celeste Arden	£2.99	
THE FANTASY HUNTERS	Celeste Arden	£3.99	
A GALLERY OF NUDES	Anthony Grey	£4.50	
THE GIRL FROM PAGE 3	Mike Angelo	£3.99	
THE INSTITUTE	Maria del Rey	£3.99	1992
LAURE-ANNE	Laure-Anne	£2.99	
LAURE-ANNE ENCORE	Laure-Anne	£2.99	
LAURE-ANNE TOUJOURS	Laure-Anne	£3.50	
Ms DEEDES AT HOME	Carole Andrews	£4.50	1992
MY SEX MY SOUL	Amelia Greene	£2.99	
ONE WEEK IN THE PRIVATE HOUSE	Esme Ombreux	£3.99	
PALACE OF SWEETHEARTS	Delver Maddingley	£4.50	1992
THE SECRET WEB	Jane-Anne Roberts	£3.50	
STEPHANIE	Susanna Hughes	£3.99	
STEPHANIE'S CASTLE	Susanna Hughes	£4.50	1992
THE DOMINO TATTOO	Cyrian Amberlake	£3.99	
THE DOMINA ENIGMA	Cyrian Amberlake	£3.99	
THE DOMINO QUEEN	Cyrian Amberlake	£3.99	

EROTIC SCIENCE FICTION

Title	Author	Price	Year
PLEASUREHOUSE 13	Agnetha Anders	£3.99	
THE LAST DAYS OF THE PLEASUREHOUSE	Agnetha Anders	£4.50	1992
WICKED	Andrea Arven	£3.99	
WILD	Andrea Arven	£4.50	1992

ANCIENT & FANTASY SETTINGS

Title	Author	Price	Year
CHAMPIONS OF LOVE	Anonymous	£3.99	
CHAMPIONS OF DESIRE	Anonymous	£3.50	
CHAMPIONS OF PLEASURE	Anonymous	£3.50	
THE SLAVE OF LIDIR	Aran Ashe	£3.99	
THE DUNGEONS OF LIDIR	Aran Ashe	£3.99	

THE FOREST OF BONDAGE	Aran Ashe	£3.99	
PLEASURE ISLAND	Aran Ashe	£4.50	1992
ROMAN ORGY	Marcus van Heller	£4.50	1992

CONTEMPORARY FRENCH EROTICA (translated into English)

EXPLOITS OF A YOUNG DON JUAN	Anonymous	£2.99	
INDISCREET MEMOIRS	Alain Dorval	£2.99	
INSTRUMENT OF PLEASURE	Celeste Piano	£3.99	
JOY	Joy Laurey	£2.99	
JOY AND JOAN	Joy Laurey	£2.99	
JOY IN LOVE	Joy Laurey	£2.75	
LILIANE	Paul Verguin	£3.50	
MANDOLINE	Anonymous	£3.99	
LUST IN PARIS	Antoine S.	£2.99	
NYMPH IN PARIS	Galia S.	£2.99	
SCARLET NIGHTS	Juan Muntaner	£3.99	
SENSUAL LIAISONS	Anonymous	£3.50	
SENSUAL SECRETS	Anonymous	£3.99	
THE NEW STORY OF O	Anonymous	£3.50	
THE IMAGE	Jean de Berg	£3.99	1992
VIRGINIE	Nathalie Perreau	£4.50	1992
THE PAPER WOMAN	Francoise Rey	£4.50	1992

SAMPLERS & COLLECTIONS

EROTICON	ed. J-P Spencer	£3.99	
EROTICON 2	ed. J-P Spencer	£3.99	
EROTICON 3	ed. J-P Spencer	£2.99	
EROTICON 4	ed. J-P Spencer	£3.99	
THE FIESTA LETTERS	ed. Chris Lloyd	£2.99	
THE PLEASURES OF LOVING	ed. Maren Sell	£2.99	

NON-FICTION

HOW TO DRIVE YOUR MAN WILD IN BED	Graham Masterton	£3.99	
HOW TO DRIVE YOUR WOMAN WILD IN BED	Graham Masterton	£3.99	
HOW TO BE THE PERFECT LOVER	Graham Masterton	£2.99	
FEMALE SEXUAL AWARENESS	Barry & Emily McCarthy	£4.99	
WHAT MEN WANT	Susan Crain Bakos	£3.99	
YOUR SEXUAL SECRETS	Marty Klein	£3.99	

Please send me the books I have ticked above.

Name ....
Address ....
....
........................Post code ....

Send to: Nexus Books Cash Sales, PO Box 11, Falmouth, Cornwall, TR10 9EN

Please enclose a cheque or postal order, made payable to **Nexus Books**, to the value of the books you have ordered plus postage and packing costs as follows:

UK and BFPO – £1.00 for the first book, 50p for the second book, and 30p for each subsequent book to a maximum of £3.00;

Overseas (including Republic of Ireland) – £2.00 for the first book, £1.00 for the second book, and 50p for each subsequent book.

If you would prefer to pay by VISA or ACCESS/MASTERCARD, please write your card number here:

— — — —   — — — —   — — — —   — — — —

Signature: _____

HELP US TO PLAN THE FUTURE OF EROTIC FICTION –

– and no stamp required!

The Nexus Library is Britain's largest and fastest-growing collection of erotic fiction. We'd like your help to make it even bigger and better.

Like many of our books, the questionnaire below is completely anonymous, so don't feel shy about telling us what you really think. We want to know what kind of people our readers are – we want to know what you like about Nexus books, what you dislike, and what changes you'd like to see.

Just answer the questions on the following pages in the spaces provided; if more than one person would like to take part, please feel free to photocopy the questionnaire. Then tear the pages from the book and send them in an envelope to the address at the end of the questionnaire. No stamp is required.

THE NEXUS QUESTIONNAIRE

SECTION ONE: ABOUT YOU

1.1 Sex *(yes, of course, but try to be serious for just a moment)*
　　Male ☐　　Female ☐

1.2 Age
　　under 21 ☐　　21 – 30 ☐
　　31 – 40 ☐　　41 – 50 ☐
　　51 – 60 ☐　　over 60 ☐

1.3 At what age did you leave full-time education?
　　still in education ☐　　16 or younger ☐
　　17 – 19 ☐　　20 or older ☐

1.4 Occupation _____

1.5 Annual household income
　　under £10,000 ☐　　£10–£20,000 ☐
　　£20–£30,000 ☐　　£30–£40,000 ☐
　　over £40,000 ☐

1.6 Where do you live?
Please write in the county in which you live (for example Hampshire), or the city if you live in a large metropolitan area (for example Manchester) _____

SECTION TWO : ABOUT BUYING NEXUS BOOKS

2.1 How did you acquire this book?
  I bought it myself ☐   My partner bought it ☐
  I borrowed it/found it ☐

2.2 If this book was bought ...
  ... in which town or city? _____
  ... in what sort of shop: High Street bookshop ☐
    local newsagent ☐
    at a railway station ☐
    at an airport ☐
    at motorway services ☐
  other: _____

2.3 Have you ever had difficulty finding Nexus books on sale?
  Yes ☐   No ☐
  If you have had difficulty in buying Nexus books, where would you like to be able to buy them?
  ... in which town or city _____
  ... in what sort of shop from list in previous question _____

2.4 Have you ever been reluctant to buy a Nexus book because of the sexual nature of the cover picture?
  Yes ☐   No ☐

2.5 Please tick which of the following statements you agree with:
  I find some Nexus cover pictures offensive/ too blatant ☐

  I would be less embarassed about buying Nexus books if the cover pictures were less blatant ☐

  I think that in general the pictures on Nexus books are about right ☐

  I think Nexus cover pictures should be as sexy as possible ☐

SECTION THREE: ABOUT NEXUS BOOKS

3.1　How many Nexus books do you own? _____

3.2　Roughly how many Nexus books have you read? _____

3.3　What are your three favourite Nexus books?
　　　First choice　　_____
　　　Second Choice　_____
　　　Third Choice　 _____

3.4　What are your three favourite Nexus cover pictures?
　　　First choice　　_____
　　　Second choice　_____
　　　Third choice　 _____

SECTION FOUR: ABOUT YOUR IDEAL EROTIC NOVEL

We want to publish books you want to read — so this is your chance to tell us exactly what your ideal erotic novel would be like.

4.1　Using a scale of 1 to 5 (1 = no interest at all, 5 = your ideal), please rate the following possible settings for an erotic novel:
　　　Medieval/barbarian/sword 'n' sorcery　☐
　　　Renaissance/Elizabethan/Restoration　 ☐
　　　Victorian/Edwardian　　　　　　　　　☐
　　　1920s & 1930s — the Jazz Age　　　　 ☐
　　　Present day　　　　　　　　　　　　　☐
　　　Future/Science Fiction　　　　　　　　☐

4.2　Using the same scale of 1 to 5, please rate the following styles in which an erotic novel could be written:
　　　Realistic, down to earth, set in real life　☐
　　　Escapist fantasy, but just about believable ☐
　　　Completely unreal, impressionistic, dreamlike ☐

4.3　Would you prefer your ideal erotic novel to be written from the viewpoint of the main male characters or the main female characters?
　　　Male　☐　　　Female　☐

4.4　Is there one particular setting or subject matter that your ideal erotic novel would contain?
_____
_____

SECTION FIVE: LAST WORDS

5.1 What do you like best about Nexus books?

_____

_____

5.2 What do you most dislike about Nexus books?

_____

_____

5.3 In what way, if any, would you like to change Nexus covers?

_____

_____

5.4 Here's a space for any other comments:

_____

_____

_____

_____

_____

Thank you for completing this questionnaire. Now tear it out of the book – carefully! – put it in an envelope and send it to:

**Nexus Books
FREEPOST
London
W10 5BR**

No stamp is required.